.50

The
DUCHESS
and the DRAGON

The DUCHESS and the DRAGON

a novel

JAMIE CARIE

B&H
PUBLISHING GROUP

Nashville, Tennessee

Copyright © 2008 by Jamie Carie Masopust
All rights reserved.
Printed in the United States of America

ISBN-13: 978-0-7394-9844-6

Published by B&H Publishing Group,
Nashville, Tennessee

Scripture taken from The King James Version.

This story is dedicated to my sister, Jennifer—who knew Serena's strength better than I did. To our deep nights sitting on the deck, dreaming and talking out this story, and to your power (Him and you together) to remain strong and faithful and passionate in the face of hardship and opposition. You are my heroine . . . This one's for you.

ACKNOWLEDGMENTS

To my editor, Karen Ball—who sweated with me over all the thee's and thou's, the wilts and the arts. I'd like to meet Drake someday too!

To the B&H sales guys and gals—whose home is the road most days, who took these books and ran with them, believing in them. I think of you often; I pray for you often. You are the soldiers on the front lines.

To the bookstore owners and their teams—who are a light and a hope to the communities where they serve. I am humbled to be a part of your ministry.

And to Julie Gwinn, my publicist, a woman who knows the pillar of cloud and the pillar of fire, who moves when He says move and stays when He says stay. You are a multifaceted jewel in His kingdom.

This is a team effort—getting out stories of God's amazing love. I thank God for each of you.

May the side of good win . . .

Chapter One

NORTHUMBERLAND

Drake's fist came down on the massive desk with bone crushing impact. Pain radiated up his arm and into his body, a body trained in the art of bland derision. A body broken now, unable to restrain the fury of this betrayal. He cursed, the sound a quiet hiss in the room. He hung his head, his straight, black hair a curtain over clenched eyes. "May he rot in—"

"Quite right." Charles Blaine, friend and neighbor for as long as Drake could remember, threw himself back into the luxurious cushions of a chair. "Dastardly business, that." He'd said this already. Twice. He repeated it for the third time, staring at the carpet, shaking his head.

Drake swung away from his friend, wishing to be alone, wishing for only the ears of these four walls that he might truly vent his mingled disbelief and outrage. Instead, he took a bracing breath and pulled himself together. He was giving his friends a start.

Control . . . control, man . . . control everything still within grasp. His stomach trembled with the effort.

With a short crack of laughter, he swung back to face his guests, his lip curling, his tone edged in the scorn they all expected. "I should have guessed, I suppose. Stupid of me, really, not to have been prepared. Not to have countered the old man somehow." His voice lowered as he looked down and away from them. "I suppose I never believed he really hated me so much as he let on."

The other two men in the room exchanged glances, obviously at a loss. How could they have any answers for him? The facts spoke for themselves, glaringly real on the scattered pages that lay against the black gloss of the old duke's ornate desk.

Albert Radcliff, the family barrister, mopped at his brow and blew his nose, which was forever running—but had been running with particular need in the strain of the last hour. By some odd twist of fate, Albert was visiting Alnwick Castle when the old duke, Ivor Weston, clutched his chest and collapsed onto the rug, gasping for air like a beached trout.

Drake, too, was home, which was stranger yet. As if all the stars had aligned and arranged the drama so that it might unfold exactly as Ivor wanted. It was fully imaginable that Ivor bargained with the devil for such a favor, some last request in exchange for witnessing a son's destruction.

A favorite pastime of the devil's to be sure.

Charles, though, must have had an angel nudging him. Drake's boyhood friend and neighbor arrived full of excitement about his most recent purchase—a new stallion, a white Lipizzan of famed parentage to add to his stables. They'd been admiring the magnificent animal in the drive when they heard shouts for help from the butler. Drake wasn't sure what he would have done had he not had his friend's bracing support. He shuddered, imagining his hands around the solicitor's throat . . . the new will

Ivor insisted Albert enact thrown into the fire, curling black and smoking, disguised as ash.

No, it didn't bear thinking of.

But Drake couldn't help it, couldn't escape the memory of his father laid out on the floor. The sound of the old man's desperate, rasping command—"New will . . . in the safe!"—rang out in the room like a death knell.

He could only watch, his hand stretched out toward his father, while waves of shock rippled through his body. But Ivor was intent on only one thing. He lifted his head off the floor and grasped his solicitor's hand in a vein-popping, eye-bulging frenzy. "It is what I want . . . nothing else will do. Find it, Albert."

Drake moved into his father's field of vision and knelt down beside him, reaching for his hand.

Ivor jerked away, placing the hand on his rasping chest, then finally turned toward Drake. Ivor stared at him—really looked into his eyes as he'd never done before. Drake recoiled as his father's mask of indifference was stripped away by death's honesty, exposing the truth of feverish eyes and compressed lips, revealing a long-awaited, gleeful vengeance.

The old duke even cackled in his excitement, a grating, harsh sound that was cut off with a gasp for air. He'd started to speak, then gave up and died—that leering smile lingering around his now frozen lips.

So sinister was the scene that both Drake and Albert backed away from the body as though it were black and stinking with the plague. They'd looked at one another for several shocked moments, then made for the safe.

And now they knew.

Each person in the room knew the depths of his father's hatred for him. By the end of the month the whole of society would learn the shocking news that Drake Alexander Weston, the only child of the Duke of Northumberland, had mysteriously, inexplicably, been cut from the will.

Albert stood, his hands shaking as he restacked the papers. He looked up at Drake, strain deepening the creases around his mouth and eyes, his age-mottled hand lying flat on the restacked documents.

"A nasty piece of business if ever I saw one. It is not the will he had me draw up years ago, my . . . lord." He choked on the title, throat working up and down under the loose skin of his neck, then coughed into a hastily pulled handkerchief. That he should now be calling Drake "your grace" instead of "my lord" was one of many mockeries yet in store for Drake.

Drake waved him off. "Never mind, Albert. I suppose I will have to get used it. I suppose I should be happy to have a title a'tall." He said the words in a clear tone, but had to turn away from their staring faces, his stomach rolling. He fought the nausea threatening his throat.

Unsure of his way, he found himself walking to one of the many masterpieces displayed on a far wall. Van Dyck's lush *Samson and Delilah* hung suspended like a scene come to life against the swirling mother-of-pearl panels of the walls. He stared at the raw beauty of the scene. Here was a man with strength, the kind of strength to bring down kingdoms. But Samson had his weakness, and Drake? Now he knew his. Tears welled up behind his eyes. He'd only wanted to please his father, to know that he was proud of the man Drake had become. But it wasn't to be. Now, all he could see was a painting that would never belong to him. A father's love that he would never have. Why? His mind struggled to grasp it. Why all the grooming and pretending? The years at Eton and then Cambridge, the best schools in England, the military career in His Majesty's Royal Navy, the constant displeasure at any show of emotion other than self-satisfaction for some material gain. All the torment he'd gone through that made him into the man he now was. He'd thought it was to make him into a duke. He'd thought it was to mold him into a man like his father.

He'd thought wrong.

Drake paced across the rich Savonnerie rug, woven for this very room and placed to complement the gleaming mosaic flooring. His father spent much of his life in this room, overseeing its most minute detail—all part of the grand scheme to reflect the power and honor of the Seat of Northumberland. Drake's gaze swept the room, trying to grasp some hidden meaning.

He remembered, as a boy, when he'd really seen it for the first time. The richness of color and texture could be overwhelming to someone unused to such luxury. He'd seen the awe on their guests' faces many times, and he'd always taken pride in the fact that someday . . . someday it would be him greeting that awed visitor; it would be his room that brought gasps of wonder from men and women who could but dream of such wealth.

A trickle of sweat ran down his back as he realized he was gasping for air. This place . . . it was breathtaking. Was there any place on earth more perfect? Alnwick Castle. It was his promised inheritance.

His.

Inheritance.

He lurched back toward the men, trying to wear the familiar devil-may-care attitude but feeling like a carefully constructed house of cards whose bottom strut had been jerked away.

His eyes were drawn to the desk where the destruction of his life lay. The new will, confident in its strong, slashing handwriting, glared at him. The desk, a work of art, made of ebony wood covered with tortoise shell and inlaid with gilded brass, mocked him. A jade sculpture of a Chinese dragon stood on one corner, ornate and ferocious in design. It used to frighten him as a child.

Now he knew there were far more terrifying things in life than dragons.

A marble quill and ink set stood now silent near the top center edge.

Weapons used to destroy his future.

A clear glass sphere sat on the other corner along with several dogs, some intricate blown glass, some porcelain, others pewter and silver—all made in the image of his father's only passion outside power and wealth: his dogs.

His father's favorite, Hunter, had received the attention and praise Drake had longed for as a child. He had been secretly glad when the dog died, but it hadn't mattered. There was little Drake could do to earn a word of praise from the stoic Ivor Weston, fourth Duke of Northumberland.

Now Drake realized it was far worse than he had suspected. His father hadn't just disliked him. He'd harbored a deep hatred for his son. The question remained: Why?

Drake stared at the pages willing them to reveal some clue. His father's handwriting, so stark and clear, proved he had been keen until his last breath. The hope that he had gone mad held no relief. Nothing could explain what he had done—expect pure maliciousness. Drake, his hands now braced on each polished edge, stared at the desk, in the room his father loved, and felt his barely constrained hurt and rage break through the barrier of his will. With a violent roar, he swept the pages and decorative accoutrements onto the floor. Glass and porcelain shattered; papers fluttered through the air like the feathers of a bird caught mid-flight by a bullet.

He swung around to face his startled friends. He'd let the caged animal out, but he no longer cared. Let them pity him. "There must be a way out of this! I refuse to let him do this to me!" Looking at the barrister he commanded, "Burn the will. We will use the other. The one you wrote up years ago. No one will know."

Albert only shook his head and looked down. "Nasty business, that. Can't do it."

Charles leapt up, clearing his throat, then made for the crystal decanter to pour a stout drink. Avoiding the broken glass, he picked his way back to Drake's side. "Easy, man," he said in a voice meant to soothe, "drink this."

Drake shook his head as if clearing it from a fog, took hold of the drink, and gulped it in one swallow. Hot talons of fire burned his throat, but he was glad. Glad of any sensation other than the dark pit of despair that awaited him. Setting the glass down on the now barren desk, he walked to a chair and sat. He closed his eyes and then dropped his head into his hands, no longer trying to make sense of it all, only knowing searing pain.

Charles cleared his throat. "Look here, Albert, is there nothing we can do? No way around the will?"

Drake looked up, saw Albert's gaze dart around the room as if it could help him. Shaking his head he said finally, "I am afraid not, the will is very clear, supersedes the other. The ducal estate and title is to be given to the, um, the cousin, Lord Randolph." His voice lowered as he corrected himself. "His grace, Randolph Weston." He mopped at his damp brow with his ever ready handkerchief as his eyes wandered over to the crystal decanter as if he, too, needed a drink.

Drake stood abruptly, "Do not call him by that title within my hearing, do you understand? Never again."

Albert nodded and continued. "Sorry, but you must accustom yourself to hearing it. It will soon be common knowledge." Albert shook his gray head and looked at the floor. "If only you had a brother, then we could at least keep it in the immediate family."

Drake's head shot up. "What was that?"

Albert reddened, a vein pulsing blue in his forehead. "I am sorry, my lord. Pointless to think, much less speak of such things."

"What is this about a brother?"

"Only that if you had a legitimate brother, my lord, your cousin would then become heir presumptive and the title and estate might go to the sibling as the next of kin after you."

"Your father hasn't a pregnant mistress hidden around the place, has he?" Charles drawled from his chair.

Drake rose and began pacing the length of the carpet. Giving Charles a scowl, he directed his question to Albert. "How so, when my father dictated in his will that everything be given to my cousin?"

"The king would doubtless override the will if a more direct heir were discovered. A few carefully placed words and documents, birth records and such, and I believe King George would look the other way and allow the sibling to inherit." Albert shrugged. "Alas, there is no other heir."

Drake stopped pacing in front of Albert and looked into the old man's face with a slow smile. "Perhaps there will be." He spoke more to himself than the others. "Yes, a dear, little brother."

Rubbing his chin thoughtfully, he felt his smile grow. Of course. It was perfect. The best part of this plan was that his father, for all his wealth and determination, would not have the last laugh after all.

That distinct pleasure would belong to Drake.

Chapter Two

The men stared at Drake Alexander Weston, Earl of Warwick, wide-eyed. He had cracked, the disappointment too much.

Drake knew that's what they were thinking and gave them the same smile he'd worn since he was ten, the world-weary smile of omniscient confidence. "Who knows of my father's death?"

The two men exchanged glances. The duke's body lay in the next room. The physician had been sent for, but little else was done as they had been so intent to carry out those last words.

Charles spoke up first. "Aside from the three of us?" He shrugged. "A couple of household servants and soon Doctor Canton. The man has only been dead a little above an hour. I thought we would notify the parson first thing in the morning."

Drake raised his hand. "No. No one is to know anything yet."

Charles stared hard at his friend. "What the devil are you thinking of, Drake?"

"We will keep the old man's death a secret—" he couldn't restrain a smile; this was too perfect—"until I can marry."

"Marry?" Albert frowned at him. "What good will that do?"

"No good at all if I marry as myself."

His friends' expressions told him they feared for his sanity.

"However, a great deal of good——" he drew out the suspense—"should I marry as my father. Even more good when I produce a child. Namely, my brother."

Albert choked on his water. Charles stared at Drake in wide-eyed disbelief. "You can't be serious. It will never wash. First off, how do you propose to keep the old man's death a secret?"

"As it has been stated many times before," Drake said sardonically, "I am, in appearance at least, the very image of my father. With a little theatrical makeup and some padding——" he shrugged, looking down at his wide chest and flat stomach—"I will look enough like him to make an occasional appearance. From a distance, of course. I am quite certain I can even fool the servants."

Charles shook his head, "And what of the servants who know? You'll never be able to keep news of this import quiet. You're talking out of desperation, man!"

"The desperate are often the most cunning." Drake wasn't in the least deterred. "Listen to me. My servants are completely loyal to me. I am certain I can depend upon their cooperation. The doctor, however, will have already been told and will have to be bought."

"But how . . . ?"

Drake ignored Charles's sputtering confusion. "I will marry immediately, as my father, and upon finding the most fertile noblewoman in all of England, I will, God willing, bring a son, a dear baby brother, into this world. A short time later, my father will die from a withering disease that has kept him ill and in bed for months. The end result will be that my brother will inherit the dukedom. I will, of course manage the estate for him until he comes of age, at which time I will turn it over to him." After finishing his case Drake looked at his friends, satisfaction filling him, replacing the despair. He almost chuckled aloud, knowing this was the final and most perfect irony of all.

"I will give up what is rightfully mine to one person and one person only. My own son."

THE DAWN, THREE days later, found Drake on the third story balcony of Alnwick Castle, having a hearty breakfast of ham, eggs, buttered toast, potatoes thick with cream, and coffee. Whenever he was home and the weather permitted, he took his morning meal outdoors: on a balcony, terrace, or one of the many garden spots. He preferred these places over the stuffy red-and-gold dining room he shared with his father on rare occasions.

This morning he was engrossed in his newspaper, calm as any other morning. And why not? Having convinced Charles and Albert of his scheme he had little doubt he could convince others. And convince them he had. He smiled in memory, the words of the newspaper in front of him growing dim. Soon after their conversation had ended, Drake called the servants who knew of Ivor's death to the study. They were given a condensed version of the plan and asked for loyalty, even as a weighty purse of leather was pressed into each hand. The doctor had been a bit harder to convince, but Drake was certain he could depend on him now that he had silenced the man's conscience with an even heavier purse. The good doctor would never have to treat another case of consumption or deliver another baby as long as he lived if he didn't want to.

The next step in this lunacy was to locate some padding, cosmetics, and the wherewithal to use them. The unaware servants were told his father had gone to London for a few weeks. Drake calculated that would give him time to prepare and practice for the appearances he would make as his father. But the greatest challenge would be to find the perfect woman who would pose as his father's wife. Ivor should fall in love while in London, he mused, and come back remarried. The question was . . . to whom?

Drake allowed his mind to travel over the faces of the women in his life—beautiful women of varied backgrounds and temperaments, but having in common the grasping, avaricious character that dominated the ladies of his set. There had been many over the years, but many more opportunities for romantic liaisons that he had flatly refused. He was as calculated in his dalliance as he was in every other aspect of his life. He could have—perhaps even *should* have—chosen one of them to become his bride by now. But he'd enjoyed the life he led too much to consider that it could change so completely.

Still, now that he had to choose one and quickly, he found himself unable to do so. Lana, his current mistress, was an earl's daughter. She would be delighted—no, ecstatic. But he didn't think he wanted to trust such a secret with her. She was too demanding, too moody, and much too talkative. He needed a quiet woman—submissive and sweet. Someone who would accept this scheme and him as a temporary husband without questioning him to death over it. Once the child was born, Ivor could be put to rest in truth, and Drake would end his relationship with the woman. He would live in London, visiting occasionally to watch over the upbringing of his son.

Or rather . . . his brother.

He chuckled. It *was* preposterous, when he thought of all the implications. But the woman would remain a duchess, living here in the splendor that was Alnwick Castle. He was confident he could find any number of females willing to accept the terms of such a bizarre proposal.

Rubbing his freshly shaved chin, he leaned back in his wrought-iron chair and contemplated his other feminine acquaintances. He really should marry a virgin. Had to be certain it was his child that inherited the dukedom. And, much to his surprise, he realized he wanted someone who would be faithful, at least for the duration of the scheme. An innocent who would bear him a child and then become a rich dowager duchess, raising her child in the quiet countryside of Northumberland.

It was more than many women of the ton had.

An infinitesimal movement from Drake's hand brought his footman to his side. Drake gestured for a refill of coffee and indicated his need of more eggs. They appeared, at the perfect temperature, in the exact amount he would have wanted on his plate and in his fine imported Indonesian cup. Drake picked up his fork, eyes on his food, and nodded his dismissal.

Sipping from his cup, he sank back into contemplating candidates for a wife when a slight rapping sound at the outside of the door to his balcony caused him to turn, a frown tugging at his brows.

"Yes?" he barked at the shadow behind the wavy glass.

A reed-like man slipped through the opening. His shoes were dirt encrusted, his clothes filthy, a grimy hat turned round and round in his hands. Drake resisted the urge to curl his lip. "What is it, man? Can't you see I'm at my breakfast?" This was hardly the sign of a well-run establishment. How had the man gotten beyond his stalwart butler? "Where is Crudnell?"

"Pardon, milord, I begged an audience with ye. I heard tell of . . . well . . . I know ye 'ad some trouble . . . t'other night." His voice dropped to a whisper, while he glanced over his shoulder. His gaze took on a greedy glint as he met Drake's eyes for the first time. "I was 'oping to get in on the blunt. In exchange for my keepin' quiet about the plot to get your fine self an heir, if you take my meanin', milord."

Drake went hot, then cold. He stared at the man. The audacity! To be called on the carpet by someone of this person's ilk. Drake turned in his chair, facing the little man.

This, too, was his father's fault. Rage returned, rushing to his cheeks and throbbing in his head. That he should be cornered by the likes of this fellow, in his own house, on his own balcony—

It was too much! Surging from his chair like a dragon awakening from the comforts of his lair, Drake stalked over to tower above the man. "You, you sodden stench of humanity, will not utter a word about anything to anyone or you will never be able to utter a word again! Do *you* take *my* meaning?"

The man backed up, cowering, but to Drake's astonishment he rallied. "I'll not leave without the same blunt the doctor got from ye. And I know how much it was."

The doctor. He should have known the old fool would be the weak link in this mess. "The doctor told you?"

"Not exactly, milord, but I overheard 'im telling 'is wife. I work for 'em. They was talkin' with the windows open, milord."

Black dots of rage filled Drake's vision. He advanced—breathing hard through his nostrils. If this little man knew, soon the whole countryside would as well. His plans to reach his own bit of heaven crumbled like the tower of Babel. "You are very sure of yourself." Drake's words held quiet menace. "Whom have you told?"

The man shrugged nervously, "Only my wife, milord—just to safeguard my protection whilst I was 'ere."

"And whom, pray tell, has your wife told?"

"N–n–no one." Then, seeing Drake advance, he amended, "I can't rightly say, she being a woman and all."

Drake roared and took another step, backing the man up to the railing. "So you think you are safe from me?"

The man glanced over his shoulder at the stone terrace below. Terror filled his eyes.

Drake felt his own power. It would be so easy . . .

He took another step, closing the gap of reason that held his hands back, and leaned over the man. The scoundrel bowed back, his waist pressed against the railing, his feet on tiptoe.

The sun felt hot on the back of Drake's neck and he watched, transfixed as a trickle of sweat beaded on the little man's brow, rolling slowly down his dirty face. Time seemed to hold its breath as Drake wavered, feeling the hardness of the tiles under his feet, seeing a spot of peeling black paint on the railing beneath his hand. A sudden breeze rose up, making his hair dance around his face. Suspended, Drake stared into the man's eyes—and felt with astonishing clarity the reality of holding another's life in his hands.

Take it—just as your father took yours.

The man's face wavered, became Ivor's, full of scorn and laughing from the grave. Drake's insides shifted, then shattered. It was gone. Everything . . . gone.

With a sudden move, Drake reared back, away from the man.

A sudden shriek split the air—an awful sound that startled Drake out of his trance. One glance told Drake the terrible truth: The man couldn't recover his balance quickly enough. Before Drake could move, the little man, eyes wide with fright, stretched out an arm toward Drake—and was gone. Toppled over the rail. Another scream, and then a dull thud.

The sound echoed across the stone terrace below and carried into the lush green gardens.

Drake looked at the fingers of his right hand, grasping into thin air. Stunned, he peered over the rail at the inert body, one leg lying cocked in a position that spoke of severe injury. A sick nausea rose from his belly to his throat. He pressed his fist to his mouth. Why hadn't he been able to grasp the man's arm? He had only meant to frighten him . . . hadn't he?

Before he had the chance to answer the questions, the echo of hurried footsteps sounded behind him.

"My lord, we heard a scream . . ."

His footman and butler stood at rigid attention at his back. Drake turned slowly to face them. "He fell. My visitor slipped over the railing and fell." The words rang as false as they were. The careful, blank stares from his servants assured him they did not believe him.

Crudnell stammered, which only added to the strange reality that was now his life. "W–w–what shall we d–d–do, my lord? Fetch the doctor?"

Fear and panic rushed in.

How strange, this feeling of fear. Drake couldn't remember feeling it since he was a small boy. It was . . . immobilizing. He couldn't think how to answer his butler. Plowing through the servants, he ignored their presence and fled to his bedchamber.

Closing the door behind him he leaned against it, panting as if he'd just run the breadth of his property.

Think, man!

There was no question that he was responsible for the man's death. When the entire tale came out—and it would, of that he had no doubt—they would hang him or worse, send him to a hellish life in Newgate Prison.

He tore himself away from the door and rushed to the dressing chamber to search for a trunk. He threw clothes and stockings and neck cloths out of his way, utterly panicked. He had never packed for himself in his life and felt impotent rage at the knowledge that he might require help finding something in which to pack his things.

No, he couldn't let the servants see him like this.

A small trunk stood in the far corner of the dressing room; he dragged it out. Opening it, he inhaled sharply. It was his childhood trunk. Something he hadn't seen for years and hadn't even known still existed. There lay the boyhood treasures he'd cherished and long since forgotten. With no time to waste, he pawed through it. Most went to the floor in a pile: a wooden yo-yo he'd gotten at a fair, a few books, a battered sailboat and some half-finished sketches. Near the bottom lay a miniature portrait of his mother.

This and a lace handkerchief embroidered with ivy and her initials, LW, intertwined in the leaves, he left in the corner of the trunk. Turning to the mass of clothing, Drake chose some practical and some formal clothes. He didn't know where he was going or if he would ever return.

A sudden pounding on the door startled him.

"Leave me!"

Footsteps padded away down the hall. Drake redoubled his efforts, cramming his signet ring onto his finger and a heavy leather pouch of coins in his pocket. He would get more money from his solicitor in London, when he could. This would tide him over until he knew the lay of the land.

Shouted voices drew his attention to the window. A carriage had just stopped in front of the castle and a tall, stately gentleman was descending. Drake peered out, half hidden by the heavy, royal blue window coverings. Justin Abbot? A dark curse escaped his lips. What was the king's lackey, a powerful member of the Cabinet Council and a person Drake only acquainted himself with when necessity demanded it, doing here now? Drake had heard that the man was in the north on King George's business, but he hadn't expected to see him at Alnwick.

For him to appear now meant certain disaster.

It had only been three days since his father's death, but it was possible Abbot had heard something and was coming to investigate. Add the incriminating evidence of a dead man on his terrace and . . .

Drake jerked away from the window, seeing that his hands were clenched so tight his nails were imbedded into his palms. He must not panic. And yet, it seemed the very earth was opening beneath his feet.

He rushed to the packed trunk and shut its lid with a bang. Oh, for more time to plan and think! There were papers in the library he would like to have, more money, valuables he could sell later if need be. But no time. He locked the trunk, his fingers fumbling in haste and frustration.

Drake hoisted the trunk. Was it possible? Was he now carrying his only belongings in the world? The hall outside his room was quiet and deserted, but he could hear voices drifting up from the stairway. Quickly, he slunk toward the backstairs. Maude, an upstairs maid, was coming up. She took a breath to speak at the sight of him, stopping suddenly when Drake shook his head and put a finger to his mouth. "You did not see me, is that clear, Maude?"

She bobbed her pretty head, eyes wide, and whispered back. "There's a man here to see you, my lord. From the king. How could he have known so quickly?"

"Let's not jump to conclusions, Maude. What's to know? Listen, reason would have it that I put some time and distance between this situation and myself. You understand?"

Maude nodded again, though her brow puckered.

"Good, now let us go down together and find a horse. I may be in need of your assistance."

Even as the two hurried down to a back entrance leading to the kitchens, Drake could hear a commotion coming from the front of the house.

"Now," Drake commanded, "as quick as you can and without being noticed, run ahead and tell Henry to saddle Talisman for me. Then lead him toward the south garden gate. If you are seen and anyone remarks upon it, let him loose and I will find him. Understand?"

Maude nodded again, "Yes, my lord."

"Very well, now go."

Drake watched as she hurried to the stable. Once out of sight, he held to the shadows of the house, making his way into the garden, careful to stay beneath the foliage of bushes and trees. At one point he thought he heard a shout coming from the house, but he wasn't certain. Pulse accelerating, he hid behind a dense wall of hedges, peering over the top and waiting for movement from the direction of the stable.

Part of him wondered if he shouldn't go back and brazen it out. Running only made him look guilty. And yet, the thought of the cold wall of Newgate pressed against his back made him happy to see Maude rounding the corner of the stable. She led his prized thoroughbred, an animal as fast as he was enduring, and Drake silently thanked whatever fate watched out for him.

He held his breath as the pair hurried through open ground. When they reached him, he gave her a quick peck on the cheek and said, "Not a word to anyone, Maude. You have done me good service this day. I will not forget you."

She blushed and nodded, starry eyed. "But when will you return? What will happen to all of us, my lord?"

Drake grimaced. What, indeed? "I do not know, Maude. I wish I could tell you, but I just don't know."

After strapping down the trunk Drake swung up to the familiar creak of his saddle. Talisman galloped several yards, then Drake turned and took one last look at the manicured lawns, the formal gardens, the imposing castle that stretched into the blue of the sky.

An inheritance lost.

Drake turned from it all, his heart leaden, not knowing if he would ever see it again, and put the spur to his horse.

He did not look back.

Chapter Three

LONDON

Drake huddled against the brick building of his solicitor's office, the sharp edges of the wall digging into his back. The hardness reminded him of the stone terrace the man had fallen to. It never left him for long, this feeling of guilt. Sometimes it was a weighty pressure against his chest that made him struggle for a deep breath. Other times, a deep sorrow, a grief so profound that he couldn't think how to go on with the ordinary business of where to eat, or whether he should stay at Charles's house, or what to do next. It was as if he'd plummeted from another world . . . into a hellish world.

Rain-soaked and cold, he clenched his teeth until his jaws ached. A high-sprung carriage with a coat of arms emblazoned on the side passed, splashing water onto his boots, adding to his sodden, heavy feel. A woman's laughter drifted from inside the carriage—that kind of laughter that was pleased with itself, confident in its invulnerability.

He used to laugh like that.

A sudden feeling, a flash of insight struck him of how it might feel to live on these cold, unfriendly streets. Truly, he could stay here all night, huddled on this corner, and no one would care.

He looked at the scene around him with new sight. Across the way a couple stood, the woman beautiful and smiling up into the handsome face of her companion. She beckoned a serving girl to come closer with the umbrella. Her bracelet entangled on the handle as the slight servant maneuvered the umbrella as close as she dared. The woman jerked her hand back, her face not quite so lovely now as she berated the servant with harsh words. Drake watched as the servant's face turned ashen and panicked. Had he done that countless times without noticing?

The theatre must have just let out, Drake thought bitterly. Servants held carriage doors open, waiting with warm blankets to ensure their betters were comfortable. All the trappings of what used to be his life.

He resisted the urge to slam his fist into the wall. If he could just get up to Albert's business quarters, he could at least gain the comforts of a fire.

It had been two weeks since his hasty flight from Northumberland. After reaching London, Drake took up residence with Charles for a few days. He'd hated to come to London, knowing his chances for capture increased with every mile he came within the king's court, but it was the best—no, the *only*—place to liquefy his assets and hear news that would either bring him out into the open or exile him from the continent.

The latter had soon proved true.

It hadn't been long before Justin Abbot returned, questioning his closest friends, saying only that he was looking for Drake. The noose drew ever tighter, and Drake knew he had to get out of London. England too. But to travel any distance, he needed more money than he had been able to spirit away. And to gain the comforts of a heavier purse, he needed to see Albert.

He had waited all day for the cover of darkness and now stood there, skulking in the shadows like a common thief, waiting for this theatre crowd to disperse.

Finally, he slipped around the corner of the building and hurried to the entrance, rain dripping from the lowered brim of his hat. He ducked into the hall and drew a deep breath. The marble floor and tall ceiling caused his footsteps to echo through the deserted place. Head down, he followed the familiar path to Albert's office.

"Drake," came a scratchy voice from an inner room, "is that you, then? In here."

"Albert?" He didn't sound well. Drake picked up a lantern, which cast a gloomy glow in the outer office, and crept toward the inner sanction.

At the sight of a single candle lighting Albert's craggy face, Drake released a held breath. His friend was alone.

"Put the light out," Albert wheezed. "Abbot was sniffing around earlier today." Pulling a handkerchief from his pocket, he dabbed at his dripping nose.

Drake studied the corners of the room before obeying. Then, setting the lantern on the floor, he took the seat across from Albert. "Are you being followed? Watched?"

"No . . . no, I was not here when Abbot came by today, but he will be back." Albert pushed a bottle across the desk. "You look frozen through. Here, have some Madeira."

Drake wished it were something stronger but grasped the bottle. He hadn't allowed himself to spend any unnecessary money and the restraint had been surprisingly difficult. He had always prided himself of the mastery of his will, but recently discovered the magnetic pull of the forbidden. The liquor slid down his throat with smooth familiarity, bringing a rosy warmth to his chest. "Do you have the money?"

Albert sighed. "'Tis not as much as you hoped, my lord. But I didn't want to cause questions by overtly rippling your financial waters. There seem to be eyes and ears everywhere." He slid a heavy purse across the desk.

Drake felt the weight in his hand and glanced inside. "This will not last a year."

Albert nervously rubbed the loose skin of his jaw line. "I shall send you more as I can. I have not been able to learn what they know, but I know they have not given up looking for you." He leaned across the table toward Drake. "We must get you out of England, my boy."

Leave England? Had his life really come to that? Drake dropped his head in his hands and drew in a deep, ragged breath. "What of the shares in the East India Company. Have you sold them?" When Albert didn't answer Drake looked up, eyes narrowed at the old retainer. "Have you managed anything else for me?"

Albert cleared his throat, his gaze darting away from Drake's scrutiny. "I have a plan to buy you some time until this debacle is sorted through. You're not going to like it, but it will get you out of the country with no one the wiser."

Drake found he had no voice, could only stare.

"There is a ship, *The Prince Royal*, leaving for America in two days. If the king's men are watching the roads and ships leaving England, you would do well to adopt a disguise of some sort. They will be looking for an aristocrat with the usual trappings of nobility. The captain of this ship is signing on indentured servants." He hesitated at Drake's dark look, cleared his throat and continued. "I know it sounds intolerable, but it may work. They will not be looking for you among the masses of poor going over to be indentured. Once safely in America, I can send you more money and, while you are away, I will see what I can do about getting your name cleared. When we know what the king is thinking, we can act accordingly."

Drake stood and paced the small room. "If you think a pardon is possible, I should stay and face the charges."

Albert's jowls swayed as he shook his head. "Drake . . . I do not think that would be wise. We need time for the facts to come out and for tempers to subside. You *must* leave the country."

Drake placed his hands on either side of the desk and leaned toward Albert. "How could this have happened? Albert, *tell* me. Am I not my father's son? Have you but to look at me to see his face? I see him every time I look in the mirror. Why did he do this to me?"

Albert looked down at his clasped hands in his lap, his lips pressed together in a thin line. "I do not know, my lord. I do not know." He paused, sudden speculation in his gaze as he looked back up at Drake. "You have just reminded me of an old rumor. I have never put any stock in it, mind you, but . . ."

"Tell me."

Albert shrugged. "Rumors are rarely reliable, Drake."

"You will tell me regardless."

"Well, your father did have two brothers, did he not?"

"Yes, Cousin Randolph's father, Clinton, dead for many years now, and Richard, the youngest brother who lives in Bristol, I believe. Quiet man, I've met him only once. What of it?"

"The tale was that your mother fell in love with Richard. She was already betrothed to your father, had been since she was a young girl, but hardly knew him. Not long after the marriage

Richard came to see them, and your father was away. I do not know the details and I certainly cannot believe it true—"

A deep dread made Drake's stomach tremble.

"—but some say you were conceived during his visit."

No! The denial echoed inside him. Impossible. He couldn't be anything other than Ivor's son. It was unimaginable. "How could anyone think such a thing? There must be more to the story." That anyone should question his parentage on the simple fact that his mother was alone with his uncle for a time was absurd.

"The only fact that gives the tale some credence is that when your father returned, he banished Richard from Northumberland and said he would never see him again. No one knew exactly why, but rumor was rife, as it always is in such cases."

"Preposterous!" But the quaking inside him grew, threatened to become a full-blown panic. He thought of his mother, a sad, pale wraith of a woman, possessing an ethereal beauty that seemed to fade each year until she was a ghost on her deathbed. And always, that faraway look in her eyes . . .

His hand, a balled fist in his lap, shook so that he had to press his other hand against it. He looked down, willing a stillness into his body. He would not, could not think of his mother doing such a thing. She would have never betrayed his father in such a manner. She would never have made her son illegitimate—*would* she?

Drake stood and paced, pulling his shattered emotions into brisk action. "So your plan is to indenture me to the colonies? I, Drake Alexander Weston, reared to a dukedom, shall become a servant?" He let his mockery show in his smile as he looked down at the older man from his full height of six foot three inches.

"My lord . . . that is, I see little alternative."

"No!" Drake turned to the desk, snatched up the half-empty bottle of Madeira and flung it against the wall.

Albert sat in stunned silence, fear lighting his eyes. Drake struggled to control his emotions. He caught a glimpse of himself in a small mirror hanging on the opposite wall. Wild-eyed, unshaven, and so angry. The man who stared back was not a man he knew. The careful control bred into him since birth was gone. In its place he saw a fire-breathing dragon capable of murder.

Yes—he saw a murderer, and it terrified him.

Breathing fast he flung himself into the chair, his hands balling into fists. "What shall I do? What would you have me do?"

Albert rose from his chair and handed Drake a piece of paper, then laid a bracing hand on Drake's shoulder. "Sign this, son. Buy some time. It is your best hope."

Drake stared at the paper. Had the world gone mad? Sign the paper. Indeed.

Fingers shaking, he took the quill from Albert's hand and dipped it in the black ink. Just as he pressed tip to paper, Albert halted him. "Sign your name as Drake Winslow. You dare not go by Drake Weston any longer."

He stared at the tip of the quill, the ink so black and ready to drip, wondering if he could do it. Then he hunched over the page and scrawled the foreign name.

"It is over," he whispered into the dark.

DRAKE STOOD WITH the rest of the indentured in a long line on the docks of the River Thames. The mid-morning shadows of the warehouses fell across them, shading the sun as it rose beyond the Tower of London. London Bridge sat in the distant west, a familiar black outline against the gray sky. How many times had he clattered over that stone edifice and thought nothing of its magnitude, its memories of such a great city. Now he might never see it again.

Turning toward the west and his new future, Drake felt a shaft of doubt for his own sanity. Two ships bobbed in front of them on the dark green waters of the Thames. One, massive and sturdy, was being loaded with supplies, her hull sitting low in the water. Next to it floated their ship. Studying that rickety craft with the eyes of a man who had financed and inspected many a cargo vessel, Drake fought the urge to slink out of line and back into the shadows.

Being indentured was the least of his worries. His shaky resolve to follow Albert's plan threatened to dissolve into the wisps of a nightmare. Mere weeks ago he wouldn't have considered trusting a barrel of tea aboard this heap and now he was boarding it himself? Ludicrous! And yet, what choice did he really have?

He looked around at his companions, dock workers and passersby, half hoping for some miracle to jump out and save him. Instead, his feet shuffled forward with the rest.

A sudden shout drew his attention and that of his companions. A constable was leading a man, hands tied behind his back, down a gangplank and back to shore. The constable jerked to a halt, his eyes sharp as he scanned the crowd. Drake ducked his head. The hat he wore was pulled down low over his eyes, two weeks' worth of beard darkened his cheeks and chin, but he was tall and stood out. His chances of being caught in such a disguise were slim, but still, sharp tension stiffened his spine. The colonies were better than Newgate.

Or so he kept telling himself.

A woman behind him coughed, a rasping sound that boded ill. His skin crawled of its own accord as he took an involuntary step forward. They were a downtrodden lot, his fellow passengers. The stench of poverty hung like a bleak aura around them. Drake shuffled even further forward, hunching down, allowing the hollow feeling in his gut to reach his eyes.

No one he knew could possibly recognize him. He scarcely recognized himself.

His mind fixated on the murder—those few moments replaying in his head with razor-sharp clarity. Sixteen long days since an interrupted breakfast and a poor man's death. Days filled with watching and waiting, but Drake knew not what he was waiting for. Sixteen days of anxiety gnawing at him till he'd lost so much weight that his clothes hung from his frame in heavy folds. Sixteen nights of fitful sleep for fear the nightmares would come. Nightmares that strove to ensnare him and pull him down into madness where murderers belonged. Truth be told, he had little need for a disguise; his mask of wretchedness was only too real.

They drew closer to the gangplank—a wet, narrow board slippery from muddy feet. The dank, fishy smell common to the Thames assaulted his nostrils; the screech of seagulls above their heads grated in his ears. A mother and two small children set foot upon the gangplank, and Drake found himself holding his breath. The youngest child, a little girl, began to cry and wouldn't move; the boy clung to his mother's skirts threatening to topple them all.

"Get a move on!" A shrill voice from behind yelled.

The woman took another step, but the younger of her children swayed. All eyes in line watched as the mother screamed and grasped a fistful of the girl's shirt. There was a collective sigh of relief as they righted themselves.

Before Drake could think better of it, he stepped out of line and was walking to the front.

"'Ey! What's to do, 'ere?"

"You cain't step ahead in line!"

Drake stilled the complainers with a look, the mantle of authority still draping him.

One woman nudged the man beside her. "Who's he think he is, eh?"

Drake leapt onto the gangplank, swinging the tiny girl into the crook of one arm. The lad looked up at him with big, round eyes as Drake grasped his hand. "Step lively now, my boy. You can do it."

The child nodded, chubby cheeks rounding in a smile. When they reached the other side, Drake jumped down onto the deck of the ship. The girl in his arm hadn't moved during the crossing, but now cried out for her mother. Drake turned to the woman and helped guide her down to the deck. He then deposited the toddler into her arms. "Your children, madam."

The woman stood, mouth open for a moment, and then blushed. "Oh thank ye, kind sir. I was so afeared they'd be drowned afore we ever begun."

Drake inclined his head, then turned from her—and stilled. Countless numbers of eyes were upon him. *Fool! How could you have forgotten? Can you not for a moment remember who you are now, what you are supposed to be?* This was going to be impossible! He gritted his teeth and turned away, following the others down into the hold to claim a bunk.

A rickety ladder, a creaking, swaying floor, a dark hold, a place where the air didn't move. This would be his new home.

It took a few moments for his eyes to adjust. He stared, heart sinking, at row upon row of double or triple-tiered bunks. Alnwick

Castle, its grandeur, its imperial force against nature and man, rose up to taunt him. Against all will, a sob grew in his throat . . . followed immediately by shame. Making a quick judgment, Drake staked his claim on an outside row with easy access to the ladder leading up on deck. Some of the others claimed a bed and then returned to the deck for a last look at England before sailing. Drake thought better of leaving his belongings unattended, so he sat on the bed and waited. It wouldn't do to court more trouble by standing up on deck for all to see him—a fugitive, a dependent on the winds of fate, a poor wretch leaving his homeland.

His new home amounted to about six feet long and two feet wide, his bed a thin straw-filled pallet on a rickety looking frame. Underneath the frame was the only space to store his belongings and the meager supplies he had purchased for the journey that would take about fourteen weeks. They were packed in here like slaves, except slaves were shackled. Drake's appreciation for freedom suddenly made itself known, startling him.

Embarrassment stole up his neck as he realized that he wanted to collapse—to lie on this shoddy iron bed and wallow in self-pity like he hadn't since he wore gowns. Instead, he took a shaky breath and steeled himself. He would make it to America, get out of this ridiculous indentured servant business altogether, and begin a new life. What he would do to support himself once the meager funds in his trunk ran out he didn't know. Still . . . news traveled slowly. Perhaps he could join the other impoverished nobility on the new continent.

He wrapped the thin blanket about him, lay back, and closed his eyes, hoping sleep—and the nightmares—wouldn't come just yet.

Chapter Four

erena stared out her bedroom window, taking in the late fall scene of her yard and street. The leaves were mostly fallen now, lying in brown, tumbled heaps, blown about by the breeze. An old, gnarled tree filled the north corner of the yard, where a wooden swing twirled, the wind its only occupant. She had swung on that swing countless times, reaching her toes up toward the sky. A sky that today was the pale blue-gray of weather coming.

She smiled as inspiration filled her. Closing her eyes, she let the colors swirl behind the darkness of her lids. The rope of the swing turned from weathered tan to a shocking yellow. The seat of the swing became golden brown. It rose in her mind's eye, tossed by the wind into an azure sky.

Then she shifted her focus to the trees—their trunks slick and shiny with her black paint, bubbles of deep green like little mossy outcroppings popping up and down their mighty lengths. The leaves were in juxtaposition—the ones still attached to their branches, the stubborn ones, growing old and brown while the dead ones on the lawn became bright, alive again in golden yellows, fiery orange, and violet reds. Their veins pulsed with a blue-green blood. The grass brightened to a yellow-green, swaying in the breeze, then she deepened the color in her mind, adding a hint of blue. Her breath caught as the world outside her window became a fairy place where princesses and dragons roamed, a place not seen on this earth.

"Yes, the light is soft but bright." She breathed the thought aloud, imagining the slant of the sunlight and all the shadowy places. Her eyes shot open, her hand pressed flat against her beating heart. Where were her paints? She *had* to get this image onto canvas before it blew away on an earthly breeze. She knew nothing this astonishing would last long in her imagination. A part of her feared it—this knowing of what she wanted and then the battle to get it down. It was always like this—elusive and frantic. But she had to try.

"Now where are my paints?" She was forever leaving things scattered about.

She turned, facing the bedroom she shared with her sister, a furrow between her brows. Mary Ann's side of the room was, of course, as neat as a pin. Hers? She grimaced. She just couldn't seem to put things back in their proper place, nor even imagine what that place might be.

She crouched down, flipped the quilt up onto the bed, and peered underneath. Ah! There was her pile of rolled-up canvas. Now, *where* were those paints? She hoped she hadn't left them somewhere, some new spot she'd found in her roamings where she had painted last. Her mother would not be pleased to find her begging for more paint.

The door banged open. Mary Ann stood at the threshold, a little breathless. "Serena, come quick! Another ship has arrived."

It took Serena a moment to comprehend that the time to paint was lost. She groaned, knowing she might not ever capture that colorful land in her imagination. A profound sense of loss touched her as she stared at the rolled-up canvas, aching for the feel of stretching it over a wood frame. But another part of her, one equally strong, wanted to help.

Serena stood, gave the canvas one last stare, and then turned to get her bonnet. "I am coming."

It was time to go. Time to leave dreams and imaginings, and do what she could to help the indentured who traveled to America on a hope and a dream.

IT WAS EVENING. The gentle rocking in the hold mocked Drake's inner turmoil. He lay curled on his side, squeezed onto the narrow confines of the cot where he spent much of his time. His arms were raised, wrapping around his head, covering his ears. His eyes were closed to the misery around him. The first few weeks of the journey proved just how stark reality had become. Seasickness was rampant. Vomit made a miserable mess of the hold, and the stench of it clung to the air, making it impossible to breathe deep. The fresh air of top deck was a distant, haunting memory. Once onto open sea, Drake had been shocked to realize that they were considered more cargo than passenger, rather like cattle than human. Basic needs and rights were now in the hands of a captain whose eyes glowed with fanatical greed. Drake knew the type— and knew the future would not be pretty for the lot of them.

Many of his fellow passengers were ill before leaving London. This combined with foul food and toilet habits added to their misery, leaving countless numbers unable to leave their cots.

Then, one by one, the dying had begun. Soon, the news came that twenty-seven people had perished. What had seemed a stunning death toll at first was now just another event in a wretchedness that left the living numb. Bodies were thrown overboard with little ceremony—those left alive hadn't the strength or spirit for formalities. The worst had been a pregnant woman unable to deliver her baby. After she and the child died, the crew didn't even bother carrying the heavy body to the deck. Instead, she was pushed through a porthole to her watery grave.

Drake curled inside himself, shunning the others in their close quarters. His fellow shipmates soon learned not to bother him unless they wanted a snarling return. He had honed the skill of verbal cuts and scornful glares long before, now it was as natural as his scowl. And as necessary.

He couldn't let them see his fear.

Each evening, as dusk approached, Drake gritted his teeth and resisted the panic. The deep of night, the pitch black, when the creaking of the old ship ruled them—that was the worst. He was afraid to sleep; for when he lost the fight, the nightmares came. It wasn't as if he'd never had a nightmare. As a boy he'd suffered them often, waking, sweat soaked, from skeletons of dead animals or fiery-eyed demons haunting him. Such nights he'd rear up, panting among his pile of blankets.

But those nightmares were nothing compared to what haunted his nights in this place.

The same and yet varied enough to never lose their terror's strength, they had the ability to wake him and leave him lying like a corpse, stilled with fear. His father, fiendishly laughed at him from the grave. Or worse, the man he'd let fall haunted him, crying from a bloody pool on the stone terrace below. Once, it was his father killing him, and another time it was his father who had pushed the man over the railing. Always the images were ghastly and Drake felt, little by little, his sanity slip away with each one.

Sleep became a dreaded thing, darkness his enemy.

When awake, Drake's mind traveled its own paths, paths his battered will could no longer resist. His memory revisited encounters he'd had with the man he'd always believed was his father. Now he doubted everything. The gossip about his mother haunted him. What he knew for certain was the hateful stares of Ivor, the contempt he'd never understood, the impotent rage underlying his actions, so incomprehensible to Drake. The questions still lingered, rearing heads that chipped away a little more and then more at Drake's identity.

Had it been Ivor's plan all along to dangle a true son's inheritance and then rip it away when the truth of Drake's lineage was revealed?

Weak, his father called him. Any show of emotion ridiculed. Any fear belittled. It hadn't taken Drake long to learn the value of becoming a shadow in any setting, as still and quiet as a piece of furniture in the castle, a ghostly form during a hunt where he secretly abhorred the killing. A silent presence at an auction of horseflesh or valuable artifacts. He was expected to watch and soak in the play of power. And he had learned his lessons well.

Then, at twelve years of age, something changed. His father began grooming him as heir. It was right and expected and everyone around them breathed a sigh of relief. Life finally took on a comforting though severe routine.

Looking back, Drake now wondered . . . Was it then that his father turned bitterness into revenge? It seemed obvious, looking back. Ivor had set upon his master plan—treat Drake as the son he'd always longed to be, waiting for the day, when he would snatch it all away.

The plotting gave his father new energy, excitement even. The subtle promises, the unequaled education, the single-minded building together of a financial empire to rival any king's—it all lead to that fateful day when father would destroy son from the grave during the reading of the will.

Who was he now? His true father, if rumor was to be believed, was an unknown uncle. The man had left him and his mother to their fate, skulking away to Bristol. How could he have done such a vile thing? Had it been Drake, he would have taken his lover and son and left England, not slink away like a dog with its tail between its legs.

All he knew was that he hated him for it.

Suddenly a sound broke through Drake's remembrance. Muffled sobbing reached him from several bunks down. The full moon lent a surreal light through the portholes, casting a ghostly gleam on the sleeping passengers. Sitting up, he searched for the sound's source. His first inclination was to turn over and ignore it, but something about the shaking of the thin shoulders, the dark tousled hair reminded him of a long forgotten memory, and he found himself going to the cot and squatting down on the rough planks of the floor.

"What is the matter, boy? Are you hurt?"

A tear-streaked face of about nine rose up from a wadded blanket that served as pillow. "Who are you?" Resentment filled the response. "I don't need nothin' from you."

Drake resisted the urge to get up and leave. Instead he sat down on the floor, settling in. "Well now, you may not, but I just woke up from a ghastly nightmare, and I was hoping you would tell me something to get my mind off it. Are you sure there is nothing you want to talk about?"

The boy sniffed and drug the sleeve of his arm across a runny, freckled nose. Propping his head on his hand he asked, "What was your nightmare about? I 'ave the same one all the time."

"Oh yes? Tell me yours and I will tell you mine."

The boy sat up, wrapping thin arms around bony upraised knees, looking half-scared and half-excited to have such a rapt audience. "The ship wrecks in a terrible storm, takes on water like the very devil and . . . people are drownin' and I . . . I'm tryin' to save my mum. She's drownin' . . . going under the waves. They always grow bigger and bigger, but somehow I'm floatin' above 'em. I–I always wake up and don't know if I've saved her or not." His voice caught but he quickly rallied, lifting that pointed chin. "Bet yours ain't worse than that 'un."

Drake smiled, feeling suddenly better than he had in weeks. "No, not worse, but equally bad. Mine involves a sea monster trying to drag me down to a cold, watery grave. Must be those beans we have been eating for our dinner. Did you have the dream tonight?"

The boy looked around and then whispered, "No, sir. I . . . I was just missin' my mother. She stayed behind with my little brothers and my sister, Ella. Pap took me and Sean with 'im to get our start." He paused and stared off into the distant moonlight. "I don't know when I will see 'er again. Or if ever I will." His voice became a whisper. "I'll see 'er again someday, don't ya think?"

"Of course you will. What is your name?"

"Danny Oliver. And yours, sir?"

"Drake—" Drake's true name hesitated on his tongue, but he held it back. Giving the boy a small smile, he finished, "Drake Winslow. Good to meet such a fine young fellow. You know, I went away to boarding school when I was about your age."

"Really sir? Can you read, then?" The lad's eyes were shining now with something far better than tears.

"Certainly. Have you had no schooling?"

Danny shook his head. "I wish I could read, though. I would most like to write. My mum says my head is full of stories. I would write them down if I could."

Drake thought back on his prized education at Eton, the private tutors he'd abhorred, something he'd taken very much for granted.

"What was boarding school like, sir?"

Everything from floggings to illicit excursions to Town flitted through Drake's mind. "Well, I attended Eton. The first two years were the worst. The older boys initiate the younger ones, you know. But then, after a time, we grew up and we became the older ones, so it evens itself out. When I was twelve my father sent down a tutor who lived with me to help me with my studies. Aside from learning to read and write, we studied Latin and Greek, arithmetic, literature, English and French and, our favorite, of course, fencing."

Danny's eyes grew wide in admiration. "Are you very good with the sword, sir?"

A bark of rusty laughter escaped Drake's throat. "Passably good, I'd say."

"I should like to go to such a school." Danny's eyes held the faraway gleam of childhood dreams. "Pap says we will have our own land in America, a place where anything is possible. Do you think that's true, Mr. Winslow?"

Drake looked into those eyes of hope and felt his spirits rise for the first time. "I hope so, Danny. I truly do hope so."

A SCREAMING WIND rose into the pitch of night, tossing the vessel into deep troughs on the turbulent Atlantic, as if they floated on naught but a pile of matchsticks. Drake clung to his pallet and tried to block out the piteous cries and prayers of his terrified shipmates. They had been on board for eleven weeks and Drake was no longer thankful he had successfully made it out of London.

He heartily wished he was in Newgate Prison instead.

At least there he would be paying for his sin. Here, he just awaited death. Would he be the next to succumb? Eleven weeks of sickness, starvation, and raspy-throated thirst made the death toll climb. Fever, dysentery, and scurvy ran rampant. Drake often rubbed a thumb against his own gums feeling how swollen they had become. His ribs poked his skin when he inhaled, a peculiar feeling, leaving him lightheaded and woozy whenever he moved suddenly. What really frightened him, though, was his lack of strength. Getting off the cot and walking to the place designated for the men to relieve themselves now brought him to a point of excruciating panting and dizziness.

A sailor came down the rickety ladder bearing a tray of biscuits. He began to pass them out, greedy hands reaching for something Drake wouldn't have conceived of eating months before. Now, his hand shook in equal anticipation. The rations, shrinking with each day, were putrid. The meat was full of worms, the water like sludge and full of worms, the biscuits infested with weevils. That men of power and wealth could treat the desolate so inhumanely was a shocking reality he now faced daily.

Life had become a horror he never dreamed existed.

As he crunched down into his biscuit Drake tried not to think about the fact that he had been one of those powerful and wealthy. Nay, not just one of them. He had been at the *top* of the powerful and wealthy. Princes from other countries acquiesced to him. And yes, he owned shares in the Virginia Company and the

East India Company, profiting from the misery of such as these sharing this dank world with him now.

He laughed bitterly, rolling a weevil around in his mouth, toying with the choice of swallowing it or spitting it out. He finished his only meal for that day in seconds and then, turning to his side, curled into a ball on the lumpy cot. His head ached from all the tortuous thoughts. He imagined drowning and the silent rest that would come with death. Maybe he was going mad. It was a grasping feeling, like he was hanging by his fingertips from the window of a high-storied building—this no longer knowing who he was, no longer knowing his place in the world. He felt like an empty skin that still had to walk and talk and eat . . . but had no soul.

You're worthless. No one wanted you and no one ever will. Just look at you. You are nothing.

Drake put his arms up over his head, covering his ears. He no longer had the strength to fight the voice that told him who he was. He could only curl up against it. Lightning flashed and thunder rolled, shaking the groaning vessel. The storm was taking a nasty turn.

Danny, several bunks away, called to Drake, fear in his tone. Drake turned toward him, desperate for a distraction. Danny had proved his salvation more than once on this hellish voyage. He saw the boy through the dim light. His thin frame draped in ragged clothes, hanging onto his cot, eyes wide. Drake's stomach turned. Watching the children endure this suffering required a different kind of bearing up than he'd yet experienced. The numbers haunted them all—only twenty-one of the original forty children were still alive.

Drake held tight to the beds on the way to Danny's cot as the ship jerked about anyone who tried to walk. Grasping the boy's thin-boned hand, Drake squeezed, panting to catch his breath so he could shout above the gale. "Is this not a grand ride, Danny?"

"My stomach hurts and I think I'm going to throw up, but there isn't anything in my stomach to come up." Danny grinned at his own joke, the skeletal smile making Drake's stomach twist harder. He remembered his breakfasts of coddled eggs and ham and toast, and how he'd thought it his due as a human, never mind as a duke. What he wouldn't give to have that golden, butter-smeared toast to give to Danny right now.

How different he could have been! Drake's chest heaved with the sorrow of it, but he rallied, became bright and encouraging, because he didn't have anything else to give Danny but hope. "Well, in that case, it's a good thing your stomach is empty. Now let us see if we can get your mind on something else. How is your reading lesson coming?"

Drake had written out the alphabet for Danny some days ago, helping the lad memorize them and the sounds they made.

"I'm up to letter *p,* sir." He put his lips together, forcing air out, making the *p* sound. He stopped suddenly as a violent cough racked his emaciated body. Drake put a comforting hand on the boy's back. When the spasm subsided, Danny blurted out, "Will you really give me a book once I 'ave it all down?"

Another dip rolled Danny into Drake, nearly knocking them both to the floor. "Of course. A gentleman always keeps his word." Drake rushed the statement, seeing the boy's eyes fill with terror as he righted them, settling the child back into his blankets.

Suddenly, a loud creaking sounded above them, which turned into a thunderous crash. Drake covered Danny's body with his own, waiting for the ceiling to cave in on them, the water to flood in. When it didn't, he looked up to see a sailor coming down the steps, water pouring into the hold.

"You there! And any other able-bodied men! We need help!"

Drake patted Danny's arm. "Hang on tight, Danny. We're men of the sea now. We can overcome this." The boy nodded, hero worship in his eyes as Drake turned from him and scrambled up to the deck, panic imbuing him with renewed strength. The ship had righted itself, but the damage to the main mast was massive. Every man available scrambled to the huge, wooden pole with its tattered sails flapping like wind-blown laundry. Drake shouldered his part of the load as they struggled to raise the beam. The wind tore at them and the weight, too much for their combined weakened state, knocked the beam out of their hands.

Again and again they tried to raise it, creaking and groaning, the men grunting and heaving, but finally, they gave up and laid it back down on the deck. They could only try again after the wind died down.

Drake's dread grew. Without the main sail it was impossible to steer the ship, which now tossed upon the gray, foaming waves like some giant child's toy. The thought of going off-track and losing time sobered them all. Rations were already slim; they couldn't afford to lose their way.

Soaked to the bone and shivering violently, Drake abandoned the attempt and, with the other defeated men, stumbled back down into the cesspool of stench that was their home.

Nothing left to them but to wrap sodden blankets around themselves and wait to see if, come morning, they were among the living.

FOURTEEN WEEKS AND five days in the pit of a vermin-infested hold. Fourteen weeks of soul-robbing hope. Fourteen weeks of living minute by minute, and then—as a rainbow appearing—a shout was heard, echoing though the hold.

"Land!"

The word lifted them out of their desolate places.

"Land . . . ho!"

It awoke them from the depths of their despair. It was the sweetest word they had ever heard.

Drake opened his eyes, scarcely daring to believe. Land. Had they really reached it? Sitting up slowly to avoid the constant dizziness that tormented him, he listened, hoping to hear the word again—hoping he hadn't dreamed it. Others around him roused, looking like walking, crawling corpses with fanatical excitement on their faces. It was true, they'd all heard it.

Staggering to the ladder he waited in the sudden line, men and women with crazed expressions and sudden energy pulsing through their gaunt frames. They climbed the ladder with legs that shook and then stumbled across the deck to the railing. Drake recoiled from the bright dawn, their new dawn, pain shooting through his head until he thought he might collapse, but his spirit rose within him, urging the frail flesh to the rail. Behind them, a glorious sunrise pinkened the sky, washing the deck of the ship in a rosy glow. But no one spared much energy to appreciate it. They focused, as one desperate being, toward the dark line of land on the western horizon. Drake tried to hold his emotions in check as his shipmates fell apart around him—women and men wept with relief, falling to their knees in raptures of joy, grasping at the rail, unwilling to tear their gaze from the land, thanking God in loud voices that belied their weakened state. They'd reached land. They'd reached their promised land.

Drake felt a tear trickle down his hollow cheek and blinked to rid the water from his eyes so he could focus on the dark blur approaching. He found his mind repeating a lunatics' litany. *Have we really made it? Have we really found it?*

Suddenly he was kneeling. The sunlight sent bolts of pain through his eyes and into his head, but he squinted, staring at the dark coastland, willing it to arrive as nausea and excitement rolled deep in his belly. Not much sea left, his mind reminded him in a muddled fog. After so many weeks on water, land seemed a new anomaly. All he could remember now was the sea. Gray, deep, dark, unfathomable water.

He pulled himself up, clung to the rail and licked his dry, cracked lips. He watched the gentle, gray-green waves lap the ship's hull. To drink full and deep of clean, cool water. What did that feel like? Thoughts of water tormented him, memories of crystal goblets brimming with it was a dreamy image in his head, not that he ever drank much water. But now, now that he couldn't have any, he obsessed about it—its thirst-robbing authority, its crystal clarity. It even dogged his dreams. That it was all around him, and he couldn't drink it had nearly driven him insane.

Daniel McLaughlin walked up and put a hand on his shoulder. "How you be feelin' now, Drake? Fever gone yet?"

Drake squinted up from his hunched position at the only man on board he had really liked, the red-headed Scotsman, and the kind of man you would want covering your back in a fight. Drake was glad he had taken the risk and gotten to know the man.

"Not gone yet, Daniel," he croaked out, "but as soon as I can get some water, I shall recover. That is all this body needs." Drake's fever had burned hot for the last three days.

Daniel grinned, showing white teeth against an auburn beard. "Some decent food wouldna hurt much either, would it now? With land in sight, I think we just might get off this floating hell and get a little of both." He swept his hand toward the hazy coastland, his voice turning soft with conviction. "Freedom and a good life are just over those waves. Hold on for a few more hours, my friend."

Drake struggled to stand upright, and Daniel helped him back to his cot. Another day, Daniel promised—just one more day.

Pray God he survived that long.

Chapter Five

PHILADELPHIA

Serena Winter stood at the bottom of the ladder in the dark hold, blinking, waiting for her eyes to adjust to the dim light and for her sense of balance to return in accord with the rocking motion of the ship. Mary Ann, younger by two years, stood just behind her. "Are there many?"

"I do not know yet. I cannot see a thing." Moving a couple of hesitant steps forward she shifted the heavy basket on her arm. "I will take this side and thee can go over there."

"All right." Mary Ann giggled. "Watch thy step, sister. Remember the last time we played nurse. Thy shoes were nearly ruined."

Serena remembered. All too well. She grimaced and nodded at her sister. This was their sixth time playing nurse, as Mary Ann liked to call it. When a ship of indentured servants arrived in the Philadelphia harbor and there were known sick on board, the Society of Friends was quick to respond. The older girls of local families had all been trained in rudimentary nursing and they rotated shifts to help the needy. Sometimes they went to the poorhouse or homes of the elderly, but Serena had a special place in

her heart for the indentured. There was a woeful faith about them that made her want to help them succeed. She knew they came out of desperation with the hope that after their term of indenture was over they would be able to make a good life for themselves in this wild, new world. But the journey and their treatment often left them too weak to even care that they had finally made it. As Serena nursed them back to health, she also cared for their dreams, praying for them, hoping for them, encouraging body and soul back to health.

Picking her way carefully between the bare cots, Serena looked for someone in need of care. Most of the indentured were up on deck waiting to be allowed to go ashore. Many had called out for water and food as she and Mary Ann passed by, but Serena ignored them. Those too sick to leave their cots down in the hold were most in need of the meager provisions she and Mary Ann had brought with them. It was hard to ignore anyone, especially the thin, filthy children, but worse was the knowledge that often-times these poor people had to wait days or even weeks until all the advertising and sales were completed and they could go to their new homes, unless the soul-drivers came—and God help them if that happened.

A groan drew her attention. Serena turned, and there, in a shaft of the dim light cast from a porthole, slept a man. Serena picked her way toward the cot and leaned over him.

Her breath caught in her chest. His longish, dark hair was lank, and a dark beard covered most of his face. Even so, he was striking—beautiful really—hollow cheeks and all. A sudden thought rose to her consciousness: *God took special care when He fashioned this man.* He was thin and weakened from his journey, sick and flushed with fever, but something about him radiated

greatness and strength. A strange sensation overtook her, making her want to reach out to him. She watched, detached from conscious movement, as her hand, small and pale, did just that. Her palm gently cupped his cheek, stroking up to his forehead, and found it burning hot. With the backs of her fingers, she smoothed his hot temple and brushed back a lock of dark hair.

Suddenly fingers as strong and tight as a manacle grasped her wrist. She reared back, about to cry out, when he mumbled incoherent words and released her. Taking a shaky breath, Serena stared. Was he delirious with fever, then? She had heard of it happening but had not seen it. She reached into her basket and brought out a cool, damp cloth, which she laid on his forehead. Taking a water bottle, she uncorked it with a soft pop and poured cool water into a tin cup. Carefully, she lifted his head. "Please, sir, drink this."

There was no response, so she tipped the cup, letting the tiniest trickle of clearness spill into his mouth. He swallowed. She smiled, caught by the moment, and tried again. He swallowed a little more, his throat moving under the growth of his beard. Again and again she fed him drop after drop of the water, exhilaration at each small success filling her, until the cup was nearly empty. Her arm ached so that she could no longer hold up his head, so she eased him back to the thin pillow and tried to make him more comfortable. Taking another damp cloth she ran it down the column of his neck and into the opening of his shirt where dark hair curled on his chest. His skin was hot and dry, heating the cloth so quickly that she had to pour a little of her precious store of drinking water onto it before starting the process again at his forehead. He grew restless, mumbling sentences that made no sense and then suddenly. "Don't call the doctor, Crudnell, he knows all. Cannot trust the man."

She had no idea what that meant, could only stare at his chiseled face and wonder if the fever would break or take him further into unconsciousness. But, more than anything she could ever remember wanting, she wanted him to open his eyes and *see her.*

After doing all she could to cool him down, she tucked the thin blanket around his shoulders and scanned the area for others. Her eyes had now adjusted to the light and she could see three more men on her side of the hold. Moving quickly to them, she assessed their condition. One was dead, the hollowness of his body showing starvation to be the likely cause. Serena pulled the blanket over his head. She would tell the captain and make sure he arranged for a decent burial. If not, the Friends would come and take the body to ensure the man had a place of rest. It wouldn't be the first time a ship's captain had shifted the responsibility. The other two were sleeping and, when awakened, were very grateful to find freshly baked bread, thinly sliced but thick with butter and water—enough water to quench weeks' worth of thirst. With healthy nourishment, Serena thought, they should be back on their feet in a few days.

Serena went over to Mary Ann's side. "How many are there?"

"Five women, one about to give birth, I think, and another with a three-year-old who is very sick. Oh, Rena—" she looked down at the floor of the hold, trying not to cry—"'tis so hard to see the little ones suffer."

Mary Ann was too softhearted to be an effective nurse, but she did her best, in between the sighs and the tears. "It is well that we are here to bring them comfort, then. Hast thou given them water?"

"Yes, and some food. They are all awake and very grateful."

"Take me to the child." Serena followed Mary Ann through the maze of cots and knelt down next to a woman and her child.

The mother lifted her head and offered a weak smile. Two of her teeth had rotted and her gums were bleeding. "Thank ye, dear ladies. I haven't been much help to little Harry here, but ye are like angels come from above. I thank God for ye."

Serena smiled at her, all the while assessing Harry. His fever was high, but he was awake and able to talk. There was no rash, which was excellent. Serena leaned toward Mary Ann. "Mostly I think they are all starved and thirsty."

Serena focused again on the mother. "Has he had loose stools, ma'am?"

"Oh my, yes. Vomiting before and the loose bowel now. Poor little chap can't keep nothin' in his stomach."

Serena reached into her basket for a jug of blackberry root tea. Dysentery was common and so she carried the tea with her on these trips. The little boy drank greedily of the sugared tea. "I will leave this here with thee," she said to the mother, "but it is for him only. Give him a cupful every two hours. I will leave plenty of good water for you and the rest of the women."

The woman smiled, nodding, and whispered her thanks as Serena moved on, Mary Ann following at her heels, to the pregnant woman.

"She says she is in her eighth month," Mary Ann whispered at Serena's back.

After assessing and talking with the woman, who was also feverish, Serena turned to Mary Ann. "She needs to be examined by Beatrice. She is such an excellent midwife. Would thee run and fetch her?"

Mary Ann nodded, relief in her eyes at the prospect of escape. "'Tis fortunate we brought Henry along as escort, else I would not be able to!"

Serena waved her away with a smile. "Yes, 'tis fortunate indeed. Let us hope our good fortune continues and Beatrice will be found at home and not out delivering a baby."

As soon as Mary Ann left, Serena's mind turned back to the man she first helped. Who was he? He seemed, somehow, so out of place here among the starving. There was an elusive beauty about him that made her imagine him in an elegant manor house, a crystal cup in his hand upraised in a toast, a troop of fawning, elegant people at his table. She had the sudden desire to paint such a scene. And him. She closed her eyes, envisioning him dressed in her watercolors. A sudden coughing made her eyes snap open. It was him. She found her feet turning, walking toward the shaft of light pooling around his bed. Mayhap he'd been caught in an earthbound spell that robbed him of his true identity.

She stared down at his face, studying it. Noting the delicate bone structure beneath the skin, she saw the deft strokes her brush would make as she painted his eyebrows, his eyelashes, his beard . . . the contrast dark and beautiful. Her gaze drifted, like a stroke of paint, down his jawline to his squared chin. A bit too thin for perfection but elegant, even delicate, with a cleft that only the careful observer would see perfectly centered under the dark growth of hair.

"How fearfully and wonderfully thou art made." She breathed the thought aloud and then turned. Had anyone heard her? She exhaled a silly smile, laughing at herself. She'd never behaved so or thought thusly in all her life. What was wrong with her?

Using great care, so as not to wake him, she sank down on the narrow edge of the cot, reaching for his forehead. It was still burning hot, making the cloth warm and dry. Exchanging the cloth for a fresh one from the basket, she pressed it against his brow, allowing her fingers to brush his temple and then back into his hair, repeating the motion until it became a gentle massage. She leaned closer still, now willing him to wake up. A fanciful thought flitted through her mind that he had been waiting for her touch to bring him back to life, that she held some power over his recovery. She smiled at herself and him, but she believed it.

His hair was black as ink, blue-black almost, and fell long and straight away from his forehead. Her fingers slid into it seemingly of their own will. Silky and inky. She imagined him with a fuller face and shaven clean. He would most certainly be handsome, but more than that, he was . . . noble. "Who art thou?"

The soft question seemed to stir something in him, for he scowled at her and answered, most imperious: "Drake Weston, fifth Duke of Northumberland, of course."

Serena gasped. "Thou art no duke!" Was he mad?

He seemed to have lost his momentary lucidity and didn't respond. Serena shook her head, staring at him for a time, then exchanged the cloth, laying a fresh one on his forehead. As she leaned back toward him she whispered, "But thee can dream of such things for a while longer, and then thee must wake up and see me."

Her husky voice sounded strange to her own ears. Her hand seemed to have a mind of its own as she touched his cheek, feeling the coarse whiskers under her thumb. It had been a long time since she had touched whiskers, and those only of her father's as he tickled her with them when she was a little girl.

The man took a long, shaking breath and seemed to sink into a deeper sleep. Her hand trailed down his neck toward his chest—

She froze. *What* was she doing? She *wanted* to touch him, and the urge had no connection to nursing. What was wrong with her? She stood, but again his hand shot out and grasped her wrist.

"Stay with me." The words croaked past dry lips.

Serena sat back down, easily conquered, reaching for the water jug for something to do. Pouring cool, clean water into the tin cup, she lifted his head to drink.

"Yes, I will stay by thy side if thou wilt drink."

He drank more this time and then dropped back onto the pillow with a sigh. She sat beside him, hands clasped in her lap to keep them from touching his face and hair, allowing herself only to watch him sleep. Her gaze fell on his lips, and she remembered the ointment in her basket. She bit her lower lip. Dare she?

A small smile formed on the man's mouth, and Serena reared back. Could he read her mind? Of course not, she chided herself. He was probably just feeling better—he'd certainly needed the water he had been able to ingest. Slowly, so as not to disturb his sleep, she leaned toward the basket on the floor and rummaged through it until her fingers wrapped around a little clay pot. It was in her lap and opened before she realized she had made her decision. She looked down at the ointment. Normally, she would have given it to the patient and allowed him to apply it himself, but this man clearly could not manage that. She dipped her finger into the pot before she could convince herself otherwise, the soothing smells of lemon and beeswax filling the space around them. Her hand stretched out toward his face, her heart pounding. What if he woke? How would she explain what she was doing?

She dabbed a bit on his lower lip and sat back to see what response he would have. Nothing. He slept on. She nodded. She was a nurse; she could do this. Leaning in again, she quickly spread the ointment across his bottom lip. He moved his head away, as if avoiding a fly, but didn't wake. Determined to finish the job, she reached for the upper lip, which wasn't quite as chapped. It was softer and curved, dark rose in color with an indention in the middle that must be sinful, it was so well shaped. Her heart pounded in her chest and her breath quickened as she spread the ointment across the top of his upper lip. She halted, realizing how close she had leaned in, how deep her breathing had become . . .

When had she closed her eyes? Heaven help her, she wanted to kiss him.

"You can, you know."

At first she didn't know if the deep voice had come from the man or some other being in the room, so deep and quiet and inside her head it was. Her eyelids shot open as she straightened. "Can what?"

"Kiss me." He smiled, but didn't open his eyes.

Serena gasped, "Thee has been awake this entire time, sir?"

One of his shoulders lifted. "I didn't think it would help my cause—" he paused pressing his lips together, as though struggling to stay conscious—"for you to realize that." Then he appeared to drop back into a deep sleep.

Serena shot to her feet, escaping her temptation and the moment, moving away from the bed to create as much distance as she could while still seeing his face. She had to get away from this man before she did . . . something . . .

As she turned, her cheeks on fire, she saw that Mary Ann was coming down the steps with the midwife. "Serena, the soul-drivers are here! They asked about these in the hold, and I did not know what to tell them. I said thee wouldst talk to them."

Soul-drivers. The name alone caused her dread. Heartless men who gathered those to be indentured off the ships and drove them house to house, farm to farm, until they were all sold. They took no regard for families, splitting children from mothers, husbands from wives. Nor did they regard humanity, scarcely feeding or caring for those who'd just survived a long, nightmarish journey.

She nodded to Mary Ann. "I will go up and speak to them." Turning to the other woman, she inclined her head. "Good day, Beatrice. Thank thee for coming. Mary Ann will take thee to the woman I am concerned about." She hurried up the stairs. If she could save these few in the hold from the horrors of soul driving, it would be some small gift. One thing she knew for certain: they would not have the man who now haunted her.

They would have to fight her for him.

Chapter Six

Frightened people crowded the deck. A tall, burly man, biceps bulging, eyes hardened, with a slashing whip hissing through the air to keep the people pinned like animals against one rail. Children wept and clung to their parents, while the adults gathered them close, their own faces mirroring confusion and fear.

Serena watched, overwhelmed by distress for the despised and desperate. They were a pitiful sight—except for one man. A tall, red-headed fellow who didn't take kindly to the treatment, as evidenced by the fact that he had engaged two of the officials in a fistfight. Serena turned away just as they caught him and pounded him to the wood of the deck. Clinging to the railing, she was able to skirt around the scene and make her way toward the ship's captain, determined to hold some rank in this world where she really didn't belong.

Captain Masters stood at the far side of the deck, his back turned away from the scene. Serena had spoken to him briefly when she and Mary Ann boarded the ship, and he'd seemed a friendly sort then. Now he appeared decidedly uncomfortable.

"Captain, might I have a word with you?"

His turned toward her as if coming out of deep thought, looking for a moment, unable to remember her.

"I am Serena Winter . . . of the Society of Friends?"

"Ah yes, what can I do for you, miss?" His gaze shifted toward the men shouting orders at the crowd. "You shouldn't be on deck at the moment. As you can see, we are, ah, trying to do business here."

"Yes, I can see that." Despite her training to be always moderate in speech, Serena couldn't keep the disdain from her voice. "There must be a better way to procure indentures for these people."

The captain straightened to his full height, looking down his nose at her. "Young miss, you haven't any knowledge in these matters." His face turned gruff and red. "What do you want?"

Oh, *why* hadn't she held her tongue. She needed this man's cooperation and riling him wasn't going to help her cause. "I wanted to assure thee and these . . . buyers that the few in the hold are not able to travel. All but one have high fevers. That one is dead."

The captain started. "Dead, you say? Gad, what a stink down there! I'll not be responsible! We've already docked, and I'm sick to death of this business."

Serena was not surprised. "Captain, perhaps we might help one another. If thou wilt assure me that those in the hold will not be moved, I will see to it that the dead man is properly buried."

A gleam lit the captain's eyes. "A little businesswoman, are thee?" At the stressed "thee," Serena gritted her teeth. The captain's eyes narrowed, and she had the distinct impression he was trying to judge her figure through the plain, gray wool of her dress and the black, hooded cape. Serena withstood the insolent scrutiny, chin raised and waiting.

"You are a pretty thing, aren't you?"

He reached out to touch her cheek, but Serena blocked his hand, leaned toward him, and took the tone of a mother admonishing a child. "Captain, I have come here to help the sick and the starving. One would think that thou wouldst know better how to take care of an investment." Her voice was quiet, peaceful even, just speaking plain truth in a way that he could do nothing but acknowledge. "Now, about those in the hold, do we have an agreement?"

The captain sighed heavily and nodded. "Sorry, miss." He pressed his lips together as he watched the soul-drivers dividing the indentured into groups. "I'm not exactly sure how I ended up in this business, you see." He looked at Serena and gave her a tight smile, then turned brisk. "I have an even better deal for you, Miss Winter. Since you are so in love with the sick ones down there, I'll sell the lot of them to you for half the price I'm getting from these soul-drivers. *You* can find them indentures. But I want them out by noon tomorrow." Almost to himself he added, "They'll probably be dead by then anyway."

With that announcement, he walked away, leaving Serena standing there, her mouth open.

What had she done? She turned, then started when she found Mary Ann and Beatrice behind her. Mary Ann rushed over. "What happened, Rena? Are they going to take the sick, too?"

"No." She looked at Mary Ann wide-eyed. "I believe I have just bought the sick in the hold . . . or promised that the Friends would."

"*What?*" Mary Ann gaped at her.

"It will be all right." Serena assured, not at all sure that was true. She turned to include Beatrice. "We will see if we can find homes for them among the Friends until they are well, then perhaps we can help them find indentures."

Beatrice, a plump, round-faced woman with a gentle face, didn't hesitate. "I will take Molly, the pregnant woman, home with me. She can stay until the babe is born and perhaps beyond that. I could use a helper, but I will have to discuss it with Foster."

Serena nodded. "Thank thee. That should help." She turned back to Mary Ann. "Father will know what to do with the rest." She hoped.

It was nearly dark when the girls got back home, rushing to the kitchen where they knew they would find their mother at this hour.

"Mother, thou wilt not believe what Serena has done!"

At her younger daughter's exclamation, Leah Winter, a pretty woman with light-brown hair and eyes, turned from the stove and looked Serena over with concern. "What has happened?"

Serena shook her head. "We are fine. It is about the indentured, is all." Serena shot Mary Ann a *don't-say-another-word* look.

Their mother nodded, smiling, soft wrinkles crinkling the skin around her eyes. "Good. Please wash up and set the table before I hear it, then. Thy sisters have been very spirited this afternoon, and I am running behind time. Father will be home any second."

The girls headed for the washbasin, knowing that doing anything else at this hour would be fruitless. Supper was always ready and waiting for their father the minute he walked in the door at six o'clock. It was a ritual not to be toyed with. And besides, they may as well tell the story to both during the meal.

With six daughters—ranging from twenty-one-year-old Serena to Lidy, who had just turned four—their father, Josiah Winter, was rather spoiled. He was waited upon, doted on, and made to feel a king from the moment he walked in till he blew

out the last candle and slipped into his cool, crisply ironed sheets. His wife ran her household like a well-commandeered ship where the simple, basic comforts of a clean home, wholesome food, and contented children were the rule, not the exception.

Not that Serena's father didn't work hard. As one of the few silversmiths in the area, he was hard-pressed to keep up with the orders from a prospering society. Philadelphia was on the verge of becoming one of the major seaports of the world and its people were becoming rich.

Serena and Mary Ann kept their silence as they took their seats and bowed their heads for thanksgiving. After two bites their mother turned laughing eyes to her husband. "I think the girls are bursting with news. Shall we let them tell it now?"

Mischief sparkled in her mother's eyes at the faintly alarmed expression on Serena's father's face.

"What is it, girls? Did something happen at the ship this afternoon?"

It took them both, with frequent interruptions and questions from the rest of the family, the length of the meal to tell the tale. At its end their father sighed heavily. "Those soul-drivers will reap their own reward and we will not spend valuable time discussing them and their evil practices. However, God has used thee, Serena, of that I have no doubt. Today, a wealthy gentleman came in and ordered a tea service. I was surprised that he paid in advance, but now I see that God has provided. We shall use the money to pay for the indentures." He stood and told Serena to get her cloak. "We will start with the Isaacs and the Tromleys. I am sure we can find families to take in the sick and help them find work when they are recovered. Come, Serena."

Mary Ann bobbed up behind Serena. "Might I go too, Father?"

He wrapped his other daughter in a hug and kissed her forehead. "Please stay behind and help thy mother put the girls down. We shall be late and thy mother looks tired."

No one argued with him; rather, the younger girls crowded around to get their good-night hugs.

Serena and her father walked silently, side by side in the frosty air, to the homes of some of the other Friends. Philadelphia was peaceful at night, and Serena treasured any time alone with her father.

"Tell me about the people and their conditions. I should like to know how best to place them."

Serena twisted her fingers together inside her warm wool muff trying to give an accurate picture of the pitiful plights she had seen. "There are seven women, but Beatrice took one home with her—the one expecting, which was so kind of her—so that leaves six."

Her father nodded, his face reflecting the white light of the moon. Serena couldn't help thinking she'd like to paint him at this moment—the way the light of the winter moon made his face bright and pale, his blue eyes glowing with solemn purpose, the thin beard circling his chin. But she turned her mind back to his question.

"One of the women has a son, Harry, who is three. They were mostly weak from starvation and lack of good water, though the child has dysentery and is quite thin. The other women should recover soon and be able to enter into their indenture. None require more than simple nourishment, I think." She hesitated. Why didn't she want to mention the duke? She ducked her head, watching her brown shoes slough through the snow as she thought of him and the name she had given him. It was so unlike her not to want to tell her father something.

"And the others? There were men?"

"Um, yes. Three. There was a fourth, but as I told you at dinner he was dead. Of the three, only one was very sick. He was delirious with fever. I did believe him close to death, and yet he showed a certain strength." Shaking her head at her wistful tone, she looked up to her father who had stopped in front of the Tromley's house.

"The other two were sound, then?"

"I believe so. They were all very grateful for the provisions we brought them."

"We should have no trouble placing them." And yet, for all his confidence, there was disquiet on his face. And a look she'd never seen before.

THE DREAMS CHANGED. Dark swirling voices tormented him; hot, sulfurous breath enveloping, melting his skin. His father's laugh grew closer, gained ground upon his mind. It was so dark where his father now was . . . and hungry . . . hungry to grasp Drake's coattails and pull him down into the pit. Drake floated in darkness, had been floating thus for as long as he could remember. Time ceased—there was only this suspended nightmarish dream.

Then there was a voice. Soft and feminine, but with strength behind it. The voice beckoned him out of the darkness, calling, making him want to reach out for it. It too had a laugh, light and full of light. His father's hateful cackle faded in that laughter's easy victory. For the first time since the murder, he wanted swim to the top and live. He would see the owner of that voice . . . he would live in the reflection of its light and laughter.

The darkness melted away into a bright nothingness.

"OVER HERE." SERENA brought the lantern around and held it up so her father could look at Drake's face. At her father's slight intake of breath, Serena swung around to look at his face, but it was hidden in the shadows of the dark hold.

"What is it?" Never had she known her father to be shaken.

"Him."

"Him?"

They were speaking in low-toned voices, as the other occupants slept. Serena had already pointed out the other men, leaving the "duke" for last.

"Last meeting, during silent worship, while my eyes were closed, I saw a man's face."

A chill crept down Serena's spine. *"This* man?"

Her father nodded. "I am sure of it."

"What dost thou think it means?"

Josiah shook his head, only asking, "Is he very ill?"

Serena reached out and touched his forehead. It was still hot, but he was breathing deep and regular. "Yes, but he seems more at ease. I will give him more water." She had left an extra flask of water and a tin cup beside the man's bed in case he woke. Her father watched as she filled the cup and then helped her lift the man's head so that she could coax him into swallowing.

"We will take him home with us."

Serena turned her head to stare at her father. They had found more than enough volunteers to take in all the sick in the hold. Her father was paying for their indenture papers, and no one expected the Winters to bear this burden also. But something

inside her soared, said this was right. "Yes, he will improve with our care."

Her father nodded. "I do believe he will. Now, stay with him while I go hire a carriage to take him home with us tonight. The others will be helped in the morning, but I will not leave here without him." He nodded at her and left.

Serena turned back to the man on the cot. He hadn't swallowed much of the water so she tried to give him more. She shifted, sliding him so that his head lay on her lap. He didn't seem interested in drinking and finally, after a few more attempts, she gave up. Stroking his hair back from his warm brow, she spoke to him in a soft, quiet voice, yearning for a response.

The ship swayed and creaked beneath her feet, lulling her into a world of water and shadows. She stared into the darkness, something deep within her straining to find the shadow's edges . . . places she'd never known existed. It called to her, making every nerve alive as Serena sensed something here with the two of them.

Something incomprehensible.

She looked down at the man. His face appeared different than the first time she had seen him, as if he'd fought some battle and won. A peacefulness stole over her, causing her to take a deep breath. She closed her eyes, breathing deeply. His scent filled her mind and her fingers began to glide through his hair, exploring the shape of his head, then his temples, then down to the sharp plain of his cheekbones. "Come back, my duke," she whispered. "I have need to see thee fattened up and shouting orders."

Suddenly she felt a touch on her cheek. Caught in the dreamlike spell, she turned into the hand without opening her eyes. As she had done, he caressed her cheek. Now his thumb ran along the line of her jaw. When fingers touched her lips, her eyes fluttered open.

"Your voice saved me."

His own was raspy and deep, but gratitude glowed in the dark pools that were his eyes. And he was even more devastatingly attractive with them open.

Serena drew a sharp breath, wanting to get up, both trapped beneath his weight and that of his words. "Thou hast been very sick." She strained to right her senses. When she started to slide out from under his head, he grasped her hand with surprising strength.

"Stay."

"I must not. My father will be back soon."

"Have we reached Philadelphia then?"

"Yes. The others have already been sold. 'Tis fortunate thee wert so ill and escaped the soul-drivers, sir." As she spoke, she slid out from beneath his head and refilled his cup. "Here, have another drink, and thou wilt hear the tale."

He smiled at her with such a look that she thought she might melt into the wood of the floor.

"A long story, I hope. I would listen to your voice forever."

Heat surged to her cheeks, her gaze dropping to the floor. Her mind told her how inappropriate it was to behave like this with a complete stranger. And yet, it was as if other parts of her—her heart, her soul, her very skin—knew him as deeply as she knew herself.

She told him about the soul-drivers, the others that were ill in the hold and the Society of Friends who were to take care of them. She told him about her conversation with the captain. He laughed, then, a deep rumbling sound that reached into her and then down to her toes.

"And what shall become of me, *ma petit chevalier?* You said your father is coming with a carriage?"

She blushed again and looked down at the lantern at her feet. She knew just enough French to understand he'd called her his *little knight.* "Yes. We will take thee home with us tonight, where thou wilt stay until thou art well. I would see thee well, sir duke."

The duke part had slipped out, as that is how she had been thinking of him in her mind, but the sudden glower on his face startled her.

"Why would you call me that?" His voice was imperious and demanding.

"Th-thou said'st it in thy fever while sleeping."

"Said what . . . exactly."

Serena took a deep breath. "I asked thy name and thou said'st it was Drake Weston, the fifth Duke of Northumberland."

Drake laughed, but this time it wasn't the deep chuckle that made her knees weak. This was a wicked, scathing laugh. "You believed me, did you?" One dark brow arched over his eye.

"I–I, no. I did not believe thee."

"Of course not. How could the Duke of Northumberland number among the white slaves on this piece of God-forsaken wreckage? Impossible. Ludicrous. Am I right?" His voice shook.

Serena felt his anger and was afraid. "Tell me the truth and I will believe thee."

Drake chuckled. "Such a pretty speech from such a—" he sighed and shook his head, his eyes growing hot—"spell-binding woman. I am no duke so you may take the stars from your eyes, my dear. I am Drake Winslow, indentured slave." The bitterness was unmistakable.

HE WANTED HER.

The girl stood speechless before him, and Drake decided to have pity on her. She had, after all, saved his life. She was the one. His light. He recognized her in a way that was deeper even than her voice.

"I beg your pardon. I haven't much to be happy about at present, but that has nothing to do with you." He smiled at her again and saw the light in her eyes change. She was so easy to read, so vulnerable and innocent. He couldn't remember the last time he had seen such open sweetness. "You have brought me back from the darkness, and for that I am forever in your debt. So come, tell me your name."

Her hands hung, loosely clasped together, against the front of a plain dress, but her face—dear heaven, her face—was lavish extravagance and no amount of plain attire could detract from it.

"Serena Winter. My father is Josiah Winter, a silversmith here in Philadelphia. We would take thee home until thy recovery. If that would be agreeable."

"From the sound of things, I would say I am fortunate you decided to pay a sick call. I would not relish being out on the road, for sale as a farm hand." He cursed. "What a mess this is! Please, would you look under this bed and see if you can find my trunk? After being delirious with fever for so many days, I feel the need to check its contents."

Serena nodded and stooped down, the top of her head at Drake's eye level. He stared at the plain, white bonnet, fingers itching to take it off and discover the promising richness of her hair, a color he'd never seen before. Streaks of golden and russet in a lush caramel-honeyed mass, all tucked neatly under the prim cap.

Coming back up, she shook her head. "I see no trunk. There is nothing under thy bed."

She jumped as he swore violently. He leaned over the side of the bed and peered under it. "Put the lantern down here, if you please."

"Thou art sure it was here?"

"Yes!" He fumbled and almost rolled into her. "Curse this weakness!" He bit the words out as he threw himself back onto the pillow. "Everything I own, and at least four-hundred pounds . . . gone."

Serena gasped. "But why would thee indenture thyself if thee could pay for the voyage?"

"'Tis a long and sordid tale and not meant for such innocent ears as yours," Drake replied in clipped condescension.

"Good heavens, I do believe thou art a duke!"

"Please, could you look around the hold for a trunk?" Drake closed his eyes. His head felt as if a metal spike was being thrust through it, and he didn't have the mental strength to spar with her.

He heard her rise and walk about the hold, could envision her peering into corners and crevices with her lantern-light. He was afraid to hope and yet, couldn't help himself.

At her returning steps, he opened his eyes. Her fingers twisted together as she delivered the news. "I am sorry, sir. I cannot find a trunk. It would appear thou hast been robbed."

The blow was almost physical. He turned his head away, fearing what he might say or do.

"I am a slave in truth, then." He shut his eyes once more, wishing the blackness would come back, that it would consume him and last forever, setting him free from the horror that was now his life.

But it would not.

His light stood before him, like some guardian angel of old, and he didn't know if he would come to love her or hate her. But he did know for certain that nothing was ever going to be the same.

Chapter Seven

After Drake was moved to his new bedchamber, the fever spiked again and he spent another two days in and out of a semi-delirious state. The house was like many other houses on Letitia Street, made of orderly, red brick with a neat exterior—a central door, large windows on either side, and a row of three windows looking out from the second story for the girls to peer down at the street, spying and making up outlandish stories about the people coming and going. Josiah, always interested in modern inventions, had installed working sash windows that slid up and down, which the girls would open to catch a summer breeze and lean out of.

There were four rooms downstairs, plastered and white-washed, with a narrow stairway between them. The front rooms comprised the parlor and the dining room. The two rooms in the back of the house were bedchambers, that of Serena's parents and another that Serena and Mary Ann shared. It was this room they'd converted into a bedchamber for Drake.

Behind the house was the kitchen and the necessary room, both separate buildings. The upstairs held one large bedchamber for the four younger daughters, which had plenty of room for

Serena and Mary Ann to squeeze in while their guest recuperated—not that Serena was getting much sleep.

Her mind was filled with him. His confused semi-consciousness told them more of who he was than if he'd been awake. Serena was put in charge of nursing him back to health, but her mother was ever careful that the door was always left open and others were about. Serena knew her mother had noticed the dreamy, blushing, stuttering state that had suddenly come upon her. Everyone had, save Lidy, and she was only four.

How mortifying to lose one's composure so thoroughly. Why, men had been calling on her for several years now and she had never had any difficulty being herself around them. It was . . . frustrating. Absurd even.

"Thou art about to wash that dish clean away, Serena." Kindness rested in her mother's smile. "Why dost thou not take him some tea? He seemed to like the last cup better."

With a guilty flush Serena put down the plate. "Yes, I believe I shall." She carefully measured out the sugar and put a drop of milk in it—just the way he liked it. Even in his weakened state he had a way of letting everyone know what he expected. "And he certainly knows what he likes!" Serena snorted.

Her mother laughed. "What?"

"Oh, I do not know. I was just thinking how we bend and scrape to his every desire. Why do we do it? After all, he is supposed to be our servant, is he not?"

Her mother laughed. "'Tis strange. But there will be time enough for him to adjust to his new status once he is well. And thanks to thee, that should be soon, and we will have him out from under our feet."

Serena knew she must have looked stricken at the thought of him leaving, for her mother laughed again and squeezed Serena's hand. "Oh my dear, thou must tread carefully. I foresee a broken heart from a man such as he." Pulling back, her mother cupped Serena's face. "I know how thou feelest, but we know so little about him. Like a handsome, dark devil he is, and not a Friend." She paused, shaking her head slowly back and forth, her eyes penetrating. "I will not see thee hurt."

Serena couldn't help herself. She wailed, "I do not know what is happening to me! Why can he not be a Quaker?"

Her mother sighed. "I know. I have spoken with thy father and we both feel this man has many secrets—and pain, even aside from the illness he now fights. He is dangerous, Serena, and will soon be gone. Thou must accept that. Anyway, what of Christopher? He should be here to visit again soon."

Christopher! Oh, how could she have forgotten? And why did she feel no emotion, no joy, no dread, no . . . anything at the reminder? "I suppose he will."

"Thee *supposest* he will?" Her mother's brows arched. "Thou art not excited for his visit?"

"Yes . . . of course. It is always good to see Christopher . . ." She shrugged. What else was there to say?

"But not so very good now? Serena, have a care. Christopher has deep feelings for thee."

Serena nodded. "I know. I fear I have little to give him back."

Her mother sighed. "There are many kinds of love, Serena. The feelings thou hast for Mr. Winslow seem powerful and over-whelming, I am sure." Her eyes took on a faraway gleam. "There was once a young man I thought I loved. I was convinced life would cease to have meaning without him. That all ended when he left town with a friend of mine. They never married. He ruined her, in more ways than the obvious. He nearly ruined me. I was so close to giving him everything, and all he gave me were empty promises."

She tilted her head and a soft, sad smile touched her lips. "Now I am grateful it was not me he asked to run away with him. Now I can look back and see the shy Josiah in the wings: honest, good, caring, and right for me. Thy father might not have inspired the height of emotion in me as did the other young man. But thy father loved in depths. Depths I did not understand at the time, but depths upon which we have built a life. Knights in shining armor are more often are cloaked in nothing but plain, brown wool."

Serena couldn't imagine her mother ever being in love with a man other than her father. "Thank thee for telling me that. I will remember."

Her mother gave her a squeeze. "Now take his royal highness his tea—" she laughed—"and we'll leave to thy father the task of teaching him servitude."

Serena's eyes widened with shocked laughter. "Poor Father."

DRAKE LOOKED AROUND the room, not particularly liking the disdain he felt for it, but feeling it none the same. It was positively sparse. Plain white walls, no paintings, no tapestries, no rug to warm one's feet on the cold wood floor. There were plain, cream-colored linen curtains and a few pieces of furniture made of sturdy oak—heavy, dark, serviceable: a simple highboy, a small chest at the foot of the bed, and the four-poster bed without curtains where he was currently reclining. But the bed was stuffed with soft feathers and conditions were vastly more comfortable than those in the ship's hold. He was grateful for the warmth, the care these people had given him, the many kindnesses. He felt almost good enough to get up and wondered how much longer he could endure the sickbed.

He was contemplating what he might do first when he got out of it when Serena glided in bearing a loaded tray and a surprisingly handsome silver tea service. She set it down on the round table with a clatter and then turned to face him, her hands held loosely behind her back, a shy smile on her face—an expression endearing and stirring at the same time. It never ceased to amaze him, this effect she had on his senses. Drake Weston was no stranger to beautiful women. Some of the most sought-after women in English society had sought after him. But none had given him the physical jolt this simple but lovely creature did just by smiling at him.

"Thou art feeling better?"

His smile deepened. He could listen to her *thees* and *thous* all day long. Her voice had such a lilting quality to it. "Yes—" he cleared his throat, still a little hoarse from disuse—"thank you."

"I brought tea and toast." She smiled again at him, this time with adoring eyes. Did she have the vaguest idea what she was doing to him? "Just the way thou likest." She smiled, handing him the cup.

A memory of abruptly correcting her yesterday flitted across his mind, and he frowned. "Thank you. I beg your pardon if I was demanding yesterday. I am unused to lying abed. It seems to have a grating effect on my nerves." He gave her the practiced smile that never failed to melt a woman's heart.

She didn't seem to notice, only waved it off with an endearing, delicate move of her hand. "Thou art forgiven." Handing him a plate she perched on the feather mattress beside him and reached out to feel his forehead. "Thy fever has broken and thy eyes look clear. I do believe thee will recover, sir."

"Please, you may call me Drake. 'Sir' makes me feel old enough to be your father."

"Drake." His name was breathless on her lips. "What does it mean?"

The jolt coursed through him again. No one had ever asked him that. He reached over and took her hand. Rubbing little circles in her palm with the pad of his thumb he said deeply, *"Dragon,* I believe. My father was obsessed with them."

"Oh."

She would be so easy to seduce. Drake drew her hand to his mouth and just touched the backs of her fingers with his lips. She inhaled sharply, and he smiled. "I don't have to ask what Serena means." He watched the play of emotions on her face. "'Tis obvious." He glided her fingertips across his lips. "And so fitting."

Serena gasped, snatching her hand away. Hot color filled her face. "What art thou doing?"

Drake released an abrupt laugh. Some part of him, some part he hadn't known was there, felt like he had known her forever. "I don't know. I fear I lose my grasp on reality and propriety when you are near." He looked down at the covers for a moment, pondering the surprising truth in his own words, then looked back at her with a grin. "But since I am forever begging your pardon, I will beg for something else instead."

He couldn't fault her the apprehension on her features. He raised his hand to his face, rubbed his jaw, looking at her. "I would dearly love to remove this beard. It itches."

Serena's relief was apparent in her escaped breath and shy smile. "I should like to see thee without it." Then, as if realizing what she had disclosed, her eyes grew round and she clapped her hand over her mouth. His deep chuckle followed her as she turned and fled the room.

Drake leaned back, pondering this enchanting creature and her effect on him. She made him feel so . . . so . . .

He sat up, the blankets falling to his waist. She made him feel as no woman ever had. It was unaccountable. And yet, he could not deny the strange feelings flooding him.

Was it possible? Could he, for the first time in his life, be . . . in love? He swore softly at himself. The bleak reality was, it didn't matter. He had nothing to offer her. He was a nothing, a nobody. Falling in love would not change that.

The door opened, and one of the other sisters came in with the shaving supplies. Apparently, Serena was still feeling shy.

"And which one are you?" Drake asked as pleasantly as possible, trying not to scare the pretty little thing away.

"Mercy, thy highness," she said with a bright smile and a curtsy. "I am eight."

Drake laughed out loud. He couldn't help it. This household was full of imps, and a body just couldn't settle into a good misery no matter how badly one wanted to.

"You mustn't call me that." He took a bite of the honeyed toast. "I am Mr. Winslow, or Drake even, and would be most pleased to hear you say it."

She looked a little nonplussed, dumped the shaving supplies in his lap, and then complied in a sing-song voice. "Drake Even, Drake Even, Drake Even . . ."

"Cease!" He softened the order with a grin. "That's enough for now, thank you. How would you like to sit and tell me all about your family? I've only spoken with a few of you, but I hear there are more."

The child was thrilled with the idea of having his undivided attention and plopped down next to him on the side of the bed. "Wilt thou finish that toast, Drake? My mother won't give me another crumb until noon, and I am very hungry." She leaned close, every inch the conspirator. "They lock up the food or Mother says she would get nothing else done. I don't really take her meaning though—it's not as if *she* would be the one eating. I can surely get my own food from the cupboards. I *am* eight."

Drake thought it wise to agree with the little sprite and handed her the rest of his breakfast. "You may have my toast, Mercy. Now, tell me about your sisters while I shave."

Mercy nodded happily and took a giant bite. Without waiting to swallow, she proceeded. "Serena is the oldest, but then you have met her. She is like our father. He's a silversmith. He makes beautiful things from silver. Serena, though, she likes to paint and makes the most wonderful pictures. Thou hast to come upstairs and see the walls; she has painted whole walls from floor to ceiling up there."

Drake felt oddly proud. "What does she paint?"

"Oh, scapes, I think they call it, and animals and people and . . . anything. Sometimes she goes to the river and paints, or she might bring her pencils to one of the picnics and sketch the people there. She is a wonder with a pencil, sir."

Being something of a connoisseur of the arts, Drake decided to suspend judgment until he could view her work, but he was undeniably curious. He waited for more information while little Mercy took another bite and chewed.

"Mary Ann is next. She is more like Mother, and Father says she's full of mischief. I like to play paper dolls with her because she has the best imagination and says the funniest things and everyone has their own voices! She can even mimic

Mrs. Crane—she is the meanest Friend—and it's so funny when she does it. Then there is Hannah. Hannah likes to read and sew and play the harpsichord. We don't have one, but our neighbors, the Lowrys, they let Hannah play theirs whenever she wants to. She helps out with their two boys, William and Charley. I hear they are 'a real handful.'"

Drake tried not to grin as he carefully ran the sharp razor down the side of his chin. He couldn't remember the last time, if ever, he had shaved himself, and it was proving a challenge. If not for the child on his bed, he'd be irritated by now. "Go on." He nodded to her.

"Well, Rachel is next. She is ten. We get along most times." Mercy sounded completely unconvinced. "I guess she is my closest sister."

Drake laughed. "When you're not fighting, that is?"

Mercy nodded and frowned. "She likes to boss me."

Drake laughed again and then grimaced as a trickle of red ran from the soap and down his cheek. Holding his finger to the spot to stop the bleeding, he said, "And then there is you."

"Yes. Can you believe Father had six girls? I know he would like a boy to help him in the shop, but he always says God gave him what he needed. But it does not seem that way. It seems like he needs a son." She shrugged at the puzzle and abruptly switched topics. "I love the outdoors. Since it is winter and cold, I cannot go out much and Mother says that makes me agitated." She shrugged. "But Christmas is coming soon and that will make up for having to stay indoors so much. Last, there is the baby, Lidy, who is really no baby at all. She is four and everybody loves her the best, which is fine, because she is the baby."

Christmas. He'd forgotten Christmas was coming. His last few Christmases had been hectic with parties and the lavish gifts that brought gasps from his friends. Then there were the women—dark-eyed Louisa, golden Flora, and Kate, the sensual redhead from Ireland, to name a few—all hoping to become the next duchess. There were other Christmas memories, too. The deep scent of pine that filled the castle, decked out in all its glory for a season of entertaining. Even though his mother was long gone from them, his father had insisted on a sensational Christmas. If nothing else, they had agreed that it was good for their growing fortune. He remembered the self-congratulatory toasts between he and his father when another investor had succumbed to their combined brilliance. How proud his father had seemed in those moments, and how desperately he'd wanted to please him.

Now he knew. It was all a lie.

And it was gone. All of it. The glittering life, the belonging to a world of privilege and respect, the envy of most everyone around him. In an instant of cold awakening, Drake realized he'd reveled in their envy, thinking himself so much better than most of his acquaintances. Sickened, the razor suspended midair, he stared at the hollow-cheeked man in the mirror.

"Art thou well, sir? Might I get thee a drink of water?"

Drake struggled to bring himself back into the room with Mercy. Back to his new reality. "What a delightful family you have," he said, but all the lightness was gone from his voice. He wiped off the last of the soap and studied his reflection in the small hand mirror. Who was this strained and thin creature peering back at him? He feared he no longer knew. But he didn't like him. He looked weak . . .

Drake scowled at the pathetic reflection.

Mercy's eyes grew as round as an owl's. With a little screech, she fled the room.

Drake called out to her to apologize, but it was too late. *Pull yourself together, man! No sense frightening little children with your foul mood.* He was wiping the shaving supplies clean when Serena burst into the room.

"Good heav—" She froze, staring at him. "I . . . um . . ." She swallowed hard. "I heard Mercy scream."

Drake shrugged. "Must have been my face. I do not think she liked it."

"I cannot see why not." Serena looked down and blushed again, but she didn't run away this time.

"I'm afraid I can." Drake answered back, hoping, wishing she would come into the room and talk to him, chase away these demons that haunted him.

Serena's surprise shone in those wide eyes. "Thou must know."

Drake motioned for her to come into the room. "Know what?"

Serena didn't come any closer, but she did clasp her hands together and say to him, in her musical, lilting voice, "That thou art truly fearfully and wonderfully made."

She left him then. Left him alone. But her words rang about the room—an entreaty, a proclamation, full and alive with hope. Drake smiled and let loose a shaky laugh. Once again, this woman, Serena Winter, a plain Quaker woman, had brought light to his heart.

Maybe . . . in this strange new world, she would prove his salvation.

Chapter Eight

What dost thou suppose he will think of meeting?"

Serena shushed Mary Ann, grateful her sister had whispered the question in her ear as the family rode in a wagon south along Second Street past Elfreth's Alley where their father's shop was located, toward the meetinghouse on Arch Street.

She glanced at the man in question from beneath her lashes. He was sitting on a rough wooden bench across from them looking big, vastly overdressed and out of place between her two youngest sisters. Just looking at him made her heartbeat double. "I do not know. He must think us odd."

Mary Ann giggled, gaining the attention of those piercing, blue-gray eyes.

Serena inhaled as his gaze locked on hers and his voice, rich with amusement, asked, "Is there something I may assist you with, ladies?" One eyebrow rose as he stared down his nose at them.

Mary Ann giggled unrepentantly, while Serena turned pink. Clearing her throat, she managed. "We were wondering what thou might think of our meetings."

Drake offered a brief smile and indolent shrug. Gad, the man was like a conceited blueblood! He reminded Serena of Lord Tinsley, one of her father's most affluent customers. Except Lord Tinsley never made Serena's blood pool and race, pool and race, in a repetitive cycle that left her dizzy as did this Englishman. How Serena wished she knew his secrets.

"I have never been to a meeting of the Friends, but of course I have heard of them and your founder, the famous George Fox. It should prove interesting."

Serena chanced to see her mother's shoulders shake in what could only be suppressed laughter and restrained her own smile. "I hope thou wilt enter into it with an open mind, sir." Her voice was huskier than she liked with her family listening.

"Of course. A mind of studious and open intent." He mocked her, his white teeth set in a patronizing smile.

Serena shook her head. "Oh, but thou must not *study* the meeting. Thou must just experience it."

Drake laughed. "A woman's advice, to be sure." He turned toward the front of the wagon and her father's back. "Mr. Winter, do you agree that a man of intelligence and of an analytical bent should lay all mental discernment aside and use emotions to judge such an event?"

Drake waited, a pleasant expression on his face, as the rest of the family held their breath in the wake of his challenge.

Serena's father considered for a long moment and then said simply, "If it is possible. Sometimes the heart feels what the mind cannot comprehend."

The family smiled, Serena's heart bursting with joy.

Drake frowned. "Ah, the heart. And what if the heart is cold . . . stone even." His voice was level and dead.

Serena's father turned and stared at Drake. "Blessed are the *pure* in heart, for they shall see God." He paused again, letting it sink into all of them. "And how might a hard heart become pure? Hearts can be broken and softened, with trials . . . and love." Her father turned to look at them, his gaze resting briefly, thoughtfully, on Serena's upturned face, and then he turned back, lightly slapping the reigns.

Serena looked down into her lap, cheeks burning. She couldn't look at him, not after what her father just implied. Why had he done it? Her parents would hardly sanction a union between her and the dark stranger now living with them.

When they reached the wide, windswept yard of the meetinghouse, Serena stood from her wagon seat, gathering her coat around her, eyes still glued to the gray floorboards of the wagon. She was about to climb over the edge and jump down as she always did when a long-fingered hand reached into her line of sight. Looking up into his eyes, she couldn't help the answering smile while she put her hand in his elegantly gloved one as he helped her down. He then offered his arm and she took it, though she knew it was wrong, that it would give rise to all sorts of questions from the Friends.

WHAT WAS THE girl's father implying? Was he offering him his daughter? He had nothing to give her. The irony stabbed at Drake. It was the first time he could ever remember wishing to shower a woman with everything the earth had to offer, and he had nothing. He'd showered many women with the desires of their hearts, but it had always meant little to him. Just a means to an end, and a happiness from them that would last a moment—a moment he'd known would come and took full advantage of.

As he and Serena walked toward the door to the church, he breathed in the crisp winter day and imagined Serena in a duchess's finery. A satin ball gown in green, to match her eyes. Jewels hanging from her ears and around her neck, dipping into the ivory hollow of her throat. White silken gloves that reached just above her elbows where the tender flesh of her upper arm would be bare until the slender lace of a sleeve began. With her hair artfully arranged and just a touch of pink on her lips . . . she would be devastating. And she had no idea, no idea the power she could wield. He pictured her dancing, close in his arms, whirling to the violins in one of the many grand ballrooms of his world.

Glancing at the top of her head, neatly covered by an unadorned mop cap, he smiled, internally shaking his head at himself. Even had he the riches, she would likely scorn such trappings as sinful. He sighed. Perhaps they were. They hadn't done *him* much good.

The entry to the meetinghouse was barren, leading to a large square room. There were rows of wooden pews on all sides facing the center. Everything was brown, none of the splendid color of the Church of England. None of the stained glass, the holy relics, the statues, the altars with their gleaming gold and silver utensils and velvet cloth. No solemn, rich priest to stand before them like a demigod. Here there were only beams of dusty sunlight streaming from plain rectangular windows. A dull, weathered floor echoed with a hollow sound as they walked, arm in arm, to their place.

Like their home and work, these Quakers were austere in their worship.

"Thou wilt sit on the men's side, with father," Serena whispered before unclasping his arm and moving away. He watched her graceful, flowing stride as she left him, and felt the warm place where her hand had rested on his forearm growing quickly cold. Josiah Winter clapped him on the shoulder and motioned for him to follow.

The seats were less than comfortable, but Drake supposed that kept them awake, at any rate. He watched as the congregation filtered in. Like solemn brown sparrows alighting on an equally brown branch, they blended in with their surroundings. Men and boys to one side, women and girls to the other. He waited, while they settled themselves, for the service to begin.

It finally dawned on him as they closed their eyes, some bowing heads showing tanned necks, that no one was going to speak. Drake closed his eyes. The minutes ticked by. *Tick . . tick . . . tick . . .* He could almost hear a clock in his mind. He forced himself to relax, took a long, silent breath as his shoulders gradually loosened. His breathing lengthened, his heart slowed, and he suddenly realized that it was peaceful here. It was like a thickness had settled in the air and then rested on him. He inhaled deeply, filling his lungs with its still calm. His mind cleared of all else. His astonishment was only eclipsed by the inability to feel anything more than this sense of overwhelming peace. The minutes ticked quickly now.

Into the quiet a voice spoke. So in tune with the serenity was the voice that Drake didn't know if it was human or in his mind, but he listened as though it held great import.

"To everything there is a time. A time to mourn and a time to laugh. A time to sing and a time to cry. A time to give thanks and a time to know thanksgiving. To each life a season for all things to be revealed. Give thanks and know the peace of thanksgiving in all things."

Drake waited with bated breath for more. He wanted answers. He wanted ease from this constant confused pain that gripped him. Maybe here, among these people, he would find something he sought. But there was no more. The person sat down, leaving Drake to meditate on what the speaker had said. The Ecclesiastic feel to the words was familiar; mayhap he'd heard it at a funeral, some long-ago acquaintance that barely registered on the important business of his life. But the end, about thanksgiving . . . he didn't know that. Did it bring peace to be thankful in all seasons? Was that the message?

Drake wasn't sure, but the remainder of the hour went surprisingly quick. At some hidden signal they all stood and shook hands with each other. Drake nodded to several men as Josiah introduced him. Looking around, he now recognized a few others from onboard the ship. They, too, must have been rescued by these Quakers.

At Josiah's urging, Drake followed the men into another, smaller room. There, laid out before them, was a long table loaded with covered dishes. Mary Ann passed by him and dimpled prettily. "Now, 'tis time to eat."

As she sailed by to help her mother, he joined the line that formed, answering those questions he could from the men around him, but all the while looking . . . feeling . . . for Serena.

He found her ladling something from a steaming pot into a bowl. She looked up, her eyes finding his, and then smiled at him, the connection like a thing of old, like something they'd been born to. Drake felt himself melt in the warmth that was such a part of her.

"Drake . . . let me introduce a friend of mine. A botanist, Mr. Bartram."

Drake dragged his eyes from Serena's with difficulty. With a slight bow he directed his gaze at the man. "Mr. Bartram, a pleasure."

Mr. Bartram had a clear gaze that searched his. "I understand thou art recently from London?"

Drake nodded. "Northumberland, actually. But most recently, London."

"Ah. Northumberland. Beautiful land. Yes, well, I am looking for an apprentice for my studies in botany and was wondering if thou wouldst be interested in such a trade? I have a homestead just west of here with acres of forestland waiting to be explored. I find I do not have enough time to do all the work myself." He smiled, obviously pleased with himself.

Drake struggled with an appropriate response while the man continued.

"Forgive me, I presume much. Thou hast just recovered from what must have been a horrendous journey and an illness, I am told. But please, in our effort to help thee and thy fellow shipmates, is there a trade at which thou art skilled?"

A skill? Well, he *had* tripled his father's estate in business ventures, making him one of the wealthiest men in the world. But what could he tell this man? "I seem to have a head for numbers. I'm afraid, aside from some general knowledge in farming horticulture—" and the ownership and management of tens of thousands of acres of farmland, he added silently—"I know little about plants."

Drake hoped it would suffice. The mere suggestion of spending his days tromping through thick forests, identifying and cutting plants, sent genuine despair through him. He needed to take some hand in the cards fate had dealt him, so he continued doggedly while the line moved forward and men began filling their plates. "I was hoping for something in business."

Mr. Bartram nodded to Josiah. "Mayhap he can help thee then, Josiah." He grinned and confided to Drake, "'Tis an artist, your host. He complains often enough about the paperwork and calculations accompanying such a thriving business as his."

Drake looked at the gentle man beside him. He could work for this man. He could live in his house.

He could spend his free time with a woman named Serena.

As if he read Drake's mind, Josiah's brow knotted and he looked deep into the younger man's eyes.

The need to reach for a plate broke the uncomfortable moment. Attempting lightness, Drake asked, "What say you, Mr. Winter? Have you need of an apprentice?"

Josiah nodded. "Indeed, I have need of help in many areas. A man is rarely able to do everything with ease. Dost thou think thou couldst work with thy hands, also? I need someone to do the more simplistic work of a silversmith."

Drake thought of the shiny metal. He had only been intent to accumulate it, never to create with it. His attempts at drawing were mediocre at best and he abandoned the arts long ago for the more manly pursuits of hunting, swordplay, horseflesh, and gaming.

He had just reached Serena, with her steaming dipper of soup. He looked up into her eyes as he answered. "Truthfully, I have never attempted anything like it, sir." Still staring into her eyes he finished softly, "But I find I would like to try."

Serena knew Drake wasn't aware how high-handed he sounded, but Josiah and the botanist exchanged amused glances. It was obvious to all that Drake was used to giving orders, not taking them.

Serena handed him his bowl of stew and smiled up at him. "What wouldst thou like to try?"

The immediate response that rose to his lips made him suddenly clear his throat. Stopping the words from escaping, he said instead in clear resolve, "Silversmithing. Your father and I are discussing an apprenticeship in his shop."

Serena blinked several times and looked at her father, "That's . . . that is wonderful."

"It is settled then," her father said, focusing on Drake. "Thou wilt come with me to my shop, starting tomorrow morning."

Drake turned, looking down at the floor, a feeling of unreality filling him. He blew out a breath, quieting the chuckle that wanted to escape.

He was a shop boy now.

Chapter Nine

rake was awakened early, fed a fortifying breakfast, and then handed a simple, white linen shirt with crossties instead of buttons at the neck and dark leather breeches to wear. He wore his own boots and tied his hair, which had grown long enough to touch his shoulders, back from his face with a strip of leather. Mrs. Winter's eyes twinkled merrily as she waved them out the door, wishing them a good day.

Serena watched from an upstairs window, a wistful smile playing across her face.

Dawn hovered over the city as Drake and Josiah Winter walked along the brick-paved streets, their breath creating little puffs of vapor in the still crispness. Josiah walked with a purposeful stride and a quiet air that Drake was loath to disturb. Instead, in the light of the fading stars, he looked over what, when compared with London, was really an infant town.

It was surrounded by rough wilderness, but there was a neat pattern to the growing city. Philadelphia, Drake knew, was the brainchild of William Penn, also a Quaker. Penn had been pointed out to him many years ago in London when Drake was only a student at Eton. The man's sense of purpose was admirable, and Drake could now only respect Penn's city. The man's careful planning was obvious in the neatly arranged blocks that stretched out from the Delaware River. The waterfront made the town a thriving seaport. Drake remembered the typical squat buildings from his arrival: wood yards for fuel, shipyards for the boat builders and mast makers, and numerous sheds and storage warehouses. Further inland, the citizens had contributed a certain creative flair to the neatly quaint houses that lined the streets, mostly of brick or stone facade. There were the usual taverns, shops and churches, several churches. The meetinghouse they attended yesterday was situated on the southwest corner of Second and Market Streets, but it was one of many houses of worship.

They turned onto Elfreth's Alley, where the artisans must practice their trades. As in London, signs swung out from brackets over the walkways. While some were painted wooden signs, many were a replica of what the establishment offered. The barber had a pair of shears, the farrier a horseshoe, the shoemaker a wooden boot. Drake smiled to see that Josiah's shop had a silver plate hanging from its bracket. "Is the plate real silver? I would think you would fear it stolen."

Josiah smiled back at him. "As did Serena. 'Tis wooden, with a special silver paint she made. It has fooled and tempted a few, as I have replaced it four times."

They laughed together as they went into the dark shop. Josiah set about lighting a hurricane lamp and directed Drake in starting a fire in the forge.

Then Josiah showed him some of his work. There were spoons, ladles, snuffboxes, teapots, coffeepots, sugar bowls, and cream pitchers. Also, standing salts, caudle cups—for serving caudle, a spicy hot wine that Drake had yet to try—and in a special, velvet-lined box were all sorts of fancy silver buttons, buckles, and some jewelry.

Lastly, Josiah explained the silver trays with the customer's "cypher" on it. "When a man has accumulated enough silver coin to keep him awake at night, he has it turned into plate." Josiah turned it around so that Drake could see the inscription. "If it were stolen with his cypher on it, then the owner could easily identify it, should they catch the thief."

Drake chuckled. "For want of a bank, it would appear a sound method. And profitable for you." A thoughtful pause. "Have you considered branching off into banking?"

Josiah looked genuinely appalled. "I do well to keep my own accounts in order, young man." He shuddered, "'Tis a horror for me to think of keeping those belonging to others." He removed some tools from the cabinet. "But with such an idea, I can see thou truly dost have a head for numbers."

Josiah motioned him over to the long wooden worktable. "Let me show thee the tools."

Drake watched in appreciation of a man's skill as Josiah took his latest customer's silver coins and melted them in a crucible until it became a shimmering pool of molten metal, any dross burning off in the fire. Mesmerized, Drake watched Josiah pour the mass into an iron mold which, when hardened, would become an ingot of solid silver.

While the silver hardened in the mold, Josiah showed Drake the other molds. There were button and buckle molds, a lead block with a hollow in it for making spoons, molds for handles and feet and ornaments that could later be soldered on. Larger pieces, like the one he was making now, would be cast in sand using wax.

"Now we hammer it out," Josiah stated with satisfaction.

The silver had hardened into a small block. Josiah hefted a heavy sledge and began to beat on the ingot. *Wham! Whack!* The table shook with the force of the blows. It wasn't long before Josiah's forehead was dripping with sweat. He grinned at Drake as he passed the sledge over to him. "Want to give it a try?"

It was harder than it looked. Drake's first few blows had the block scooting all over the table. Patiently Josiah moved it back and showed him how to hold it and where to aim the blows. After a few minutes Drake could scarce catch his breath. Would he embarrass himself by giving up? Thankfully he managed to hammer out enough that Josiah took over.

"I want it a certain thickness," he explained. At noon, they stopped to eat their cold dinner, packed carefully into tin buckets by Mrs. Winter. The rest of the afternoon Drake watched, admiring Josiah's skill as the ingot of solid silver became a tea tray. It was rough, but the form was that of an artist. Drake knew enough about art to see the perfection in its proportions and shape.

"Tomorrow we will appliqué the fancy work."

Drake grinned at the man's enthusiasm. "I have the feeling you would like to stay the night and finish the project."

Josiah nodded. "In my younger days, I might have made such a mistake." He clapped Drake on the shoulder. "Time and experience has taught me to be home by six for my dinner."

DRAKE FOUGHT THE darkness, a gaping black pit of despair that opened on occasion, most times at night, right before he succumbed to sleep. Or during the night, coming alive in his dreams. Worst of all, though, was when it invaded in broad daylight, a place he thought safe. Regardless of timing, it always threatened to engulf him, to drag him under until he feared what would become of him if it overtook his will. Weeks had gone by, but it was all so useless! He had been working at the forge—sweat-dripping, head-jarring work that tested his physical strength while leaving his mind free to do the one thing he didn't want to do: think.

Were he at a desk, working with the comfort of numbers and schemes, there he would be confident, sure of a measure of worth. But here—behind this metal that blinded his eyes, this smoke that scorched first his nose then his lungs—here he was just a man struggling to turn molten metal into buttons for the wealthy.

And not very nice buttons at that. Drake scowled at the little round lumps of silver, raking the straggling hair that had come loose and hung in his eyes back into his queue. The brass mold should have made it simple. All he had to do was pour the silver into the mold and wait for it to harden. He had been hopeful all the way to the point of gently tapping them out onto the smooth worktable. The results stared back at him. Nearby mocked the examples Josiah had set out for him, perfect by any standard.

Drake wiped his blackened hands on his apron, resisting the urge to throw his latest attempts back into the fire—or better yet through the window at the condescending rich who made up most of Josiah's clientele. He ground his teeth together thinking how he had been one of them.

Just this morning a wealthy gentleman entered, just arrived from the mother country and prattling on about the land he was to control. Drake had surreptitiously eyed him from behind the huge bellows against the wall of the forge. Dressed in the height of London fashion, with white powdered periwig, bright red satin breeches, a red and gold-trimmed waistcoat, and high-heeled yellow shoes with silver buckles, he had commanded immediate attention.

Like a gaudy tropical bird among pigeons.

Lip curled, Drake watched him treat the noble Josiah with carefully metered distain. After working and living with Josiah these last weeks, Drake truly believed a better, more upright, honest man did not live. Drake itched for his previous power and position. What he wouldn't give to provide this sneering Englishman his due. The fool was only a baron! As a lion with a rodent, Drake would have toyed with the idiot until he had him reduced to a stuttering fool. Then, with the precision of a rapier thrust, he would have delivered the death blow. Something that would have really cost the fool.

Instead, he seethed with impotent fury. After the man placed his order and left, Josiah looked at Drake as if reading his very soul. "Be merciful, son. God esteems the humble. I would rather have the Maker's esteem over that of Lord Tinny."

Drake wanted to rail over the statement. Everything within him wanted to tell Josiah who he had been and how he could have bought this whole city if he'd wanted to, but instead he nodded, coming under the teaching of a truly great man, and silently meditating on Josiah, the kind of man he was and the things he said, the rest of the morning.

Josiah often said things that made little sense to Drake, but he recognized the greater purpose. It was so opposite from how he had been taught to think.

Josiah's voice broke into Drake's thoughts. "How are thy buttons coming along?"

He turned and, with a half smile, tried for humor. "Like buttons for drawers. Not to be seen on the outside, certainly."

Josiah chuckled and motioned him to the room in back. "But thou hast done wonders with my accounts. I think I made more profit last week than in the whole of the month before. Come, we will eat our dinner and then try again."

As they were eating they heard the tinkling of the little bell attached to a string on the door.

"Father?"

Drake's heart tripped at Serena's voice.

"Back here," Josiah answered.

Drake glanced down at his bare chest. The forge could be incredibly hot, and he had discarded his shirt long before. At least the leather apron he wore covered most of his chest.

Serena entered the room—then came to a sudden stop. Her eyes met Drake's, then dropped. They had had many such meetings in the last weeks. Quick moments of electricity that, for different reasons, neither one knew quite what to do with.

Her words came out in a gush of breath. "I brought thy dinner. Mother said thou forgottest it." She frowned at the laden table and then their full mouths. "*She* must have forgotten . . ." The amazement on Serena's features shifted to understanding, and she looked up at her father. "Mother is with child, is she not?"

Her father smiled and turned to Drake. "Leah has an excellent memory, except when expecting a babe." He winked at Serena. "Especially in the first three or four months, is that not right, daughter?"

Serena's smile was beautiful as she set down the basket. "Remember the time she left Mercy at the apothecary's shop while expecting Lidy?" She turned her enchanting smile on

Drake. "Mother was so horrified at what she had done, but when we finally found Mercy, the poor apothecary had stuffed her with candy to keep her from asking any more questions. He told mother he was sure she would come back for her eventually and that she had probably earned a much-needed rest from the girl's curiosity."

Josiah chuckled heartily at the memory while Serena continued.

"Mercy calls it one of her most exciting adventures and adds to the story every time 'tis told." Eyes bright with the memory, Serena turned to her father. "How far along? When will the baby come?"

Drake marveled at such excitement. With six girls, how could another mouth to feed be such welcome news?

"Thy mother says sometime this summer. July, I think." He paused, as if considering something, then changed the subject. "I need to see Mr. Jenkins, the blacksmith, concerning a project I am working on. Wouldst thou stay, Serena, and show Drake how to make buttons?" Turning to Drake he explained, "If she had the strength, she would make an excellent silversmith. When she was little, she would beg to come to work with me every day, one morning even showing up in my work pants and apron. Remember?" He smiled down at his daughter and gave her a quick kiss on the forehead.

Drake paused in taking the next bite. What it must have been like to have such a father-child relationship.

Josiah looked back at Drake. "With thy strength and her talent, I foresee wondrous buttons." Then in a lower voice for Drake's ears alone he teased, "Remember thy lessons in humility today. Thou mayest need them."

Drake looked at the open joy on Serena's face, so shining and alight, and thought that any lesson from one such as she would be welcome. But he raised one brow and said, "One must bear one's cross."

They both ignored Serena's puzzled look. Josiah patted Drake's shoulder and rose to leave, but offered one last, soft suggestion. "Bear it with thy shirt on, son."

To Serena he said, "If any customers come, Drake can enter their order. I've turned the books over to him."

Drake followed him out, then obediently put his shirt on, tying the apron over it before going back into the small room where Serena was busy clearing the table. He braced one hand on the upper frame of the door and leaned into his arm, stretching his aching shoulder muscles as he watched her work.

And fought the overwhelming urge to take her into his arms.

SERENA TOOK A deep breath. She could feel his eyes upon her, could feel the heat from his stare, making her clear her throat and search for something to say. Turning from her task she looked at him, struck by how male he was. Remembering what she had said in the hold of the ship about seeing him fattened up, she smiled. She'd been right. It was a glorious sight.

At the forward thought, she cast her eyes down. The image of him, though, burned in her mind's eye. In the past few weeks the combination of her mother's cooking and the exercise of the forge had given him a new body. Wide, muscled shoulders, substantially defined upper arms, and a new thickness to his chest had caused her mother to ask Serena to make him a new shirt.

Working on it had been pure pleasure. She didn't understand why. She barely liked sewing, but just the thought of that shirt lying on his skin after being made by her hands . . . well, it made her struggle over each poke of the needle, wanting it to be perfect. With a shaky breath, she lifted her gaze back to his. "I see thou wilt be needing another shirt soon. Father's never last long with such work."

"Your father told me to put it back on."

Serena nodded, turned, and began repacking the basket with leftovers. Brisk activity was always diverting. Smiling over her shoulder at him she grinned. "I know."

He walked closer, leaning over her to reach a dish she'd missed. She straightened to get out of his way and succeeded only in slamming into the solidness of his chest. Serena turned her head and looked up into Drake's face . . .

They both froze.

SERENA'S FATHER TRUSTED him alone with her.

That single thought warred with the intense desire to kiss her. With her face just inches from his, he drank in the creamy skin, the green and brown flecks in her eyes, the golden brows, the soft, pink lips. Just one brush of her lips, he told himself, would quench this growing thirst for her.

He knew it wasn't true, that one kiss usually led to wanting more and more. But he couldn't seem to help himself. Every muscle strained to grasp her to him. His imagination replayed what it would look like to see her fiery hair down and around her shoulders, and even though he was supposed to be the one world-wise and self-controlled, he felt as eager as a young man with his first love. He'd never longed for a woman the way he longed for her.

"Serena," he whispered as he bent toward her. How he loved the sound of her name.

She turned, wide-eyed, but with acquiescence evident in the way she strained toward him.

He lowered his head, keeping his gaze locked to hers, anticipating the rush of her breath when she finally released it. Her lips were soft, hesitant and compliant, wanting to follow and learn. Her breath was sweet. It was heady, teaching such innocence.

He had not known such sweetness existed.

She seemed entirely willing to go where he led her. Her movements matching his, her hands sliding up his chest to rest on his shoulders. He groaned, eyes shut, splitting in half with desire and guilt, trying to hold on to the reasons they must stop.

He broke free from the kiss, but then, instead of backing away as he'd planned, his lips moved to pepper kisses along the side of her neck and throat. Her blouse didn't have any buttons . . . ah, the Quakers, maybe they had the right idea after all. He pulled the top bow slowly, unable to think beyond wanting to see more of her in the dusty sunlight.

Suddenly, she reared back, gasping, staring at him wide-eyed. "Thou mustn't . . . *we* mustn't!" She dragged in a long breath and stepped away from him. "Please, forgive me."

Drake's mind and body rolled with the turmoil so that he didn't at first comprehend. Was she taking the blame? Shaking his head he looked at the floor. What a fool, trying to make love to a saint. He would burn in the abyss for certain now.

"No, Serena, it's my fault. I beg your pardon."

He looked up to see her reaction and caught his breath. She was just so beautiful. He had never seen her blush so thoroughly, but her eyes were steady and remained fixed on his. Such a mix of innocence and passion.

In a rush she turned them to another direction. "Art thou ready for thy button lesson?"

SERENA ESCAPED TO the workroom. With more energy than needed, she stoked the fire with the bellows until it roared, much like the turmoil within her. She took scraps of silver and placed them into the iron skillet and then into the heat of the forge. It was calming to focus on the beautiful silver, watching it become a puddle of liquid metal. It shimmered and shone in the light of the fire, showing all the shades of black and gray and white as it changed. It seemed a living thing and, as always, she was a little mesmerized by it.

She sensed Drake coming up behind her. "Is it not beautiful?"

Drake peered into the fire, a look of perplexity on his face. "I want it to be."

She could feel his inner turmoil, the confused need to make everything fit. "Thou art not happy here." It was a simple truth. She turned, searching his face. "Dost thou wish to be back home?"

He started to speak and then stopped, shook his head and looked into the fire. "You could not possibly understand. I am not the man you think me, Serena."

"I may not understand, but I can try. I want to know—" she put her hand on her heart—"here. I do not know why, but I . . . feel thy anguish."

"I certainly hope that is not true."

His tone caused tears to well in her eyes. "Thou thinkest me foolish."

Drake came to her and took both of her hands in his. "No. No . . . I think you are sweet and lovely and enchanting and . . . very innocent."

She raised her chin and glared at him through her tears. "I'm not the saint thou thinkest I am."

He smiled. She doubted even he realized how natural that condescending, patronizing smile was to him. How it made her want to shake her fist in his face. Instead, she reached up on tiptoe and touched her lips to his, wanting more from him, but somehow knowing it would only come this way.

"Not a saint, eh?" He smiled against her mouth, and she pulled back, cheeks aflame. She hadn't gotten very far away before he caught her and gathered her up close into his arms, his lips claiming hers, the force of his will in the kiss.

She was swept away as before, but this time she felt the thoughts of right or wrong slipping, drowned in their heat. All her reasoning why she could not fall in love with him faded as she lost herself, floating on the sensation of his mouth against hers.

Minutes passed . . . exploring minutes . . . discovering minutes.

Time stood still, and yet it seemed so short when he pulled suddenly away and gasped out, "My God!"

These words were no curse. They were more a prayer.

Suddenly Drake laughed, and Serena's spirit soared that she had caused him such joy as that sound carried. She had banished the ghosts in his eyes, if only for a little while. He smiled, and it was one Serena had not yet seen—pure and real—not meant to mean anything different than what it was.

"What magic you weave. You always pull me out of the darkness."

A chill went down her spine. While she reveled in his words, she knew something was not as it should be. She could never be his savior. But how could she say so aloud? How could she break this spell that bound them, even with the truth?

She looked at her hands. "Shall we make buttons?"

"We should most assuredly make buttons."

They turned back to the silver, and Serena saw that it had become a liquid puddle in the middle of the skillet, the impurities burned away. She focused on the task as she showed Drake how to fill the molds. "Thou madest them too full before, 'tis all." She compared his earlier work with the perfect ones she'd made, setting them side by side on the worktable and leaning over them.

Looking up at him, a wisp of hair tickling her forehead, escaping her cap, she nodded toward the buttons.

"Thou hast done much greater things than this, I think. Thou mayest learn this art . . . but even if thou never does, I know thou art worthy . . . of so much." She teared up, not able to keep her convictions buried in her heart where they belonged.

Drake exhaled, looked up to the ceiling of the shop and then back at her. "How did I find you?"

DRAKE DRANK IN her presence, his hand reaching toward her. Her body came flush with his chest, as if a mooring place. He breathed the scent of her hair. He reveled in the feel of her comfort. With her he no longer felt like a worthless man trying to do something he couldn't. With her in his arms, anything was possible, even a happy life as a silversmith.

Her talent was obvious. He leaned toward her ear, clasping her close. "*You* should be your father's apprentice. It is obvious you love this work."

She reared back and smiled up at him. "Were I a man, there would be no question. As it is, I am not able to truly learn the trade, though I spend as much time here as I can. My father is lenient and suffers my company without complaint."

"He would do better with your company. You are more suited to this work than I."

"Is it terribly trying to learn? I know my father would not want thee apprenticed to something thou art not able to do."

"I am not so confident of that," he murmured. "I think your father has other lessons in mind for me. Besides, I have signed on for the next two years. It is a short term, I know."

Serena shook her head with a breathtakingly sweet smile. "My father will take very good care of thee."

"His motives are pure, of that I will agree. Now—" he peered over her shoulder at the molds—"have these hardened sufficiently to let them loose?"

Serena laughed, taking his hand and leading him to the table. "Never hurry the process, dear one. Let us remelt thy buttons and make spoons whilst we wait."

He doubted she even realized she had used the endearment, but it warmed him like a blaze of light in this pit of darkness where he stood.

Serena. This serene woman. She made him feel . . .

Like he wasn't alone anymore.

Chapter Ten

It was Sunday again and meeting time. Drake was never asked if he wanted to attend; it was assumed that he did—or at least, he supposed, that he would. And it *was* peaceful. He had adjusted to the long silences, had disciplined his body to sit still and straight on the hard wooden bench for exactly one hour. He was even intrigued by the softly spoken "testimonies" occasionally given. The words always had a ring of truth behind them that resonated with something inside him. But he didn't understand some of the other aspects of their religion.

And most of all, no matter how welcoming they had been, he never felt like he belonged. He was too strong, too colorful against their plain quietness. Too old and too world-weary for their simple sweetness. He'd eaten from the tree of knowledge of good and evil too many times to go back and pretend a simplicity he didn't feel. And yet he felt pursued—not by anyone he could see, but by a feeling that there was someone he couldn't see in the quiet meeting room with them all. Someone who knew him, knew everything about him, and still wanted him.

Often at night, as he lay in his bed, when his body wasn't so exhausted by the day's work that he fell into an immediate sleep, he gave way to the cynicism over the ironic twist God or fate had dealt him. This world he now found himself in could not be more opposite to the one he'd known all his life. Yet it had so much to teach him. He wasn't always sure what or exactly how . . . but he knew he was changing, like his old skin was being molted off and a new, more tender skin emerging. A skin that felt everything with keen awareness.

The only thing he knew with any certainty was that all his inner wrestling ceased when he was with Serena. With her, he was able to believe that life had meaning. With her, the haunting ghosts dissipated.

The meeting ended and Drake stood and stretched, much as the other men beside him. He had met many of these Quakers and had they been fighting men he would have welcomed any of them at his back, so completely loyal and honest they were. But they were not fighting men, would never raise arms for their country or their brother, which was another of the many mysteries he found himself thinking on.

Today a new fellow he had never seen before had joined them. Tall and lean, with straight white-blond hair that was long and combed back from a broad forehead. His piercing blue eyes had locked onto Drake's upon meeting. Drake read both intelligence and a questioning assessment in them. Nodding to the man now, Drake turned and followed Josiah into the fellowship hall where they had their weekly pitch-in.

Serena's laugh startled him, causing him to turn sharply. He had only heard her laugh like that with him, but there she stood, with the man he'd noticed, her hand on his sleeve in an old and familiar way.

"Christopher Kingsley," Josiah supplied from behind his shoulder.

The man was always reading his mind, and it was disconcerting. He had always prized himself on his ability to be aloof and unreadable. "Who is he?" Drake knew his voice held the tone of a jealous suitor, but there was no sense hiding it from Josiah.

"A farmer. Lives in the Shenandoah Valley of Virginia. His parents came over from Germany with a land grant in the valley, but died before reaching it. Christopher inherited the grant and settled there. He comes to Philadelphia once a quarter to take care of business matters."

"That's not the only reason he comes, is it?"

Serena smiled up into the man's face, and Drake felt it all the way down to his stomach. Jealousy, he decided, was a wretched feeling.

"Thou seest the truth of it."

"And what does her father think of the good farmer?" The sneer behind the word *farmer* cast Drake in a bad light he knew, but it came out nonetheless.

"He is a good man. A man of our faith and a man she has known for many years. I think he would make her . . . content."

Drake turned to Josiah, eyes wide. Serena's father so rarely sounded unsure of anything he said that it came as a shock that he might not be certain of this. "But not ecstatically happy, perhaps?"

Josiah sighed and for a moment looked older than his forty-some years. "A challenged life," he hesitated, "can be more rewarding than a contented one. But a parent is loath to see a child endure suffering. 'Twould be a sacrifice."

He looked into Josiah's eyes, understanding jolting through him. "I would never hurt her."

"Until thou art well settled within thyself, thou wouldst. Even whole, I think so."

Anger filled him, had him blowing air through his clamped teeth. Drake looked over at Serena, saw the way her dusky green eyes glowed as she spoke, the way she gestured with her hands . . . all so known to him, so beloved. He looked back at Josiah, his voice low and harsh. "You wrong me, sir. She is . . . she is all that is light to me. Do you understand? She is the only hope I have." It sounded pitiful. His eyes almost swam with the emotion of it. Here, in this crowded room, with strangers possibly looking on, he had come as close to declaring what lurked in his heart as he ever would.

Josiah's eyes did fill with tears. "She can help thee, son. But thou must seek deeper and further for Truth. Only the One who made thee knows how to fill thee. Serena will fail if thou puttest her in that place." Josiah's eyes blazed with certain truth.

Drake couldn't endure the intensity. He had to get out of there! He spun and headed for the door. Serena tried to stop him as he swept passed her, but he shrugged her off as he tore out of the room.

Air . . . he needed the fresh, cold air so that he could feel his lungs and rid himself of this sensation that he couldn't breathe. Taking great gulping breaths, the fog of it surrounding him, he stood outside in the yard of the meetinghouse and forced himself to calm down. When his heart slowed, he started walking.

He walked the streets of Philadelphia, seeing and yet not seeing the largest city in the colonies for an hour or more, trying to outpace the haunting words that he would not, could not examine too closely.

He walked along the shore of the Delaware River and marveled what man could do in a few short years. Where once there

was wilderness and Indian camps, now giant ships moored, swaying majestically at the docks. Warehouses and shipyards lined the
shore. Neat and freshly painted houses and shops filled the streets,
sitting like little jewels in the crown that was Philadelphia.
Finally, he found himself in an alley looking up at a sign that
made him laugh despite the heaviness of his heart. *Man Full of
Trouble* tavern, complete with a sign of a man carrying his wife
piggyback. Shrugging, he went in.

He couldn't ask for a place more fitting to his current mood.

Inside the brick building was a semi-dark room, with crude
wooden tables and chairs. A long bar ran along one end, but
Drake choose a quiet table in a back corner. Josiah had been
paying him a small wage aside from room and board, and Drake
was glad he had brought some money with him.

It wasn't long before the man behind the counter came over
and asked in a friendly voice, "What might ye be havin' sir?"

Drake ordered an ale, counting out the coins in his pocket.
It was strange, having to concern himself with the amount of
coin on his person. Never in his life had he had to be frugal.
Now . . . he could soon run out.

Halfway through the brew the door burst open to admit a
tall, red-headed man. Drake barely glanced up, so deep in morbid
thought, until he heard the booming voice. "Drake Winslow? Is
it you, then, man?"

Drake looked up into the face of Daniel McLaughlin, the
Scotsman and his one friend from the voyage over. He stood and
shook Daniel's hand, getting a hearty clap on the shoulder in
response.

"Daniel, I didn't expect to see you again. How are you?"

The Scot sat down and motioned for a drink from the bar-
keep. Lowering his voice, he leaned in. "I have a tale for your ears,

the likes of which you willna soon forget." He grinned from ear to ear. "But first, where did you end up? If you don't mind my sayin' it, I thought you might be too far gone by the time we reached the shore, and that's the God's honest truth of it." He motioned at Drake. "But you look fit!"

"I am, thanks to an angel of mercy. She nursed me back, but I have yet to decide whether to thank her." Drake gave him a self-deprecating grin.

"Sounds like love to me. What's her name?"

"Serena Winter. A Quaker, if you can believe that. Her father has taken me on as a silversmith apprentice. I'm currently residing with them."

Daniel whistled low. "You had better luck than most of those poor souls we traveled with. Have you heard anything of the others?"

Drake shook his head. "Just the few who were sick in the hold with me. The Quaker families have provided for them as well. Come now, what happened to you?"

Daniel grinned lopsidedly and leaned in. "Actually, I've been looking for you. I believe I have something that is yours, my friend."

"What's that?"

"A medium-sized brown trunk."

Drake sat up eagerly. "Does it have money in it? About four hundred pounds?"

Daniel whistled again. "I knew there was more to you than met the eye." He shook his head. "Sorry to say it dinna come into my possession with money in it, but—" he dug into a pocket and pulled out a heavy, gold signet ring—"I'm betting this is yours, is it not?"

Drake's fingers wrapped around the ring, gripping it, afraid to look at it. "Yes. Tell me everything, Daniel. I will hunt down the blackguards who robbed me."

Daniel settled back into his chair. "Well, we dinna all get the treatment a man such as yourself got in the hold thar, with a pretty lass hovering over you. The rest of us were herded up like cattle by the slave drivers."

Drake nodded. "Serena told me about them. A wretched business."

Daniel nodded and grinned. "Oh yes, wretched indeed, but I got my say in the end. There were four of them, big meaty, brainless sorts. I tried to pummel my way out on top deck of the ship, but they got the better of me. Divided us into four groups, they did. A Mr. Joseph Linney was my group's boss, which I don't mind telling you was a gift from heaven above."

Daniel laughed, taking a long pull from his cup and slapping his thigh.

"He drove us west of the city, farm to farm, through little towns and villages. This land is amazing, Drake, untouched and wild, just waiting for a man to tame. They drove us hard, though. We were getting weaker and hungry all the time—none of us looking our best and dinna he like it that way."

Drake shook his head in disgust.

"Like I said, he wasna too bright. I soon devised a way of looking a little mad, a condition that would worsen should any prospective employer come to look us over." Daniel struck a dumb face, one eye roving to and fro while the other looked glazed.

Drake laughed quietly.

"A little talent I picked up in my school days. Always sent the lasses running home with delightful screams."

"I'll bet it did." Drake interjecting, laughing despite the sorry tale.

"So, finally, it was down to just me and Mr. Linney. He was getting a mite put out with me and suspecting my game. He told me he would find the worst, most despicable job in the next town and just give me away as I wasna worth any more of his trouble. About that time, I noticed a fine trunk on the back of his horse. It looked familiar and I guessed it might be yours. So, being the crafty Scotsman that I am, I concocted a plan to steal it back and escape any plight the good Mr. Linney had for me.

Drake shook his head with a smile. "Would that it had been filled with not only my money, but the proceeds of all the indentures."

Daniel nodded. "I had hoped to find something to sustain me. When we stumbled into the next town, sure enough, as I hoped, we headed for the first tavern. I'm counting on Linney's powerful thirst for whiskey to aid me, you see? Once there, it wasna hard to goad him into trying to out drink me, and by the time night fell, the man could barely stagger across the street to the boardinghouse. I took the trunk under my arm and half carried him to his bed. Making like I was the slave driver and he the idiot indentured, I instructed the woman who owned the place to lock him in till midmorning as I wanted to sleep in."

Drake leaned back in his chair, laughter shaking him. "You didn't!"

"Aye, I must confess brilliance struck."

"And the landlady was, of course, charmed by your good looks and charming manners and believed you," Drake drawled out, shaking his head in admiration.

Daniel shrugged. "It wasna too difficult. Soon as I had my room, I quickly went through the trunk. When I found the ring, I knew it was yours. I don't know how Linney got ahold of it, but at the time I was glad. I did not think it could hurt my cause to borrow some of your belongings, and don't you own some fine things! It wasna too hard to act the spoiled Englishman on my trip back to Philadelphia. I kept my mouth shut, stared at everyone like an English blueblood—a gesture of which you are a master, if you don't mind my sayin'." He grinned. "It worked like a blessed charm. I had people scurrying to do my biddin' within a day of practice."

Drake frowned. "You didn't meet any other gentry and try to pass yourself off as me, did you?"

Daniel leaned in. "Nay, but come, man, tell me. Are you what that ring says you are. Are you an English nobleman, then?"

Drake shook his head. "No, Daniel. I was never more than an illegitimate boy who believed he would someday be a duke." A harsh crack of laughter escaped him. "But that's another long story and I want to hear the rest of yours. I am happy my belongings came to your aid. Pray continue."

Daniel took a long drink, wiping the foam from his upper lip with his sleeve. "I don't know as I could have done it without your fine belongings. I owe you, Drake, God's truth I do. And that's about the end of my tale. I made my way back here hoping to find work and you. Imagine my surprise to run into you here."

Drake looked at the ring, sliding it on his finger. It felt right, a familiar and comforting weight, but he knew it no longer belonged there. "We're both fortunate. Where are you staying?"

"Last night I slept in a barn. I'm down to my last shilling—" he nodded at his ale—"and drinking that."

"Here." Drake dug into his pocket and slid some coins across the table. "To get you through until you can find work. I might be able to help with that. The Friends are extremely well connected and have a soft heart toward the downtrodden. What sort of work would you like?"

Daniel shrugged. "Smithing don't sound bad. Do you like it?"

Drake raised one eyebrow as a harsh laugh escaped him. "It took me three weeks to learn how to make buttons. I'm afraid my skills lie elsewhere. But I will see what I can find for you." He stood up and drained his mug. "I need to be getting back soon, so let us quit this place. Take me to my trunk."

SERENA SUPPRESSED ANOTHER yawn, eyes watering. It was hard to concentrate on what Christopher had to say when she was so concerned about Drake. Where *was* he? Would he come back? Her father assured her Drake just needed a little time to himself. After all, they *had* kept him tight under their wing since they'd met. She couldn't blame him for wanting to be on his own, but still . . . what was he doing so late on a Sunday evening? And why had he rushed out and brushed her off so at meeting?"

"Serena? Didst thou hear me?"

Christopher's patient smile was belied by the concern weighing his features.

"I am sorry, Christopher. Thou hast caught me woolgathering. Please, go on."

"I was telling thee about my new barn. But then, I can see that thou art not very interested in such things. I apologize. It grows late. I should go?"

There was much in that question. They had been friends for a long time and Serena knew that one day, when Christopher felt his farm was ready to support her, he would ask her to become his wife. Looking into his startlingly blue eyes she realized Christopher had come to his own conclusions. He had already heard the story about Drake. Serena struggled with an honest response. Toying nervously with a fold in her skirt, she suddenly stilled her hands and took a deep breath. "I am sorry."

"Sorry? For what?"

"I–I have, of late . . . found myself unaccountably attached to my father's new apprentice. Pray—" she looked up at him, her brows drawing together—"believe me when I say I didn't mean for it to happen."

"He is not a Friend, Serena. Hast thou thought this through? Thou wouldst be excommunicated."

Serena had hardly dared dream of Drake asking her to marry him, but the excitement that rushed through her body at the thought of being his wife eclipsed all else. "I only know what I feel for him. I am sorry."

Christopher stood and raked his fingers through his hair. For a second, Serena saw him as others might—tall and lean and attractive, strong, sure and good. He would make someone a very good husband someday. "Perhaps I am dazzled by the unknown. Please, hold me in the Light."

Christopher did not look very happy with that speech, or her request to hold her in the Light, to pray for her. But he nodded quickly, put on his hat and said, sadness and levity bracing up his words, "Thou knowest where to find me if thou needst me for any reason, Serena." He reached out to touch her cheek, his thumb skimming the line of her jaw, his eyes pain-stricken, then turned and walked off the front porch to his buggy in the street.

She watched him go into the darkness, his shoulders set, back straight, and a bittersweet feeling assailed her. Was she making a mistake? She could call him back. He would marry her if she gave him the slightest indication that she returned his feelings. She watched with a sick feeling while he climbed into his buggy, but the words to call him back stuck in her throat as untruth.

As he rode away, Serena saw a dark form standing in the shadows of the old oak tree. Her heart gave a leap. It was Drake. Had he heard her? She took a step toward him.

"You should marry him." His voice was like the deep of the night—dark and velvety, filled with danger. She inhaled the thrill it evoked in her.

She continued her steps into the shadows, stood in front of him, and gazed up into his dear face. The wind blew through the giant old tree he was standing under, allowing the glow of the moon to reach his face only occasionally. It was a cold light, washing out all the color in the world, leaving them looking at each other in shades of gray, casting the sharp planes of Drake's cheekbones into harsh relief, making him seem a creature of the night and more dangerous than she'd ever seen him look.

The coldness of the light reached his eyes, sending a shiver up her spine. Why would he look at her so when all she wanted was to smooth away the stark set of his features and see him give her that melting smile. Instead she replied, "Yes, I should . . . but I do not think I love him."

Drake's gaze roved her face like a whispered caress. "You are not sure?"

Serena tipped her head, longing to see past the shadows of his eyes. "I thought I might grow to love him . . . someday. I thought I *should* love him. I respect him."

"That is more than most marriages are based upon. You could do worse."

"I have said as much to myself many times, and even more of late."

"Why send him away then?"

Serena's gaze dropped to Drake's chest as she shook her head. She couldn't say it. Just the thought set her cheeks aflame.

"I know how you could tell for certain."

There was a wicked smile in his voice that sent another shaft of thrill through her. She shivered. "How?"

"Have you kissed him?"

She took a sudden indrawn breath. "No, of course not. W–why should I kiss him?"

He reached for her then, pulling her close, grasping her face between his palms. "Because if he cannot make you feel like this, then you will never love him."

She waited as his lips hovered over hers, the moon itself seeming to pause in its revolution looking down upon them with the stars in sudden interest. Serena wanted this—wanted him—with an intensity she hadn't dreamed she possessed. He held her captive with the black depths of his eyes. There lay a road to a place of sensual abandonment, but a way fraught with the rocky cliffs of uncertainty and adversity. Acceptance meant surrendering this life for the unknown. Dare she accept his challenge? Dare she throw her lot in with a man who was still, in so many ways, a dark and dangerous stranger?

His breath moved over her face, and she strained to reach him, to touch him. The relief when his lips finally touched hers was profound. Like the last time, she swam in a maelstrom of whirling emotions. Unfamiliar sounds came from her throat because of the force of his mouth as she gave free rein to the desire to press into him. She breathed him in, wanting to be as close as she could, clinging to his broad shoulders.

Suddenly he broke the contact. Hands gripping her arms, he gasped out a challenge. "Can he do that? Have you felt that with him?"

Her senses spinning, she tried to make sense of his words. "Who?"

Suddenly he was a savage stranger, giving her a shake. "Can he make you feel like that?"

Christopher. He was asking her about Christopher. Her breathless answer was immediate. "No . . . never . . . no."

Drake spun from her, walking in long, angry strides toward the back of the house. Serena put her hands to her hot cheeks, tears welling up in her eyes. Christopher would *never* make her feel as Drake did. Christopher never made her feel anything very much at all. But what of all her mother said? What of her life as a Quaker and brown-cloaked knights? Yes, Drake promised her much—not the least of which was a lifetime of such kisses. She could have it. Have him, a life with him. She only had to do one thing.

Give up everything.

Chapter Eleven

tanding in the moonlight alone, awash with feelings Drake had stirred to life, Serena found another new emotion coursing through her.

Anger. Pure, white-hot anger singed her heart.

How could Drake leave her like that? Alone with whirling emotions, with feelings that wanted to fly?

Whatever he was, whatever he proved to be. He would not get away with it!

With determined steps, Serena made her way to her old bedroom. She didn't stop to think—no more thinking—about anything. She turned the knob and walked into his room, shutting the door behind her with a soft click. She leaned against the solidness, her heart thudding in her chest so that she knew he must be able to hear it.

A shaft of moonlight spilled across the bed outlining his movements as he sat up. "Serena, is that you?"

She nodded, unable to move, and heard, more than saw, him get out of bed and slip into his pants.

"Come here." Though a whisper, his gentle voice commanded her.

She walked to him, her eyes adjusting enough to make out his frown.

"What are you doing here, Serena?"

She lifted her hand to his face, touched his cheek, running her thumb on the rough stubble of his jaw—then dropped her hand to her side. "Thou canst not just leave me like that."

He caught her hand in his, his gaze searching her eyes in the moonlight. "You cannot be here, love. Your parents are mere steps away."

"And deep asleep."

He chuckled deep and low. "Temptress. What did I do to deserve this test?"

She knew he wasn't asking her, which was good. For she had no answer for him. "I love thee, Drake." It was the hardest—and yet the easiest—four words she had ever spoken.

He groaned, dragging her into his arms. His chest came up against the wool of her plain, gray dress. "I fear I am forbidden fruit," he sighed into her hair. Her hands grasped him in answer.

"I would know such fruit. For always."

"Oh, sweetness, you know not what you are saying. It can be so dark here, with me."

"I'm not afraid."

Even as he gave up and kissed her, he murmured a warning. "You should be. You should be."

SHE WAS DRIVING him mad.

Drake pulled off the cap she always wore and threw it far into the darkness where it lay, glowing like a talisman. He unraveled her heavy hair from its knot. Long, more golden than red in the moonlight and to her waist, it swirled around them like a living thing, more glorious than he dared dream, silkier than he had imagined.

The light made the rose of her lips stand out, begging to be kissed. Drake could not resist the invitation. Just a few moments of this passion and then he would stop it as the madness it was and send her back to the attic with her sisters. Where she belonged. Safe from him.

He could not, much as he might want to, take Serena to the completion of this folly, most assuredly not in her parents' home. He would not betray Josiah's trust in him, even if, as he looked at this woman's ethereal beauty, it felt a slow death to deny them both.

But he knew she deserved so much more than an illicit affair. When the time was right, he would make it perfect for her. Somehow, he would make a perfect life for her.

He kissed her, letting his mouth linger over hers, then broke off the exquisite contact. "Tell me what you want from me, Serena."

She looked up at him, her gaze saying more than any string of words could.

"You love me?" He needed to know for certain that she understood what that would cost her. "More than anything?"

She pounded her fist on his chest, angry now. "Thou knowest I do!"

He cupped her head in his palms, running his fingers through the silky strands of hair. "You would give up this life? For a bondservant's?"

"Yes!"

He stopped her from trying to kiss him again, intent that she fully understand. "I have so little to offer." His thumbs caressed her cheeks as if to ease the roughness of his tone. "But I would freely give you what I have."

"I only want thee." Her breath was a soft whisper on his face. He allowed himself to be submersed in her, the feel of her skin so pliant under his searching fingertips, the soft sounds escaping her throat, the feel of her lips. His hands found the delicate bones at her collar, stroked the slim shoulders and then down her back.

He inhaled deeply, wanting to make this magical feeling last, so thoroughly did it chase away the blackness that engulfed him. His hands spanned her waist, outlining her ribs, feeling the rise and fall of her breath, feeling her delicacy and appreciating the form of a woman in a way he never had. So feminine and sweet.

"Like none other in all creation," he murmured into the curve of her neck. He felt her smile.

His lips had just found the hollow in her throat when the door burst open and light intruded upon the room. A sinking sensation brought him crashing back to the tiny bedroom. Serena was still too dazed to yet realize what had happened, but he knew the moment comprehension dawned. She stiffened and moved back from him, her hand to her mouth. He turned, ready to accept responsibility—and meet a father's righteous wrath.

At least he still had his pants on.

Her mother, mouth gaping, stared at the two of them. Her father looked like the grave.

"I see thou hast made thy choice." He directed this at Serena, apparently knowing his daughter's heart and the part she'd played in this scene. Before she could reply, he turned to Drake. "Thou wilt take responsibility in this."

Drake nodded. "Of course. We will be married."

Serena stepped forward. "It was my doing, Father. I came to him."

Leah stared at Drake, slowly shaking her head. "Do not marry her unless thou truly loveth her. We can forget tonight and find thee other work."

Drake knew what she wanted from him. A promise, a reassurance. This was a mother, a woman who knew what committed love looked like. "Have no fear, madam; I shall cherish her all of my days." Some of the old sarcasm had crept into his voice, but he wished it hadn't. He meant it to the best of his ability to believe it was possible.

Serena smiled into her mother's strained face, her happiness apparent in her shining eyes. "Thou must not worry."

Josiah sighed. "From the looks of things, we must make haste." He turned to his wife. "How soon can they be wed?"

Leah lifted her hand, the gesture hopeless. "We must seek a clearness committee concerning matters. Serena, upstairs with thee." She nodded to Drake. "Good night."

Drake bowed his head and realized he meant it out of deep respect, not to be perfunctory. "Good night, madam."

They closed the door taking the candle—and the light of his heart—with them. Drake turned toward his empty, rumpled bed, waiting for the despair to come . . . but it did not. Serena would be his wife! For better and worse, she would know him, the good and the evil.

For the first time in a long time, maybe ever, he prayed. A whispered plea in the darkness. "Do not let me hurt her. Please . . . God, do not let me hurt her."

AS SOON AS the girls had left the breakfast table the next morning, Josiah asked Drake the question that had kept him and

Leah up all night. "Drake, what feelings dost thou have for the Friends?"

Drake gave himself time to truly consider his answer. He did not want to respond lightly to what he knew was a serious inquiry. "I have the utmost regard and respect for them, sir. I have met few people in my life who are as kind, honest, and selfless as the Quakers I have met here in Philadelphia." He sat back in his chair and continued with feeling. "I have watched you help the poor, the sick, the destitute, the prisoner and the slave. I know firsthand your kindness and I know it saved my life. You live, instead of preach, what you believe. Living among you has given me . . . new sight." He smiled a little sadly. "I was brought up to believe the world owed me gratitude just for being born into it. In the short time that I have known you, sir, you have changed how I look at humanity. 'Tis no small thing, I assure you. And I am grateful for it." Nodding at Leah, he included her. "I must apologize for taking advantage of your trust in me last night. The responsibility lies solely with me."

"No, not thy fault alone, Drake." Serena put down her heavy silver spoon and looked to her father. "I went to him. He did not invite me there."

Her father nodded. "I am not surprised. Thy feelings have been clear to us for some time, Serena." He focused again on Drake. "I am glad for thy admiration for the Quakers. But I would like to ask thee an important question. The commitment is not a light one, and I would not voluntarily ask it except that my daughter loves thee. She has chosen to make thy life her own."

He glanced at Serena, a mist glistening in his eyes. "If thou shouldst choose a different life than that we have chosen, I fear, in the end, we will lose her. And so I ask thee, Drake, wouldst thou join the Society of Friends and embrace our life?"

Drake stared at the man that he would be honored to call father. A man he felt more respect for, in their brief acquaintance, than he'd ever felt for his own father. A man he wanted to please . . . but was destined to disappoint.

"I am sorry." He put as much sincerity into the words as he could. "I have thought about this, and find I am not ready to commit to a particular religious belief. I feel there are many unanswered questions that I must discover on my own, not by another's opinion or even most excellent example. But be assured in this. I will continue to seek out God. And I will not let the life I choose hurt Serena." Even as he said it he knew it was a promise that he should not make. How could anyone predict the future? His own had been so certain, and now look where he was . . . what he was.

With sudden clarity he realized he wasn't being fair or truthful with Serena. She didn't know him, all that he had done in his life. And he couldn't tell her. Would never tell her.

She didn't even know his real name.

Yet he was asking her to give up everything—her family, her friends, her way of life—for a stranger. He looked at her in concern. How could she still love him if she knew everything there was to know about him?

"Serena, I know my decision makes yours difficult, impossible perhaps. I will leave, find another situation, if that is what you wish."

Josiah reached out his hand across the table for Serena to grasp. "It will be hard. I wish I could take the excommunication for thee, but if thou choosest to marry an outsider, thou wilt be asked to leave the Society of Friends."

Serena grasped his hand, looking from her father to Drake, and then back at her father. "I . . ." She looked down. "I know."

Leah spoke up, her voice tight. "Josiah, they have spoken their convictions with truth. We cannot ask for more. Come, we will leave them alone to discuss it."

Serena's parents left the room and shut the door behind them. Drake stood and walked around the table. Taking the seat next to Serena, he took her hands into his and squeezed lightly. "Love, there are things you don't know about me. Things that might not please you."

She looked into his eyes. "I know there are secrets hidden in thy heart. I had hoped thou wouldst tell me." She gave him a wavering smile that melted his heart. "But I must say this: I would not force thee into marriage because of my recklessness last evening. Do not take me as thy wife out of duty."

Drake wavered. She was giving him a way out, and a part of him screamed that he should take it. Not for himself, but for her. What kind of life could he provide for her? "I am not a Quaker, Serena. Nor am I a silversmith. I am . . ."

"Yes?" Her eyes urged him to confide in her.

"I am a man between lives." He shook his head. "I feel I am without purpose really. I could take on your Quaker beliefs, but I know that would be wrong. I would wake up years from now and be miserable and perhaps even resentful. I cannot do that to either of us."

"Thou must not want me then." Her voice was flat. Her eyes full of pain.

"The only thing I know for certain is that I want you." He gripped her hands. "If it had not been for you, I wouldn't have survived the fever. Death was beckoning me and you came, you gave me hope. I owe you everything. But I have nothing to give you . . . except my body and the sane part of my mind. My heart and my soul, they are . . . shattered I fear, but they are yours also, if you want what is left."

Serena's face reflected all the innocent love she felt for him—and the confusion. "I want nothing more. But to leave the Friends . . . my family . . ."

Drake released her. "You must consider it all. *You* have to decide." He closed his eyes and kissed the top of her head, then rose. He allowed himself one last lingering look, taking in the way her neat, plain cap fit her head so well, then he left her there, alone.

It was the hardest thing he had ever done.

Chapter Twelve

erena watched him go, wanting nothing more at this moment of confused distress than to paint his tall form.

She rose and went upstairs to gather her paints, her thick canvas, and the wooden frame that she would stretch it over. The walk to the shore of the river seemed short, the grassy patch she always went to when she needed to be alone was easy to find and waiting for her, like a comfortable spot on the earth made just for her. She sank down, arranging her supplies just so. A flat, square board served as her palette.

She tilted her head to one side as she mixed her paints, enchanted as always with color, how it blended and changed into precisely the shade in her mind's eye. She knew just the shades she would use, even though she was still unsure of the subject. Sometimes it came to her like this, an explosion of color, of mood, but no real idea what to paint until she lifted the brush to begin. Today she would have blues, lots of blues, from robin's egg to deep sapphire. She mixed the paint, slowly adding purples and reds as they beckoned to her. A deep green. Some orange and several shades of bright yellow. And then brown. A big glop of brown in the middle of her board.

She gazed out at the river, its gray-green tones and the gray-blue of the sky . . . not right and painted so many times before. Turning from that, she looked at the buildings on the wharf, whites and blacks, stable and solid and so . . . man-made. No. Not today. Closing her eyes she beckoned her imagination . . . and saw Drake. Saw his face and then his back. With a sudden breath, she knew.

Taking up her brush, she began. It took shape quickly. Men's coats and women's skirts, all brown, all with their backs toward her, the backs of their heads showing some small color of skin under somber hats and bonnets. So much brown, she had to replace the glop on the pallet several times. Then came the black. Stark outlines surrounding the browns, so harsh and so hard, it was easy. It was known.

Cleaning her brush, she felt a lingering pulse of anger and wondered why and how it should be. She'd never felt anger toward the Friends before. Taking up the brush she dipped it into the richest hue of blue, the one screaming decadence. With small, delicate strokes she made another coat. Long, strong lines of color filled one side of the canvas. Purple, deep and bright, edged the blue, then some red, here and there, so loud against the other.

It was taking the shape of a man.

His face was unclear and she struggled, wanting to capture Drake, but unable to see how his face should be, what he might be feeling. She wanted his face to be as bright as the coat, but it wouldn't come. It was only a soft blur on the canvas . . . handsome . . . dark . . . but shrouded, half-turned away from her. She stared at it. Why couldn't he be everything she believed him to be? Bright, full of life, and loving her . . .

But it wasn't to be.

She set down her paints and tools and stood, leaving the work to dry in the wind. The breeze blew tendrils of her hair free of its cap, which she unpinned and tossed aside, letting her hair unravel and wrap around her. She contemplated the sky, watching as a thin cloud made its way eastward. She looked back at the painting . . . sat back down, reaching for the yellow.

The top of the canvas was bare, white and stark. She stared at it, deep in concentration, her brows knitted together. Her whole being strained, wanting this piece to be greater than anything she'd ever done. She wanted it to represent what she felt for God. "Help me!" Her cry was carried on the soft wind. "I want to capture Thee."

She closed her eyes as she did in meeting, coming at last to the place of peace. "Help me capture Thee."

Behind her closed lids she saw it. A sunrise, a new beginning. Yes! Taking up the yellow-drenched brush, she slashed it across the top of the canvas. "Bigger than the rest. Better than all of this!"

It started yellow and bright, as she thought it should be, but soon, she added the orange and then the red, turning the scene passionate. A sun, swirling and magnificent, a sky like none she'd ever seen, drenched in color. A horizon that ended in the purple, seeming to go on forever . . .

Suddenly spent, she sat back from the painting, staring at it. It was beautiful. The best work she'd ever done. It didn't matter if no other eyes but hers saw it, for she knew this wasn't her work alone.

"How great Thou art."

She stood, staring at the man in purple. "I love him. It shouldn't be so, but I do." She looked up into the sky, seeing a dim pink near the sun. "I have to love him."

She turned, leaving the painting at the shore to dry but picking up her precious paints that were so costly, and then walking toward home.

The walk home was strange, as if it might be her last along this path. She watched the dry grass flatten against the earth. She saw the street where she grew up, each pebble and stone, each wood and brick house. And a little cry rose to her throat knowing that home . . . was no longer her home.

THE NEXT DAY Drake didn't come to meeting. They had all silently agreed there was no longer any point to showing him their way. Serena rode in solemn silence with her sisters, her still-innocent sisters, who looked at her with big eyes, knowing some great heaviness weighed on their family but not understanding what caused it.

Serena donned her Sunday dress thinking this might be the last time she did. She smoothed down the gray skirt, tying the ribbons at her breast, pulling the cap down over her hair. She climbed into the gray wagon, faltering in her steps as her father looked gravely into her eyes, as her mother turned away to hide a face distressed. They had rode to the church, slower than usual it seemed, every blade of grass more green in the churchyard, every weathered board of the church building watching her, so real it hurt just looking at it. This would be one of those memories that would never fade.

Serena sat in her usual place on the hard bench, waiting, panting almost, in her apprehension that the painting hadn't been real, that God would speak to her and stop her from this thing she'd set her heart and mind to do. The meeting started as usual, all with closed eyes and opened hearts. Serena clenched her eyes tightly, her head tilting back, her throat exposed, wanting Him to stop her and yet, with a pounding heart so loud they must hear it, hoping He wouldn't. The minutes ticked by and slowly, she felt the discipline of letting her mind and emotions empty, of letting His presence replace the fear. A deep, all-encompassing peace filled her and she smiled.

I will never leave thee, nor forsake thee.

The thought shattered her, bringing quick tears to her closed eyes. It was the answer underneath all the questions. As sure as the sun in her painting had come to her. As sure as her love for Drake. This was her choice. A choice she would have to live with and all its consequences, but He would not leave her alone in the wake of life's decisions.

As she sat there pooling in the comfort of it, a voice spoke out. It took her a moment to realize it was one of the Friends and not her own mind.

"Dark is the path that leads to the understanding of good and evil. Take heed against it! Take heed against it!"

The voice rang out and echoed in the quiet of the place, but Serena could feel the heads lift, listening and nodding at the rebuke, taking heed. A darkness came over her. Had she heard wrong? Was it her own wicked heart telling her what she so desperately wanted to hear? Doubt engulfed her, her head bowed deeply until her chin rested on her chest. Which to believe? What should she believe? Her heart began to pound with fear and dread.

She saw her painting against the blackness of her closed eyes, saw the yellows stand out, becoming more and more alive, then suddenly it all faded.

All that was left was Christopher's face . . . and the brightness of his hair.

DRAKE WAS ON a mission.

Earlier in the week, while in a local shop buying supplies for Josiah's business, he'd heard the name he'd been subconsciously listening for wherever he went.

"Joseph Linney! That you, dearie?" A big man near him turned, his face breaking out into a grinning leer as he swung the woman into an embrace. She reminded Drake of the women found in the stews of London, gaudily dressed, with her bosom hanging mostly out of a sagging neckline.

Linney buried his scraggly beard into her neck, her giggling all the while. The shopkeeper cleared his throat in disapproval, causing the woman to playfully push Linney away, though still wearing a pleased smile. Linney ignored the owner and leaned forward to whisper something into her ear. She gave a gasp of delighted surprise and a quick nod.

Probably told her of his new, ill-gotten wealth, Drake thought, disgusted. He watched the pair from under the brim of his black hat, keeping them in sight as they paid for their purchases, then walked arm in arm out of the shop. Drake would have liked nothing better than to confront the man then and there, but he knew better than to be so foolish. Instead, he followed them.

It hadn't been difficult. Linney was more interested in the plump woman on his arm than in any seeming danger. They'd gone to a small house, a shack really, on a street Drake had never seen. It would seem that even in a William Penn town, poverty and the stench of poverty had found a place.

Drake watched, hidden by the corner of a building, while they entered. He needed to know if it was Linney's house or the woman's but was loath to wait until they finished their unsavory business. Josiah expected Drake back soon.

But luck smiled upon him, as a young lad of about ten years ran by. Drake called out to him, smiling. "Boy, a moment of your time."

The child looked startled and a little afraid.

Drake held out a silver coin, watching his face turn excited but still wary. He walked a little closer. "Yes, sir?"

"Who lives in that house?" Drake pointed to the house in question.

The boy followed the direction of Drake's arm and then scowled. "That's Mr. Linney, sir."

Drake had to wonder what atrocity Mr. Linney had done to deserve such a sullen tone in the boy's voice. "You're sure, then?"

"Oh yes, I'm sure. Been there for months." He spit to one side and then locked his gaze on the shimmering coin in the middle of Drake's palm.

Drake tossed it to him. "Thank you, boy. There might be other rewards of the same if you will keep an eye on the man. Just watch where he goes and what he does, you see?"

The boy nodded, squeezing the coin as though it might drop and be eaten by the dogs that roamed the street before he could get it back into his hand. He smiled up at Drake. "Thank you, sir, I will. But where will I find you to report his doings?"

"I'll find you. What's your name, lad?"

"Jimmy Bowman, sir. Glad to be of service." He grinned and bowed, a cheeky action that had Drake smiling back. "Have a care, then." Waving, Drake turned to leave.

All that day and into the next, he considered his course of action. Every day that went by would mean more of the money spent. With that surety dogging him, he'd managed to track down Daniel for reinforcements and to identify the man as the same Joseph Linney who was the slave driver.

Daniel was only too eager to help.

Now, with Serena and her family safely off to meeting, he could finish this business. Drake explained his plan to Daniel as they walked. "He should still be abed, giving us the element of surprise. Two against one, it shouldn't be difficult."

Daniel lifted the corner of his shirt revealing a black pistol. He winked at Drake with a grin. "Just in case."

Drake shook his head slightly. "Don't use it unless absolutely necessary. I just want my money back, not the man's death on my conscience."

Daniel gave him a sharp look, understanding lighting his eyes, he sighed. "Enough of them already, eh? I know, friend. I too, was in the army."

Drake nodded once, short and final. He let the subject drop. As they neared the street they slowed, edging closer to the buildings looking out at the quiet lane. It was still early for most of the street's inhabitants to be up and about, which was exactly as Drake had hoped. "Let's go."

The two crossed the mucky road, the smells of beef fat and waste disposed feet from their doorways made the street a sloth of stench. The door was a simple clapboard type that would be easy to crash through, but Drake preferred stealth.

He indicated the need for silence to Daniel, who nodded, ready to apply his shoulder to the wood. Drake reached out and tried the latch. Sure enough, it was unlocked. The door creaked as Drake eased it open. He and Daniel stood still and listened. No sound.

They could see there was another room at the back of the house. They picked their way across the main room to what Drake hoped was the bedchamber. That door was open a crack, giving view to the corner of a bed, a big foot sticking out from beneath the covers.

Drake smiled. "On three. One . . . two . . . three!"

They burst into the room, Daniel toward the foot of the bed, Drake at the head. The man didn't wake. Daniel nodded at the snoring form. "That'd be him all right. I'd recognize that face anywhere."

Daniel hadn't bothered to whisper, and Drake smiled as Linney frowned and moved in his sleep.

Daniel pointed. "Drake, on the bureau . . . is that your box? I remember seeing him take it out of your trunk; he was holding it like it was a newborn babe, he was."

Drake turned, strode over to the shabby furniture, and took up the elegant wooden box, so out of place in this room. He opened it, his heart sinking. Daniel left the foot of the bed and came over, peering around Drake's shoulder. "Anything left?"

Drake was shaking his head, about to reply that there was very little, when a creak came from the bed. Both men turned to find the huge Linney standing there naked, a wicked knife clutched in a meaty hand—and coming straight at them.

Chapter Thirteen

rake turned, the wooden box still clasped in one hand as the knife slashed toward his chest. He dodged, shocked to feel the blade catch his shoulder, the pain immediate and searing. He threw down the box, coins scattering like hailstones across the wood floor.

Daniel had recovered and dove toward the man, fisting him in the stomach. Linney's white, fat belly quivered as he let loose a roar of rage and a flow of curse words. He rounded on Daniel, and his eyes widened. "You!"

Drake took full advantage of the slave driver's momentary distraction, kicking out toward the man's knee, and was rewarded by hearing it snap. With a roar of pain and rage, Linney faltered, looking at the two of them as though trying to decide whom to attack with his knife.

A succession of quick jabs to the ribs, and then Linney's arm held and twisted, and Drake had the man disarmed, the knife skittering across the floor. Daniel proceeded to pound the man with a fist into his face and then another quick jab to his shoulder, spinning him toward Drake. Drake picked up with another punch in the huge man's face, snapping his neck back, but only momentarily.

They bounced him back and forth until they were all breathing hard and sweating. Finally Linney slipped on his stolen loot and fell to lie at Drake's feet. Drake placed a foot on the man's middle, while Daniel casually pulled out the pistol and trained it to his chest.

"Where is my money?" Drake bit out the words, pushing against the man's stomach, trying not to look at his body.

"I ain't got your money. Who are you, anyway?"

Daniel laughed at him. "He's an English lord, you fool. You've picked the wrong man to rob this time, Linney."

Drake went along with the dramatics. "Is this all of it? Have you spent it?"

Linney looked afraid for the first time since awakening. "I didn't know! I thought it was the captain's. I swear I did. Don't have me hanged for it, I beg you."

Drake backed away. "Put on some pants. Then collect every coin and return them to the box. Anything you've bought with it, too. Gather it up and let us have an accounting of your ill-gotten gains."

Linney scrambled to obey, eyeing the gun still held on him, shrugging into ill-fitting pants, then running about the room, scooping up coins and finding a few more on the bedside table. It was a pitiful amount.

"I can't gather up what I've spent it on," he admitted to Drake, unable to look Drake in the eye, holding out the box.

"Let me guess," Drake drawled out his disgust, "women and liquor."

Linney nodded. "Caught up on the rent, too. And some food, but we ate most of that."

Drake peered into the box. Not enough to sustain him and Serena for a month. He felt black rage try to overtake him, but he managed to fight it off. He'd been through worse, and some money was better than none.

His acceptance of his misfortune astounded him.

Still, he needed to deal with the thief. "Leave town and never return . . . or I *will* see you hang." Drake backed from the room.

Daniel gave the man one last shove, sending him to the floor. "That's for the women and children on the ship. You would be wise to abandon such a business."

Linney nodded. "Yes, sir. I'll be leavin' today. No more slave drivin', I swear."

With that unlikely promise, Daniel and Drake took their leave.

Daniel shook his head as they crossed the street. "I'm sorry it wasna more, Drake."

Drake tilted his head back, looked up into the sky, and sighed. "Me too, Daniel. Me too." He turned and grinned at his friend, clapping him on the shoulder. "But it's enough to buy you a decent dinner, eh? Thick steaks and enough ale to blot out the memory of a naked man with a knife."

Daniel laughed. "There's not enough ale in Philly to do that, man. I fear we're scarred for life."

Drake chuckled. "It was fun though, was it not? I haven't been in a fight in too long a time. I think I needed it." He paused, looking at his friend. "Thank you, Daniel. You're a good friend. I appreciate it more than you know."

Daniel shrugged. "Wasna anything. The sight of Linney though . . ." He shook his head and laughed again so hard he stopped walking, tears in his eyes. "That might be givin' me nightmares for years to come." After their laughter had died down, Daniel peered at Drake's injury. "But how's the shoulder?

My dinner can wait. You should get that cut cleaned up. Never know what the fool's been using his knife for."

Drake glanced at the shoulder. It had stopped bleeding but was aching like the devil. Daniel was right. He should have it looked to; infection was nothing to court. "Dinner tomorrow, then. At the same tavern we met at before? Man of Many Sorrows, wasn't it?"

Daniel nodded, then stopped. "I'd rather have an invitation to the Winters' house. Gainful employment . . . all those pretty daughters . . ."

Drake smiled. "I will see what I can do. But keep your hands off the pretty daughters. I've already gotten myself into some trouble in that arena."

Daniel's grin was wolfish. "Didja now? Not the nurse, was it? The angelic one that saved your sorry hide."

"Aye. The nurse. The angel. The temptress."

Daniel clasped him on the arm as they prepared to part ways on a street corner. "Go let your nurse patch you up then, Drake." He turned to go, waving his arm. "And win me a dinner with the telling of how brave I was."

Drake watched him go. Daniel was a good man. A good friend. It was a relief to be friends with someone without hidden motives, without the constant politicking. He suddenly realized Daniel was his closest friend next to Charles Blaine.

He'd known Blaine since childhood. Theirs was a friendship born of innocence, before either of them knew anything about power and wealth, only boyish pranks and mischief. Daniel was that kind of friend as well, and Drake was thankful. It was amazing. He was leaving with less than an eighth of his stolen money, he had a nasty gash on his right shoulder, and yet all he felt was the satisfaction of a grand adventure.

Truly, this had been one of his best days—and he wondered that it should be so.

SERENA HADN'T REALIZED how closely she'd been watching for Drake's return until she caught herself clinging to the front window, her heart lifting at the sight of his long stride coming down the lane. But something was wrong. He walked slower than usual and seemed to be breathing heavier. Serena ran out into the yard to meet him.

Alarm assailed her at the red stain on the bright white of his shirt. "Thou hast been hurt. What has happened?"

Drake came up to her, pulled her roughly into his arms and kissed her. He whispered against her lips. "A flesh wound is all. Will you patch it up, love?"

Serena reared back. "Thou wert fighting."

"Aye. A bit. But I've retrieved some of my gold." He held out a beautifully engraved wooden box. It was small but deep, with delicate carving on the lid. A hunting scene.

"What is it?"

"Do you remember when I asked you to find my trunk, while I was sick on board the ship? Well, I've recovered the trunk and some, a little, of the money."

"Someone stole it? And thou foughtest them to get it back?"

"My friend Daniel was with me and it was an easy conquest. Only my own foolishness won me a wounding."

"Let me see." Serena led the way to the back of the house and the separate building that was the kitchen.

Once inside the small, warm room, Drake leaned against the counter and pulled his shirt over his head. He winced as the sleeve pulled against the cut, then held it out for her to examine. "You wouldn't have any brandy, would you?"

Serena shook her head then stopped and thought a minute. "Wait here, I will go and get something from the neighbors. They will have something."

Drake watched her go, her straight spine intent with purpose, the back of her pale neck, slim and elegant, the white cap covering her glorious hair. He closed his eyes and thought of her hair all around her, like a living veil . . .

When she returned bearing a dark bottle, he had to clear his throat before he could speak. Her face was close as she grasped hold of his arm, then tilted the bottle with careful precision over the wound.

It burned, deep into his flesh, but he was so busy watching her face that he barely felt it.

Serena. How to describe her? He wanted to memorize this moment, knowing that they would change, hoping that they would grow old together but knowing that she would never look exactly this way again.

Her skin was ivory, with a rosy tint here and there, a flush on her forehead and cheeks and chin. Eyebrows like wings of reddish gold swooping out, giving her a regal mien when she was serious, and an elfish delight when she was happy and laughing. Her face was oval, her chin a little pointed, and her lips, her lips were the coral of a shell he'd seen once, thin with a delicate curve at the top of the upper lip. No dimples. No, she had lean cheeks and high cheekbones, a rather wide forehead accentuated by the scraping back of her hair to fit it all in the cap.

Suddenly she looked up at him. "What art thou doing, sir?"

Drake smiled, allowed all he felt for her to glow from his eyes. "I am remembering you just as you are now, so I'll have that picture in my mind for years to come."

She stared at him, a deep smile coming into her green eyes, happiness and something else that she'd recently learned—a flirtatious, admiring look—curving her lips. "I would like to do the same."

Drake offered a wicked grin for her answer. "Then you shall. Are you finished with that bandage?"

Serena nodded, looking shy and eager at the same time. She tied the two ends together, making a perfectly fitting bandage over the cut. "'Tis only a flesh wound and should heal in a few days." She washed her hands in a bowl of water, dried them on a muslin towel and then turned to face him, so unsure now, her hands loosely held behind her back, her head down.

"Come here, Serena."

She moved closer, then lifted her face to stare into his eyes.

"Look at me."

She took a deep breath, her hands still safely behind her back, her eyes roaming over his face. He felt himself flush, surprised that he could be embarrassed by something so simple as a woman's scrutiny. And yet, it was as powerful as anything he'd ever imagined.

He watched her study his hair, his eyebrows and forehead, his nose. He grinned then, unable to suppress it, knowing he had such an aristocratic nose, the nose of his Celtic ancestors. She smiled back, her breathing deeper now. Her gaze traveled across his cheeks like she was studying the hollows and planes of a map, then they stopped at his lips. Her lips curved into a slow smile as she took another deep breath.

Pressing her lips together she seemed to force her gaze lower, to his chin, studying the stubble as it grew in a thick patch down his throat. He truly hated shaving and only managed it every other day.

She didn't stop, as he thought she might, as he had. No, her study continued down to his shoulders and then his chest until he thought he might explode—

Serena backed up suddenly, eyes wide, cheeks flushed. "What art thou doing to me? What power dost thou have over my mind and heart?"

Drake shook his head. "It is the same for me, love. I am undone."

She stared into his eyes, so many emotions in those beautiful depths: fear . . . longing . . . tenderness . . . more fear. She swallowed hard, the slim column of her throat working. "I do not know what to do. I have painted it. I have gone to meeting and . . . I thought I knew, but . . ."

Drake wanted to take her into his arms and reassure her. He wanted, more than anything, to kiss her doubts away and tell her that everything would work out perfectly, but he couldn't. Only she could make this decision.

He pushed away from the counter, slipped his shirt over his head and walked toward the door. Turning, he gazed at her, standing there in the late afternoon sun. "I would give up everything to be with you, Serena."

It was the truth and that was the best thing he could give her.

He turned and walked away.

Chapter Fourteen

Serena stood at the back of the strange church, the reality of what she was doing chipping away at her happiness, causing the butterflies in the pit of her stomach to feel more like bouncing lead balls instead of a bride's wedding jitters.

There were few to witness their marriage. Gone were all the Birthright Friends that Serena had known since childhood, the foundation of her life. Gone was the guarded fence of her church, leaving her a colt, running free, seeing the world anew with wide, blinking eyes.

Her father had been required to explain their marriage to the Quakers at the monthly business meeting, and Serena hadn't needed to imagine their reactions. They had come, knocking at the Winters' door, shocked and dismayed, squawking at her like chickens whose eggs were snatched away.

At night, lying next to her sister's warm and familiar body, the naysayers' voices rattled about in her dreams, causing her to toss and turn, knowing that little by little the life she'd always known was slipping away. Her mother had finally told them that Serena had heard enough. It was decided. She would be "read out of meeting" and banished. The weight, like a heavy blanket thrown over her head, damned and dampened what she knew should have been the most joyous of times, the planning of her wedding.

Her smile wobbled, but she forced it upright. She had always pictured it so different, playacting with her dolls as a child and then, older, in her imagination. Her dream wedding had always been set against the backdrop of the plain meetinghouse with all the Friends in attendance, faces wreathed in smiles, broad foreheads glistening with the sweat of a summer's day, the bridegroom saying his vows, she saying hers. Then the Friends speaking out their blessings, their convictions for such a couple . . .

But no. This was Drake, and it was early, gusty spring, a time when thunderstorms reigned. And she loved him with everything in her set apart to love.

Mary Ann stood up with her. The rest of her family filled the first row in the pew of Christ Church, a Protestant Episcopal church on Second Street, similar to one Drake would have attended in England. That her parents had entered such a sanctuary in their plain, brown shoes appeared a blunder. But they had. For her.

Drake arranged it all. The license, the church, even a simple dinner and room of their own afterward at a nearby inn. All was in readiness for their beginning. He had no family present, a fact that saddened Serena, but Drake had brought his friend from the voyage, Daniel McLaughlin, to stand witness with him. A charming man who expressed interest in an apprenticeship with Serena's father—and had looked overlong at Mary Ann.

Little wonder her father said he had help enough.

With quiet intent, Serena lifted her chin and started down the long, decadent aisle, with its crimson runner of carpet, into the echoing emptiness of the room's vaulted ceilings.

He was waiting for her, looking devastatingly handsome. Dark-blue silk clung to his shoulders, falling into the graceful lines of a coat. His waistcoat was a shade lighter with matching and darker shades of swirling embroidery, a striking white neckcloth fell in neat, starched folds. His hair, dark and unbound, was swept carelessly away from his forehead, waving, framing his face . . . a face and form that was every inch the nobleman he swore he was not. Looking into his eyes, heavy with the promise of a life she could only imagine, she walked on, little but shaky breaths and the conviction of her heart carrying her.

She loved him. She loved him. She loved him.

It was her wedding march.

The sunlight filtered over them into myriad colors, split by the opulence of the stained-glass windows. Streaks of bright light haloed the altar and Serena inhaled suddenly, feeling as if she was walking out of drab browns and grays into the brilliant colors of life. An intoxicating excitement rose to her throat, threatening sobs. She held them back and inhaled instead, blinking out the tears, reaching him, reaching out for his hand. The strong warmth of his hand clasped hers like a root grafting with a young plant.

Serena looked up into Drake's eyes, ready to make any vows necessary to make him her own.

DRAKE LOOKED DOWN at his bride, pride nearly crushing him.

She looked the picture of virtue in a gown the color of dark cream. Her hair sat atop her head in a shining red-gold mass of thick braids and curls. A band of small pink rosebuds haloed the curls, their stems a tightly intertwined crown. There was no cap now. Her face was pale and glowing, her neck as graceful as any swan's he had ever seen on the lakes of Northumberland, her delicate collarbones as elegant and stately as the jewels of a queen.

What he wouldn't have done to give her the magnificent London wedding she deserved. He would relish seeing her in rich satin and jewels, the envy of the civilized world. But Serena would never be in London . . . would probably not *wish* to be, he realized.

Gazing at her beauty, her tranquility, he had a blinding realization that caused him to grasp more tightly to her hand and almost falter as he turned toward the minister: Had he not left all behind, he never would have found her. For the first time, he had something to be thankful for in the wake of his ruined existence. Had he stayed in London, he would have wed one of the haughty women of the ton, a woman in whose eyes he would have seen a hunger that was never satisfied. Instead, he was marrying a woman of quiet strength and faith, all of which gave the very air around her peace.

Was she not worth a dukedom?

Yes. A thousand times yes. That and more. She was worth all that he had gone through to have her.

The ceremony began with the sacraments of communion, something the Friends had rejected, believing that the sacraments of the cross were lived out each day, not in a ceremony. Serena faltered a little when given the ornate golden cup of blood-red wine, but only for a moment. She knew this was only the first of many new things she would now have to embrace.

Her vows were simple and stated with a strong voice that surprised her as she promised to become Drake's. His vows were similar, but stated with such heartfelt conviction that she was, again, moved to tears. Then he pulled a stunning silver ring from his pocket.

She stared at him, lips open, trying to remember to breathe.

He looked down, shy for a moment, then he leaned closer.

"Your father helped me make it," he whispered for her ears only as he slid it onto her finger. She stared at it in awe, never having seen anything so lavish. A silver band that grew in thickness toward its center where the tall silver setting held a huge, square, glittering sapphire with smaller diamonds mounted around about it, the guardians of greatness.

"But I have nothing for you!" She couldn't help feeling devastated at both his generosity and her lack. He smiled, pulling a simple silver band from his pocket and handing it to her. As she studied it she realized it wasn't really simple at all.

This was her father's work.

Burnished silver with an elegant edging, perfect in its simplicity, perfect in strength. She stole a look across her shoulder to her father, who was beaming, a sheen of tears in his eyes as he gave her a quick nod.

He was giving them his blessing. *His* blessing. Something she'd doubted until now.

At the ceremony's end, Daniel clapped Drake on the shoulder and gave Serena a big kiss square on the mouth, causing her sisters to giggle, wide-eyed, behind their hands. Her parents hung back at first, and then her mother rushed forward to hug them both. Eyes twinkling, MaryAnn slid a paper-wrapped package into Serena's hand and whispered into her ear, "For tonight." At the same time,

Serena heard the clinking of coins and saw out of the corner of her eye as her father pressed a heavy leather bag and a folded paper into Drake's hands. "Don't argue—a wedding gift."

It was done. She was now Serena Winslow. Everyone filed out of the church, leaving her and Drake alone together. They rushed out into the cold New England day—and the beginning of their lives. They stood, just outside the doors of the church, hands clasped tightly, and looked up toward the sky as the wind blew against them.

"We should hurry. A storm gathers."

Serena laughed up into her husband's—her *husband!*—face. "Is it not wonderful?"

Drake shook his head, smiling, the wind tearing at his hat. "The gathering storm?"

She made a great sweep of her arm, giddy in her happiness. "Everything. The storm . . . the night . . . the power of it all." They watched as the web-like clouds, thin, wispy and dark, raced across the lighter gray sky behind them. Suddenly sleet fell from the sky, thunder rolling in the distance. Drake took hold of her hand and they raced to the inn.

"Heaven help me," Drake shouted above the noise, "I have married a thunderstorm lover!"

She laughed in glee as they ran to the music of the thunder, the flashing of the lightning igniting the sky as if in celebration.

The inn was cozy, well warmed, and thankfully, close to the church. They were shown immediately to the private upper room reserved for them. Serena ran, laughing, to the fire, shaking the rain off her cloak before draping it over the back of a nearby chair where it lay dripping, making a puddle on the hardwood floor. She looked up at him, knowing her face was wet and rosy from their flight.

Drake was busy giving instructions to the serving woman
and shaking out his overcoat, but his eyes never left his bride's
face. He kissed her lightly on the lips as he passed her on the way
to hang up his wrap on a peg on the wall. "Let's see about some
food, shall we?"

Dinner was soon brought up. Drake directed the place-
ment of the meal and ordered the wine poured with an authority Serena was fast becoming accustomed to and knew was as
natural to him as breathing. She leaned her chin onto her palm,
watching him from the small table set up for them, their faces
reflected in the flickering firelight, hers in grinning fascina-
tion as the serving woman curtsied her way out of the room in
apparent awe.

"How dost thou do it?"

"Do what, my love?"

"Command such fearsome respect in others."

Drake motioned toward the food and grinned back at her.
"If you will sup, madam, I shall tell you all of my secrets."

The heated timbre of his words caused her to shiver. "Secrets,
my lord?"

He seemed not to notice her flirtatious tone, and Serena had
to wonder if that, too, was as natural to his ears as the trickling
of water is to river rock.

He handed her a glass of wine. "Drink. It will relax you."

She took a sip. "Tell me, why do they all bow and scrape in
thy presence?"

Drake shrugged out of his waistcoat, tossing it on the bed
as he sat down across from her. He loosened his cravat, a picture
of an elegant gentleman at ease. "I have found that if you expect
certain standards and speak with the authority of one who is used

to expecting those standards, people generally—" he shrugged—
"do what is expected." He smiled, one side of his mouth quirking
in a way that left Serena a little breathless.

"Very philosophic of thee. May we eat, my lord? I am
famished."

Drake frowned, but the smile stayed in his eyes. "You tease
me, I know, but . . . call me anything but that."

A glimpse of pain, quickly extinguished, gave her heart a
pang. Determined to banish it, she said playfully, "Anything?
How about *Kitten?* Or *Peaches?*" She laughed as he came around
the table and pulled her into his arms.

Kissing her quiet, he murmured. "How about *husband*.
I think I might like the sound of that."

"Hmmm, husband. It fits thee." She leaned back, his strong
arm supporting her waist. "I like it that I am the only one who
may call thee that."

"Let me take your hair down." His fingers dug into the
coif, finding pins and tossing them on the table before she could
protest.

"Should we not eat first, husband . . . while it is still hot?"

Drake ran his fingers through the long tresses, freeing them
from their braids. "I want to sit across from you thus. It is a glorious thing, your hair."

"Vainglorious, dost thou think?" Mock concern filled her
voice.

Drake laughed. "I doubt you have a vain bone in your body,
but if you did, no doubt your hair would be the femur."

"Femur? What is that?"

"The largest bone in the body." His hand glided down the
side of her body to her thigh. "Here." He leaned her back against

his ready arm and then kissed a trail of sweetness from the slim column of her neck up to her chin, then her lips.

Her eyes fluttered shut. "What wilt thou do with me tonight?"

He chuckled, deep and mischievous in response. "You will see." Abruptly, he righted her and then sat her in her chair. "Eat, madam."

They ate in silence, each anticipating the advancing darkness of night, their eyes catching and holding over the flame of the candle slowly dripping in the center of the table, seeming to Serena like an hourglass counting down the minutes.

Serena finished first and took a long, slow drink from the wine, tasting it on her lips with the tip of her tongue. She watched Drake through lowered lids, the air humming with the tension of tightly coiled springs.

"I never tire of looking at thee." What freedom, to speak her thoughts aloud.

A flare ignited in his eyes, telling her he liked hearing such things. She gave a little jump when he suddenly stood. Swallowing, she watched him toss back the remainder of his wine and come around to her side of the table. Her heart was pounding as he reached for her arm. It rose of its own accord to drape about his shoulders and held onto him as he lifted her.

"Hast thou had much experience in these matters?" she whispered against his chest.

"Enough to know what you might like. But you will not appreciate that yet."

"What does that mean?"

Drake sighed in mock exasperation. "Do you want me to talk to you or kiss you?"

Serena shrugged a shoulder and gasped as her sleeve slid half way down her arm. Looking down she saw that he had undone the ribbons on the front of her gown. "However didst thou do that?"

He answering grin was wicked. "My vast experience."

The next hour was a haze of pleasure to Serena. She had not understood how two could become one, until he made sense of it. Their breaths intermingled, their hearts pounding in urgent accord. Sensation became a new kind of direction, with touch its map. Before, she had only been able to look at him and she had thought that wondrous. Now, she used all her senses to explore him. She reveled in the essence that was Drake, the taste of his mouth, warm and rich with the wine. His scent, a mix of her mother's soap from his wedding bath and his own unique fragrance, delighting her. She breathed him and knew him and lost herself in the world that he showed her. She gave all that she had, her trust complete.

It was nearly painful, loving him thus.

ASTONISHING.

Drake had thought himself experienced. How humbling to learn he had only known the physical, never this joining of souls that had somehow, miraculously happened with Serena. What magic did she possess?

In the face of her sweet generosity, he felt the hard edges of his self-possession crumble. There was no room for the shroud of protection he had worn as effortlessly as his own skin for as long as he could remember. In the face of her love it melted, giving way to flesh and flesh, blood and blood. Left in its place was a sense of awe that this act of loving could be so humble—and yet so core deep.

He would never look at marriage the same way. Those few he'd seen that had seemed so connected . . . now he knew. Now he knew love. And nothing would ever be the same.

Chapter Fifteen

A week had passed since their wedding. A week of dreamlike floating where nothing seemed very real. They'd moved in with her parents, taking up residence in Drake's bedroom until they could save enough to start out on their own. But now, as Serena gazed out the thin-paned window, clinging to the frame, watching her family drive off to meeting, she felt a pang of sadness. It was the first meeting she had ever missed except for sickness.

Drake stood behind her, his hands at her waist. "Are you sorry?" he murmured into her hair.

She leaned back against his chest and shook her head. "It feels strange though . . . like I have grown up and started my own life. And yet . . . I do not feel that different."

"You are afraid?"

She nodded, unable to speak. He rubbed her upper arms with his hands and then turned her around to face him. "I have asked much of you. I am sorry for that." He smiled. "Come, let us think happy thoughts. I have a surprise for you."

Looking at the gentle smile he gave her, she felt the weight lift and smiled up at him. In his arms, everything felt right. "What is it?"

Drake led her into what was now their bedroom and over to his trunk.

"Daniel retrieved this for me." Taking out a velvet pouch Drake pulled the drawstring open, reached for her hand, and shook a massive ring into her palm.

"If I sell this ring, I may have enough to buy us our first home."

Serena picked up the ring and studied it. Heavy, of shining gold, she stared at the insignia in Latin and above it, a fire-breathing dragon, the fire represented by brilliant rubies inlaid in front of the dragon's open mouth. A shiver went down her back as she looked up into his eyes, the solid weight of it in her palm feeling like an inescapable trap. "It is thine?"

Drake's nod was brief and unquestionable, his eyes shuttered. "My father gave it to me."

Serena reached out and took his hand. Slowly she slid it on his finger, marveling at how fitting it looked. "Thou art of noble birth, then. Tell me."

He took the ring off, unknotted the black silk cord that drew the velvet bag together and pulled the cord out of the seam. Taking the ring he slid it onto the cord and then tied it around Serena's throat, making a long necklace. "I was lied to, Serena. And now this ring is mine to do with as I please. I am not an aristocrat. Believe me when I say I am as common as you. More so, even."

Serena shook her head vehemently, feeling the heaviness of it lie against her breastbone. "Thou must not sell it. It is thy heritage, from thy father."

He tossed the velvet bag back into the trunk and turned, studying her, then took her by the shoulders. "It represents a promise broken, nothing more. You, a home for us, that is the future. I want to provide for you. With this ring we can begin to make our way in the world, on our own." He tucked it securely inside her bodice, his flat palm resting on her heart. "You are my future."

Serena saw his need to be the man, the provider and protector of her, and gave in. "Very well. But I do hope thou wilt not regret it someday."

His answering smile lifted her spirits. He kissed her briefly. "Let us go for a walk and see if there are any houses for sale."

Catching his excitement, she clasped his hand in hers. "We could stop at the post office to see if any notices have been placed."

They walked the quiet side streets of Philadelphia in the overcast spring afternoon, hand in hand, laughing and happy. There were some buildings being raised in a business district, but seeing nothing for sale in the way of housing they wandered over to the post office.

"It is doubtful we can go in on a Sunday," Serena said as they approached the door.

Just then, a thickly built man with round spectacles came out and turned to lock the door behind him.

"Good sir," Drake called out. "Might we have a word before you leave?"

"Eh?"

Drake hurried them across the street toward him. "Good day, sir." They shook hands. "I am Drake Winslow and this is my wife, Serena. We are recently married and looking for a house to buy. Might you have notices in the post office or a newspaper we could buy?"

Shrewd eyes assessed him and then Serena. "Winslow, you say. Come in, come in." He turned the handle of the door and hurried them inside. As they walked back into the post office, the man turned suddenly. "Too bad the name is not Drake Weston. I have an important letter from England for a man by that name." He raised his brows. "I have been searching for him. One doesn't ignore a letter of such importance, and it is my job to see that it gets delivered, but no one seems to know of a Lord Weston of Northumberland."

Looking suddenly at Serena, the man gestured to a back corner. "If you would be so kind, madam, there is a newspaper on that table. You may find an advertisement in it for a home to buy."

While Serena went to fetch the paper, the man turned to Drake. "You wouldn't know of a Drake Weston, Earl of Warwick, would you, sir?"

Before Drake could answer, Serena returned with the paper. She hesitated and then, with sudden purpose, pulled the necklace out of the bodice of her gown. Holding out the ring she became breathless. "Sir, I could not help hearing and . . . might thou knowest if this would be the Earl's signet ring?"

Drake gritted his teeth as the man's round face lit up. He waited in sinking resignation as the man studied the ring.

The man glanced up from his study of the ring, a frown between his eyes. "Where did you come by this, madam?"

"My husband gave it to me, just this morning." She looked at Drake. "We were hoping to sell it to buy a house. Do you know the insignia, sir?"

The man shook his head and handed the ring back. "I am no expert in matters of insignia, but as postmaster here, I have had occasion to see several and would have to say that this ring belongs to a peer of the realm of His Royal Majesty, King George II." He turned to Drake. "Sir, either this ring is ill-gotten gain or, indeed, I have your letter."

Drake didn't try to conceal his outrage at the man's audacity as he bit out a reply. "The ring is mine."

The postmaster nodded, a small smile on his lips. "I thought as much. Would you like your letter, my lord?" He reached behind him and pulled out a yellowed envelope.

Drake ignored the outstretched hand. Turning away, he strode out the door.

SERENA TOOK A long look at the letter and then snatched it from the man's hand. "Thank thee," she whispered, stuffing it safely in her cape pocket. Then she turned away before he could change his mind and left the room.

It was gray and turning cold, looking like it might rain, as they walked away from the post office. Serena hurried to keep up with Drake's long, angry strides.

Touching him on the shoulder, she stopped him. "I am sorry. I had to know and thou wouldst not tell me."

He didn't answer, just walked away from her faster than before. She half ran to catch up to him. "Please understand, it might have been my only chance to know."

He stopped and faced her, gripping her shoulders in the middle of the cold, wind-swept street. "You do not know what you have done! It is too soon! They will know I am here now. Word will get out and—" His hands tightened on her upper arms.

Stricken as much by his tone as his words, she pulled away. In a voice that shook with anger and fear, she demanded, "Know what? What art thou hiding?" She raised a hand to his chest and stepped closer. "How can I know when thou wilt not tell me?"

"Serena . . . do not make me tell you." The anguish in his voice made his words thick. He took her elbow in a tight grip, urging her into the deep shadows of a tall building. Looking around to ascertain that no one was about, he cupped her face between his gloved hands. The wind had pulled loose tendrils of hair out of her knot and it danced across the backs of his hands. He pulled her to him, his actions fierce. "Don't ask this of me. I can't bear the thought of seeing regret in your eyes."

Serena pulled back. His irises were so dark blue they seemed black—deep wells of pain and guilt. Dread snaked through her. "How can I help thee if thou wilt not trust me? Drake, I am thy wife. Thy pain is now my pain. Let me bear it with thee."

"You do not know what you are asking." He turned away from her, half facing the stone of the building they hugged.

Serena put her hand firmly on his arm and insisted. "I want to know."

Drake swung around, his face ravaged, his voice menacing. "I *killed* a man, Serena. With my voice and size and power to intimidate, I as good as pushed him over the rail of a third-story balcony . . . and when he reached out his hand . . . I didn't save him . . . I let him fall. I. Let. Him. Fall."

Silence followed those bitter, pointed words. When he spoke again, he was quiet, terse. "And then I ran. Ran to the colonies as an indentured slave."

She stared at him, not able to utter a word as shock straightened her spine.

"Are you glad now? That you demanded an answer? Now you know what you married. A murderer and a man haunted by the surety that someday his misdeeds will catch up to him."

"Why? What had he done? Why didst thou not save him?"

"I don't know." He shook his head, looking down at her gray skirt, touching the tiny, perfect threads of a seam. "Except," he looked up into Serena's eyes, "that he represented everything I hated."

"But thou didst not push him over . . . didst thou? He fell and thou failed to save him. Was it not an accident?"

A harsh laugh tore from Drake's throat, and he reached up and gripped her hard by the shoulders. "No. You wanted to know, and so you will know the truth of it. I heckled him to the edge of that rail. I had the man scared out of his wits and I pushed my advantage completely. I showed no mercy, Serena. And then I ran."

She blinked. Her eyes overflowed until tears coursed down her cheeks. She shook her head back and forth in silent denial, but he pressed on. "I have to live with the horror of what I have done every day . . . and now, so do you."

"Oh . . . God help us!"

With that, she turned and ran from him, her feet flying out from beneath her skirts, her footsteps thudding down the cobblestones of the street. An ill wind began to blow.

IT WAS BACK, more fierce than ever.

That black void he had spent his shipboard days dodging and denying and defying. It mocked him now as he stood on the precipice looking at it—so complete—gaping endlessly, it seemed, into a dark nothingness that could swallow him up body and soul in an instant, leaving only the echo of a man named Drake. He felt the rush of his breath.

Why couldn't he get enough air?

He was drowning in despair, certain the void would be victorious now. Now that he had lost Serena.

His legs gave way. His back slid down the harsh brick of the wall until he squatted against it. His head dropped to his knees and he wrapped his arms around his head, blocking his ears to the voices—voices that no longer had any fear of God, knew their state as fallen and damned, grasping any they could to take down with them. Like great dark birds, their bodies encircled him in a cloud, each word attacking as a sword's thrust.

She hates you now—just as your father hated you.

No one will ever want you. Murderer! Murderer!

You should have never been born . . . Kill yourself! It's what you deserve.

Drake felt the dragon inside awaken, uncoil, and surge to the surface where it met the barrier of his will, of his flesh and bone. It rolled, roaring inside him, strong, stronger even than the despair. He closed his eyes . . .

Dare he unleash it? What kind of madness would it lead to? Darkness fighting darkness.

Fire burned in his belly as he surged to his feet, fists clenched by his sides, searching for the source of the invisible voices. He cursed his tongue for the way he had told Serena the dark tale, cursed a misbegotten life that had led him to this moment, and cursed God for abandoning him to it all.

Let the dragon reign. It was all he had.

BLINDED BY TEARS, her side aching and breath rushing in and out, Serena ran. It had begun to snow, soft and light and melting as it fell in the spring air, but Serena couldn't delight in the wonder. Her only thought was home and some sense of firm ground amid the sinking sand of her life.

She fumbled with the door latch, her hands shaking as she jiggled the handle up and down. Taking off a glove she finally achieved her goal and shouldered her way into the warm quiet of the house. Mindlessly she pulled off her bonnet and let it slide to the floor as she walked to the bedroom. She shut the door behind her and flung herself on the bed, letting the sobs she'd been holding back overtake her.

What had she done?

Slowly, like a heavy weight dropping through layer after layer of tissue paper, the truth lodged into her mind. She had married a stranger . . . a murderer . . . and God knew what else. She certainly didn't. The image of her husband enraged, shaking her, took hold of her thoughts.

He is dangerous. He will hurt you. If you anger him enough, he might even kill you.

She shook her head. "No. He wouldn't." But the doubts remained, roiling inside her with sickening certainty. For the first time since her marriage, she was afraid she might have made a horrible mistake.

The wind picked up, whistling about the window, lending to the eerie feel in the room. The pretty snow was turning into a storm.

She curled on her side, careful now to stay on her portion of the bed, to keep his side unrumpled. She cried until she had cried herself out and lay staring at the wall, unable to think, unable to feel.

She heard the front door open and sat up, quickly wiped the tears from her cheeks. It might be her parents returning from meeting . . . or it could be Drake. She tensed.

The knob turned and Drake's form filled the doorway. He had a way of filling up a room with his presence that always made her breath catch, but this time she looked at him with fear.

"I beg your pardon. I just came to get my things."

Serena stared without understanding, sitting straighter on the bed in a slow daze. "Your things?"

"Serena." His voice was raspy and dead. "You must want me to leave."

She drew a shaky breath, her eyes wide. "Leave?"

He went around to the far side of the bed and pulled out the trunk from underneath. She watched as he began packing his meager belongings. It only took moments, it would seem, to end something intended to last a lifetime.

Like their marriage.

He hefted the trunk under his arm and looked down at her. "You will be better off without me." He lifted her hand to his lips and kissed the backs of her fingers, then closed his eyes and lowered her hand, letting go.

She felt the warmth from his hand, a living thing, seep into her skin, melting her shock. In a moment all the lessons of the Friends came to her mind—lessons on honesty, sin, rage, and murder. In the same moment, she saw this man, whom she loved with her whole being, intent on leaving her so that she would be unsullied by his past.

She knew she should let him walk away . . . that she should spend the rest of her live in safe solitude, in the quiet, unassuming browns and blacks of the life she'd always known. The cost of the full spectrum of life's color hit her. But as she looked into his eyes, all she knew was her love for him—a love that didn't care what he'd done or what he might yet do or how wrong his whole life appeared to be.

"No! Don't go. Do not go . . . Drake." It came out as a soft pleading. She reached out her hand toward him. How could she have doubted what they had? It was too strong to be denied. "I love thee." It was a helpless plea.

He stood there, his face on the verge of crumbling . . . muscles quivering throughout his whole body. For what seemed an eternity he weighed her words, testing their validity. He finally set down the trunk and pulled her from the bed into his arms, sighing heavily into her hair. "I will make it up to you . . . to God. From this day forward I will do only what is right."

She looked into those fierce eyes, seeing determination and pain, a battered person resolving to be righteous.

"I will be a good husband. I'll work hard, provide for you and any family we have. I'll be a devoted father. I . . . I will be kind and . . . patient . . . like your father. I will be like your father."

"Being good, even as good as my father, will not undo what thou hast done. Thou must pray for forgiveness and then seek restitution with the man's family." It was hard to say, but she knew they must face the truth of it.

He slid to the floor in front of her, dropped his head against her stomach. "I have prayed, many times. I just don't know if anyone is listening. Why should He listen to someone like me?"

"God is always listening. He knewest what thou wouldst do when He made thee in the beginning of creation. And still He made thee. He knew all the sin man would commit from the beginning to the end—then He made restitution for sin by allowing His perfect Son to take it upon Himself. Thou hast repented, thou art forgiven. 'Tis so simple and yet hard for us to truly grasp." Serena sighed. "The other, though, I am not certain. I know not how to recompense for a man's life."

"I cannot go back!" he rasped. "I am tormented by it, but I've no desire to hang."

Serena gasped, feeling as though a lance had been driven through her heart. "They would hang thee?"

Drake looked up at her, his eyes bleak. "It is possible."

She wavered. "But thou didst not really intend to kill him, didst thou? Tell me true, Drake. Didst thou *mean* to push him over?"

Drake shook his head. "I thought to scare him, that is all. Something changed . . . I don't know what happened, but I was so angry, I couldn't see or think. I have very quick reflexes, honed by years of swordsmanship. After going over and over it in my mind, I know I could have grasped his hand and saved him . . . but I didn't. And I do not know why."

He grasped the fabric of her skirts in his fists. "I am sorry— so sorry. If I could go back and make it right I would, but it's too late. I need more time, Serena. Maybe someday I can go back and face the charges, but not yet, not when I have just found you."

Serena shivered at the idea of them going to London where Drake might be hanged, leaving her a widow and a stranger in an unknown world. Or worse, his going back alone, she not knowing if she would ever see him again. Suddenly she knew she couldn't demand it of him. She didn't want to risk his life any more than he did.

A rattle at the door brought them out of the moment. Drake stood, and Serena straightened out her skirts and smoothed back her hair. "I'll go and help mother with dinner." She clasped his strong hand in hers and squeezed it. "If we need to leave Philadelphia, I think I know of a place we could go."

He half-smiled with a frown between his eyebrows. "Where?"

"Dost thou think farming would be more to thy liking than silversmithing?" Her eyes were hopeful.

"Serena . . ."

"I have a friend, in the Shenandoah Valley. He has more land than he can currently farm and, I think, would sell some to us and help us get started."

Drake's countenance darkened. "This friend wouldn't be Christopher Kingsley, would it? Did he not want to marry you?"

Serena shrugged and looked down. "He may have at one time, but he knows I love thee." She pleaded with her eyes. "Drake, 'tis beautiful there, buried in the mountains. We . . . thou . . . wouldst be safe there."

Drake shook his head. "I do not like it."

"We could begin our own life there—together."

Drake felt the dragon within retreat to its lair, folding in its wings, settling back, far back into him. To sleep again. It was borrowed time . . . but he was willing to take it, to keep the monster asleep.

"I will consider it."

Chapter Sixteen

THE SHENANDOAH VALLEY

The Great Trading Path—or Great Warrior's Path, as some called it—was more of a deep gouge in the earth than a path. The surface was worn down ten inches or more in spots and muddy from the spring rains. Muck sucked at Drake's shoes. Wilderness—dense, leafy screens on either side—flanked them, its green arms reaching toward them, trying to reclaim the trail man had carved through its belly.

The group of six trudged through the mire. Serena paused to wipe her hand along her forehead and readjust the grip on her walking stick. When she didn't move, Drake stopped the packhorse and two-wheeled cart he was leading, went to her, and placed a hand on her back.

"Water?" He held out the flask, and she nodded, taking it and drinking, clearly not caring that water ran down her chin and neck.

"It should not be so hot in May." She smiled up at him, her hand shielding her eyes.

"Rest a minute. We will catch up with them soon."

Serena gave him a grimacing smile. "I had no idea the trail would prove so difficult."

Drake could only agree. This land astounded him. From the time they had left the outskirts of Philadelphia and hiked into the lush vegetation of the forests, Drake felt he had entered another world. In places the undergrowth was so thick they had to hack their way through with swords and cutlasses. Birds squawked at them from the trees. Squirrels and raccoons scurried across their path, stopping to stare with round unblinking eyes, as if they had never seen a man before. Deer startled easily, their turned-up tails fluffy white, a beckoning target as they disappeared into a thicket. The woods smelled of moss, grass, and wet earth, the air moist and unusually hot.

Serena took another drink and passed the canteen back to Drake. "There. I am better now."

"You could ride awhile. The horse seems well enough to hold your slight weight."

"No, I'll not add to the poor beast's burden unless I truly fear collapse." She grinned and took a deep breath. "Let us be on our way, husband, or we shall find ourselves in the forest at dark. That thought alone should spur me on."

Drake kissed her quickly and nodded. He had to agree with her: It would be far better to be in town by nightfall.

Here was the wild land he had heard tales of back in England, fraught with the perils of hostile Indians and wild creatures. Sometimes, especially at night, he felt the fine hairs on the back of his neck rise, sure that someone or something lurked in the dense brush, watching them. Drake gripped the comforting butt of his flintlock musket, felt the steady slap against his leg of the English cutlass he'd traded for, and set his teeth. He watched the trees, listening to the life of the forest, alert to any danger. His nerves hummed, his muscles stood out and ready, and he was amazed to discover he felt better than he had since the night they had read his father's will. Here, he felt a man, with the strength of his arms and the quickness of his senses their protection.

Truth be told, he found it exhilarating.

Five days into the wilderness and Drake felt he was finally finding himself once again. Well outfitted by Josiah and released from all debt, it was truly a new beginning for them. Drake insisted he pay Josiah back with interest as soon as he could; Josiah insisted he would do no such thing as they were family now. They had left the issue in a stalemate.

With the proceeds from selling his ring and the meager savings they had accumulated, they thought to have enough to get a start. Drake traded the clothes of a nobleman for clothes better suited to wilderness living: buckskins, moccasins, and simple linen shirts. Serena's clothes were already appropriate, but they purchased a warmer coat for the cold winters in the valley.

Leah insisted on going through her store of blankets, linens, dishes, and the basic tools to cook and clean and do the laundry. By the time she was done, they'd loaded their small cart to the brim. Josiah gave Drake a gun and an ax to build their cabin with. The thought of building Serena a cabin had filled Drake with excited anticipation. He wanted nothing more than to get out from under her parents' security and provide for her with the labor of his own two hands.

Going west to Lancaster, they'd trudged through the dense forest and then turned southwest to cross the Susquehanna River at Wright's Ferry. At its shores they met up with a party of four Scots-Irish, three men and a woman, also headed to the Shenandoah Valley.

Davis Lyle, Thom Patrick, and Henry and Delana Trimble were looking for the same thing Drake and Serena sought—cheap land. But their differences soon became known as the four became more and more themselves, course speech and manners surfacing. They constantly bickered and belittled each other. In the face of Drake's cultured speech and manners and Serena's quiet innocence, the others turned from friendly to watchful. And then their eyes had turned to mistrust and hate.

Finally Drake noticed how the men's eyes watched Serena.

He became more and more protective of his wife, trying to shelter her from their companions' influence, wanting to be rid of the four but having no real excuse to leave them until York. From there, he and Serena would travel the rest of the journey to Christopher's land alone. Hopefully their letter had reached him and he would be expecting them.

SERENA CAUGHT UP with Drake. "Are we close to York?" She couldn't disguise the anxiety in her voice.

"We will not stop until we get there." He smiled encouragement. "Come, climb up on my back for a bit of piggyback. You're light as a feather, and I would see you rested if we get lucky enough to have a bed to ourselves tonight."

Serena laughed at the wicked sparkle in his eyes. They had been too exhausted to appreciate a night together since starting out, so it was little wonder he was hopeful. Scrambling up onto his strong, broad back, Serena giggled. "I have not done this since I was five. I am not too heavy?" Before he could answer, she leaned in and blew into his ear. He groaned and attempted to slap her on the backside.

"None of that, my dear." Hoisting her up into a better grip, they went along.

They heard the town before they saw it. The others had been there for some minutes, waiting on the outskirts.

"Looks like the missus found herself a right comfortable seat."

Serena didn't care for the odd tone in Thom Patrick's voice. She slid down to the ground, gazing at the village in the twilight. "I hope there is an inn. I am famished."

Delana Trimble huffed. "Don't be counting on it, miss. Nor a bed to yourselves. We'll be lucky to all share a room."

Serena exchanged a look of trepidation with her husband.

Drake whispered down to her. "No. I will find you a bed, my dear." His hand came to rest possessively at the small of her back as they walked into the town.

It wasn't hard to find the inn, alive with music as it was. The Golden Plough Tavern, or so the sign read, was a large building with red shutters and a red painted door. The bottom half was made of timbered logs with white mortar chinking; the top half was red brick with timbered crossbeams.

Serena watched as Drake spoke with the innkeeper. The man was shaking his head but then suddenly did an about-face and showed Serena directly to a private room with a large feather bed.

"Whatever didst thou say to the man to change his mind?" She flung herself back into the feathers. The mattress sunk down, encompassing her in the softness. Drake's face appeared above her.

"I have amazing powers of persuasion, remember? Just wait, the best is yet to come."

Serena giggled. "What hast thou done?"

As if in answer to her question, there was a knock on the door. A young girl came in bearing two steaming bowls of deer stew. Another, even younger, with hair so light it was almost white, appeared behind her carrying a bottle of wine and two cups. Even more astonishing was the boy who followed with a bucket of steaming water, a large bowl, and a cloth with a sliver of soap tucked inside. Serena's delight escaped on a gasp.

"I can *wash?*" Looking at her beaming husband, she shook her head. "Truly amazing."

The food was tempting, but the steaming water beckoned. Serena smiled in happy contentment as she poured water into the deep bowl, dipped the cloth into the water, and lathered it with the precious piece of sweet-smelling soap. She could feel Drake's eyes on her as he busied himself pouring wine and setting out the bowls for their dinner.

Head thrown back, she washed her face and neck, dipping the cloth as far into the bodice of her gown as the neckline would allow. She longed to strip naked and really get clean, but there wasn't enough water and she wanted to save some for Drake. Instead she rinsed, poured fresh water into the bowl, and soaped up the cloth again before walking over to Drake, a half smile on her lips.

He sat still on the edge of the bed, eyes closed as she ran the cloth along his face, jaw, and then neck. Unbuttoning his shirt, she opened it and cleaned the rugged planes of his chest, then ran the warm wetness over his shoulders and onto his back, dragging the shirt off as she went.

They were both breathless, the food forgotten. "However didst thou manage all this?" She spoke with her lips close to his as she reached around one shoulder. It was the first time she had taken the lead in their lovemaking, and she found it powerfully affecting.

"Some things are better left secret." He rasped out, eyes closed.

Serena gazed at his features. He hadn't shaved since they'd been on the trail, and dark whiskers covered the lower half of his face. His dark hair was blue-black, shiny as a raven's wing. Long black eyelashes lay against lean cheekbones. She wanted to see his eyes and on an impulse kissed one eyelid. His lips, almost too red for a man, curved into a smile, but he didn't open his eyes. Serena tried again, this time touching the outer eyelid with the tip of her tongue. His response thrilled her.

With sudden strength he pulled her down on the bed. "What are you up to, madam minx?" She always forgot just how strong he was until he handled her. Arms like manacles wrapped around her, caging her against him.

"I want to play." She squirmed out of his grasp. His eyes finally opened and Serena caught her breath. There was such a look of happy love coming from them. She sat up and, movements slow, sought to mesmerize him. She uncoiled her hair from its knot, letting the strands wrap around her shoulders the way he liked. He watched in worshipful silence, then reached for her, the dance begun.

MUCH LATER THEY ate the cold stew and drank the warm wine, still wrapped in one another's limbs among the feathers.

"We should sleep, love. Another hard day on the trail faces us in the morning."

Serena nodded sleepily against his chest. "We are about half-way there? Another five or six days?"

"Hmm," he answered almost asleep. "Another eighty miles to Frederick Town, but we must cross the Potomac first."

"And then how far to Christopher's?"

"Shouldn't be more than a day's journey from Frederick Town. In a valley between the Blue Ridge Mountains and the Appalachians." He smiled against her. "It should be a sight."

ON THEIR TWELFTH day of travel, near dusk, but with enough light to see, they came upon Christopher's cabin.

Made of stone, dug out and picked up off the surface from the surrounding earth, it was strategically nestled near the Shenandoah River on a small ridge, its backdrop the rising wall of the Massanutten Mountains. Drake took in the grove of poplar and chestnut trees standing to one side of the cabin, providing a warmer shade than the mountains. At their feet spread a carpet of abundant wildflowers blooming with early color. Chicory with its blue-fringed petals stood proudly on long spindly stems, seeming to wave at them in welcome. Purple spiderwort and common mullein dotted the landscape. Nearer the cabin was a cluster of showy orchids, bloomed out in purple and white.

Serena drew a breath of delight.

Further in the distance lay evidence of Christopher's years of labor. Freshly painted outbuildings, some large and some small, squatted in the background. There was the squawk of chickens in a coop off to one side of the house and fluffy, soft-eyed sheep in a neatly fenced pasture beyond the main yard. It was a picture, really, like a painting come to life.

"This is Christopher's homestead?" Serena voice was filled with astounded admiration.

"According to the directions in his letter. We have arrived." Drake's gaze scanned the area in grudging admiration. Why the man hadn't asked for Serena's hand long ago puzzled him. He was obviously well set to provide for her.

Before he could consider this any longer the door burst open and a middle-sized dog bounded out to them, barking. Christopher's commanding voice stayed him.

"Thou hast come!" he announced with unabashed excitement, his eyes only for Serena as he rushed to greet them.

"Christopher!" Serena ran to him and threw her arms around his broad shoulders. He swung her around in a circle—his joy to see her plain. Finally his eyes came to rest on Drake.

He walked over and shook Drake's hand. "How was thy journey? The trail can be rough in the spring, I know."

Drake assured him it was nothing they couldn't handle. He tried to be generous and likable, but all he really wanted to do was slam a well-aimed fist into the man's pretty face.

Serena was still smiling up at Christopher. "I had no idea! From what thou described I thought thou wert barely eking out a living here."

Christopher looked at his feet, a red flush filling his broad forehead—just the right amount of modesty, Drake noticed.

"I did not want thee to be disappointed. 'Tis not town life out here, Serena, though the valley is filling up. There are more and more Friends. We have even built a meetinghouse in town, and the Scots-Irish are flooding into the valley."

Serena lifted her face to the sky and inhaled. "It may not be civilized—but it *is* beautiful. The mountains, they practically hug thy house, the stream sings closely by, and thou art well protected and provided for by thy hard work." She gave him a soft, happy smile. "I can see thou hast worked very hard here, Christopher, and I am impressed."

Drake's fist curled tightly against his leg. Forcing a nod of agreement, he asked, "How long have you been homesteading your land?"

Christopher shrugged, waving them toward the house. "Three years—a little more. I was one of the first in the valley. Oh, and I am happy to report that a tract of land to the south of mine has been recently vacated. There is even a half-built cabin on it. It is wonderful providence!"

Drake wasn't sure how fortunate it would prove to be next-door neighbors with Serena's ex-suitor, but he said nothing. He just endured as Serena was led into the house and shown around. He gritted his teeth during the inspection of the well-ordered kitchen. He ground his teeth and felt the beginnings of a head-ache as they toured the cozy sitting room that offered an astonishing number of large windows. The light they provided made the room bright and cheerful. Most houses were quite dark, especially out in the wilds. But Christopher had apparently made lighting a priority. Seeing the view from this room, Drake couldn't blame him. It was stunning.

Next, Christopher motioned them toward his bedroom, insisting they use it, helping Serena carry in her trunk. Drake was about to finally force the word *no* past his restricted throat, everything in him rebelling at the suggestion of Serena in this room, when he heard her cry of delight.

Against the back wall was a large bed covered with a colorful quilt. There was nothing particularly special in the design of the bed, plain wooden frame that it was, but what Christopher had contrived for a headboard was astounding. Three windows hung side by side, making it seem like a wall of glass. On the other side stood nature's ever-changing, awe-inspiring painting. This evening, the mountains rose majestically with a bluish, purple hue, rising in peaks of haze. Behind them, sinking into their stony depths was the beginnings of a beautiful pink-and-purple sunset. In all his travels, Drake didn't think he had ever seen anything so lovely—and it must always be so.

Serena ran to the side of the bed to gaze in astonishment out the window. "However didst thou do this?"

Christopher's face shone. "We Quakers are so plain in all we do . . . but God's creation is anything but plain. I did not think it sinful to revel in . . . a little. And," he paused, his voice low and strained, "I thought you might paint from here."

Serena's eyes shone with understanding and regret. "Not sinful . . . perfect." She turned to Drake and held out her hand. "Can we do this? In our cabin?"

Drake could only nod, his throat so choked he feared he couldn't speak.

She grasped his hand and held it tight, watching the sun sink against the mountain peaks. "Christopher will help. Wilt thou?"

She turned to him, just as Drake did. Drake hoped she hadn't seen the quickly masked pain on Christopher's face. The realization that Christopher had made this enchanting place with Serena in mind struck him with a physical force. While he felt some compassion for the man, he also felt the need to do something to brand her as his own in front of him.

"Of course I will help," Christopher said with forced cheerfulness.

"But if we take thy room, where wilt thou sleep?" Serena asked in concern.

"Come, I will show thee the rest of the house."

The invitation seemed for her alone, and Drake sensed this man wanted a moment alone with Serena.

"Go on." He half-hoped she would refuse and stay with him. "I'd like to enjoy this sunset a few minutes more."

Serena searched his eyes for a couple of seconds, then turned toward Christopher and linked her arm with his.

Drake heard her happy chatter and occasional laugh as they climbed the ladder he had spied earlier to what could only be the loft. He waited while the sun faded into darkness, hardening himself to what he had stolen from this good, honest man.

The strike of guilt was a new feeling, proof he must have changed some, as even a few months ago he wouldn't have cared how this man felt. Minutes later they called him to the kitchen and the inviting smell of dinner cooking.

The kitchen was spacious. A large worktable stood against the wall next to a massive stone fireplace—big enough to stand in and well stocked with cooking utensils. A smaller table and chairs for dining sat across from the hearth under another window. But the best part must have been the pantry lined with long wooden shelves. Serena went into raptures of delight when she saw it. Drake made a mental note to copy it, too, in a cabin of their own.

Christopher had prepared a meal of venison stew. He served them while asking questions about their trip, Serena's family, and their decision to become farmers.

Drake sat, ate little, and endured.

After dinner, the dishes were cleaned and wiped, and then Serena stated her desire to wash up before bed. "The river will not be too cold, will it?"

The Shenandoah River was a short distance away, but still Drake insisted on accompanying her. Christopher did not object.

Drake watched in silent absorption as Serena waded into the dark waters, giving a little shriek when met with the coldness. Staying close to shore she quickly scrubbed herself, her teeth chattering so badly she could barely talk to him. Drake had to grin at her stubborn insistence to wash her hair. After her quick bath they headed back toward the enchantment of the stone house.

Night soon enveloped them. Thunder sounded far off in the distance, echoing across the faces of the rocky walls of the surrounding mountains, but there was no rain.

Serena turned to him. "We really made it." She did a silly little twirl toward him that held him in an enchanted spell. It almost hurt, looking at her so happy and loving her so much.

Wrapping her arms around his waist she hugged him from behind, stopping him. "'Tis a wondrous place. I feel at home here."

A squeezing took place in the region of his heart. *Christopher's* home made her feel at home. All he had to offer her was the wilderness and the possibility of a half-built cabin. And that at the invitation of another man's help.

He wanted to curse. He was bone-weary of taking charity and letting others help and provide for them. He had a sudden vision of his palatial castle in Northumberland, one of many estates he would have inherited as duke and the home where he grew from child to man. He imagined Serena in one of his elegant carriages pulled by plumed horses adorned in the colors of his livery, red and gold. On the sides, emblazoned on the glossy black doors of the carriage, was his crest, a golden fire-breathing dragon set against a field of red—the motto underneath reading "ad defendum praedium": defender of the treasure.

They would drive slowly up the long hill, flanked on either side by tall, elegant trees that gave way to very formal, very

English gardens. His home sat atop a flat hill, beyond which were the steep cliffs leading down to the sea—the sea that had sung him nighttime lullabies, crashing against the rocks, water cascading in a cadence that swept him into boyish dreams.

Alnwick was a massive stone edifice—formidable, condescending, a stronghold against man and any device formed against it.

He would watch Serena's face in eager anticipation as they swept through the gatehouse and neared the circular drive. He would revel in her look of astonishment. His heart leapt inside him just thinking about it. They would stop and silently behold the splendor of the front facade. He would help her from the carriage with its plush velvet cushions, then lead her up the stone steps to the immense front door. She would be dressed in a jewel-encrusted, French silk gown the color of the green flecks in her eyes. Diamonds would adorn her ears, and one of the many magnificent family heirlooms would encircle her sweet neck. She would reek of his wealth from the top of her upswept hair to the tips of her glittering satin slippers. His riches would adorn her.

His butler would open the door before they even had the chance to reach the ornate knocker. Bowing low and resplendent in the duke's livery, Crudnell would welcome them into the foyer. Gilt ceilings, so high one had to squint to see the fine artistry, would greet her. A massive spiral staircase to the right, an elegant salon done in pale satiny ice blues and silver beckoning to the left. Speechless in her wonder, Serena would glide through the house, Drake showing her *his* riches, the majesty of a duke's glory—his provision.

But that was all a dream. A dream that would never come true. His stomach rolled with the crashing of it as he pasted a false smile on his face and reentered reality—the hospitality of a farmer in a stone farmhouse.

A house that enthralled his wife.

THE NEXT DAY they toured Christopher's land, seeing first-hand all the hard-won improvements. If they had put Drake on the rack, he would have been more comfortable. Fields skirted the rocky edges of the base of the mountain, some newly planted with corn and some furrowed and waiting to be planted. Spring was a busy time for the farmer, and Drake was itching to get started on his own land.

Looking over at his wife, he felt a surge of satisfaction that she was his. She sat atop a pretty gray mare, riding astride as there was no sidesaddle. Surprisingly, she rode well, swaying naturally to the rhythms of the horse. The sunlight shone on her face and the wind whipped her hair loose, letting curling strands roam wild about her shoulders. Her eyes held a sparkle he loved. She fit so well here.

His gaze shifted to Christopher atop a big black horse and his smile faded. Christopher was pointing into the distance and telling them where he would place his mill. When he looked at Serena, his eyes were nothing short of adoring. Though he remained ever polite and respectful to both of them, Drake knew Christopher would like nothing better than to be rid of him and claim Drake's bride for his own. The desire to get her safely away from the blond man hummed through Drake's veins, making him churlish and impatient. He had never felt such possessiveness before. The strength of it surprised him, along with the power of this jealousy that rode his heels, lacing his every nod and attempt at conversation.

"We will stake the claim tomorrow," he interrupted. It wasn't a question; he just wanted to make sure Christopher knew his intentions.

The blond man nodded, a knowing look in his light-blue eyes. "Lord Fairfax owns the land. 'Tis only a matter of filing and paying, and that can be done in Frederick Town. But not everyone bothers. Most of the people who come for land carve their initials in the trees and stake their claim that way." Christopher smiled. "Much like an animal that sprays the perimeter of his territory. I fear it is somewhat primitive out here." The pride in his voice belied the words.

Drake knew the name for such people: squatters. He had dealt with such on his own estates and was appalled to think of himself among their number. "I prefer to pay for a deed."

Serena spoke up. "But we can stay with thee while our cabin is being finished, can we not? I do dread the thought of sleeping in the open."

Another stab at Drake's inability to take care of her. Even if she didn't mean it to be so, it made him grit his teeth.

Christopher smiled. "Of course. I want to show thee so much. I am working on a mill and hope to become the area's means of grinding wheat and corn grown here in the valley." His clear eyes settled on Drake. "After I help with your cabin, perhaps thou could help with the mill."

Drake knew of no way to discourage such neighborly thinking and so only nodded once.

They turned their horses toward the house just as the sun was fading behind the western mountain range. Serena abandoned herself to joyous laughter as they galloped through the valley.

She looked from Drake to Christopher. "It has been so long since I have ridden. Shall we race home?"

Christopher seemed hesitant, but Drake's eyes caught and held hers in quiet challenge. "After you, madam."

THAT WAS ALL the encouragement Serena needed.

With a dig of her heels she and gray were off. Serena leaned in low, her face pressed close to the horse's powerful neck. "Come on, girl! Let us show them what we can do."

It was as close to flying as Serena knew she would ever come. The earth was soft from recent rains, and she could feel the clods being kicked up behind them as they sailed toward the barn. Down shallow hollows and then back up over tiny inclines they raced on, the horse's breathing in tandem to the drumming of her heart. Less than a half-mile away she could just make out the hazy outlines of one of Christopher's outbuildings on the horizon. Giving in to temptation, Serena turned her head to assess her position.

Drake was to her right and directly behind her, laboring to prod his packhorse into a steady run, looking disgusted with the beast. And Christopher . . . Serena faced front for a moment and then twisted to see over her other shoulder. Catching sight of him some distance back, she watched in dawning horror as Christopher's horse went down into a dip in the ground. He cried out and then Serena saw him fly from the horse's back. Turning back around, she hauled on the reins. The mare blew great puffs of air with the effort to stop. Drake raced by, a look of confusion on his face.

"Christopher's fallen!" she shouted to his back, hoping he could hear her.

Turning, she drove her heels into the gray's sides and galloped to where Christopher lay. All she could see was the shining of his blond hair in the grass. As she approached, her stomach turned. His leg lay in an odd position and he wasn't moving. Reining in, she slid from the horse's back and ran to him.

She couldn't let herself look at the leg; it made her sick and fearful. Instead, she knelt by his head and stroked back his hair. "Christopher, canst thou hear me?"

He moaned, turning his face toward her.

"Thank God." She lifted his head into her lap and looked up, searching the landscape for Drake. He was almost upon them.

The pounding of hooves stopped and Drake rushed over. "Is he hurt badly?" The question was cut off abruptly as Drake saw Christopher's position.

Serena concentrated on keeping Christopher lucid. "Art thou in pain?" She cupped his face between her hands, and when he opened his eyes, Serena could see nothing *but* pain in them.

"We need a splint," she said to Drake. "If thou canst straighten the leg, I can bind it." Looking back at Christopher she kept her tone calm and firm. "Christopher, thou must stay awake and help us. Does anything other than thy leg hurt?"

He moaned. "Knocked the breath from me, but no. I think it is just my leg."

Serena slid his head back on the warm grass and ran her hands along his neck and arms, feeling for broken bones. She gently traced each rib, prodding him. All the while, Drake was scouting for something to brace the leg with.

When he came back she looked up in relief to see him clutching a stout branch stripped of leaves.

"We'll need some rope, or something to tie down the leg." Drake's grim expression told Serena how worried he was.

Her nursing experience flooded back and brought a kind of calm to the situation. Standing, she lifted the hem of her skirt and then grasped hold of her shift. The homespun ripped easily as she tore the bottom off and then, with the help of her teeth, tore the piece into strips.

Going around to Christopher's head she helped him sit halfway up and then sat behind him, allowing him to lean back against her chest. Wrapping her arms tightly around his upper torso, she held on tight and directed, "I will steady him. Thou wilt have to straighten the leg."

When Drake hesitated, Serena encouraged him. "I haven't the strength to do it. Just straighten it out in front of him—carefully, but as quickly as thou canst."

They all took a simultaneous breath, and then Drake pulled the leg straight. Christopher let out a shattering yell. Panting, he pressed into her, and Serena stroked his upper arms. "There now, the worst is over."

She looked to Drake. "Canst thou feel where the break occurred?" There was worry in his eyes, and Serena could only silently agree. If they didn't set the leg properly, it wouldn't heal right. That would cause a lifelong limp or, worse, a crippled leg. Drake felt along the lower portion of Christopher's leg. When Drake's fingers pressed just above the knee, Christopher nearly came off the ground.

"Here. I can feel it."

Serena edged out from under Christopher, lowering him back to the ground, and knelt down beside Drake. He put her hands on the spot. As gently as she could, Serena felt for the break. Sure enough, one part of the bone was sticking out enough that she could feel the edges of it through his skin. Serena bit her bottom lip.

"Christopher, is there a doctor to be had? I can set it, if I must, but if there is a doctor . . . " She trailed off hopefully.

Christopher's eyes were still tightly clenched. He opened them and looked at Serena. It took effort for him to talk, but he managed, "Back in Frederick Town. Eight hours on a fast . . . well-rested horse."

None of the three horses were particularly well-rested after being out all day, and night was fast approaching. They sat in thoughtful silence. Finally, Drake spoke.

"I will take the mare. She's the heartiest of the three. I'll have the doctor here by morning." His lips firmed and the concentration line in the middle of his eyebrows deepened. "We must get you home to bed though."

They spent the next hour splinting the leg and creating a makeshift cot from tree limbs and the remainder of Serena's shift. It worked rather well, and they were able to drag Christopher across the thick grass as though on a summer sled.

The half-mile to the house was a slow and painful ride for Christopher, filled with bumps and turns that were impossible to soften. Drake pulled the cot-sled while Serena led the horses. It was dusk when they reached the front door, the sun sinking fast over the crest of the mountains. Christopher's face was pale in the fading light, a sheen of sweat making it glisten. Drake carried him to the bed, Christopher trying not to cry out, then helped Serena make him comfortable. It didn't take long for Christopher to fall into an exhausted sleep.

Serena followed Drake out into the kitchen, filled a canteen with fresh water, and wrapped some cornbread and cold venison in a cloth, tying it into a neat bundle. He hadn't eaten since noon, none of them had, and he would need strength for the long night ahead.

Drake checked the musket, loading it with powder and ramming it down, and then filled his pouch with more musket balls, wanting to be prepared for anything.

He reached for the dinner pail. "If all goes well, I should be back by mid-morning." He pulled Serena into his arms and kissed her, both of them hanging onto the contact for a few stolen seconds. Drake picked up his musket and canteen of water and was gone.

"Be careful," Serena whispered after him, her heartbeat still loud in her ears.

Chapter Seventeen

The house was quiet, the wind gently fanning her cheeks through the open door. When Drake was out of sight, she turned with a sigh, her hand clutching her skirt, and went back to the bedroom to check on Christopher. She sank down on the edge of the bed beside him, searching his face for signs of fever or delirium. Her hand went to Christopher's tanned forehead and she brushed back the silky white-blond hair.

She felt horrible—guilty—her stomach in knots. Her foolishness had brought them to this. He hadn't wanted to race, didn't have the thirst for adventure that both she and Drake shared. She should have known better. In a place like this, where the line between life and death was as fragile as spun glass, where such isolation from any source of help could mean starvation, pain, long hours of suffering alone without anyone to hear or know cries for help and death even. It was a land where one had only one's self to depend upon; she should have known better.

Christopher stirred. He turned his cheek into her hand and his voice rasped out. "Do not look so grim, Serena. This was not thy fault."

He had read her mind. It wasn't the first time. His uncanny ability to read her had shown itself often during their long friendship. But this time, enveloped in the dark aloneness, still wrapped in the emotions of near tragedy, the connection from it electrified the air around them. Shaking her head, she gripped his hand. "It *was* my fault . . . my foolishness . . . this is not a place for girlish whims; it is a place for survival and I have hindered thine."

Christopher shook his head on the pillow. "No." And then with more emphasis, "No." He squeezed her hand. "What better place for dreams? Serena, listen to me. Of course there are risks here, but so there are in Philadelphia . . . or London even. Thou couldst be run down by a carriage on the busy streets." He smiled. "Thou canst live in the fear that something bad will happen. Nothing good will ever come without risk. Thou knowest I speak the truth . . . thou married Drake."

His words hung in the air—thick and alive with meaning.

"That did not seem like such a risk."

"Did it not?" His eyes searched hers.

With gentle pressure he pulled her closer until she could see the moonlight reflected in his eyes—the clear, focused eyes of a man who knew himself and what he wanted. She would find no demons here.

"Thou gavest up everything to be with him."

He forced her to see the truth—*his* truth. Pulling her closer, his eyes blazed with his need of her. The realization that he still loved her was a stunning shock. Was it true?

Standing, her breath ragged, she rushed from the room out into the yard. She ran to the nearest tree, leaned against it, sliding down until she could feel the hard ground beneath her, feeling the rough solidity of bark against her back. Eyes clenched shut, she let the night breeze cool her hot face.

After a moment her breathing slowed to normal and she opened her eyes. There, in the soft glow of the moonlight, lay what she had given up. Christopher had told her in a hundred ways how much he loved her. In the solidness of a home that would keep her warm and safe and dry. In the fields, hopeful with young spring plants. Her gaze wandered over every evidence of his labors. The hearty livestock, the fences and pens, all were proof of careful planning for their life together.

Eyes opened, she saw it as he must have every day. All the little details becoming blindingly clear. The thoughtful closeness of the stream so that she wouldn't have far to go for water. The cellar, hard-won from thin soil and solid rock. He must have imagined the harvest from her vegetable garden while he dug it out, the preserves she would put up to keep them nourished during the winter. The nearness of a town—and a church. He had been so excited over the building of the meetinghouse, a place for their family to worship.

With relentless insight, she saw his dreams. Dreams he had shared with her time and time again in his quiet unassuming way and still, now that she was here, wanted to share with her. Just today he had spoken of his plans for a mill, assuring a future for their children.

A planned inheritance.

It was all suddenly so clear. She wanted to wail. She hadn't known . . . hadn't understood the depth of Christopher's love for her. What must it be costing him now? To see her and Drake so happy and loving together. His broken leg was nothing compared with the pain she caused him every day just by being here. And yet, he had wanted them to come. Why? Was he hoping to lure her away from Drake? Had she made a terrible mistake by bringing them here?

"I am so sorry," she breathed aloud.

That last thought left her chilled to the bone and shaking, the cool night air blowing against her, pressing her into the tree. "What have I done?"

She closed her eyes and let tears fall onto the plain dress that was still as Quaker as she was. Desolate, she breathed deeply, seeking God's presence, seeking the Light. "Show me Thy path, Lord."

DRAKE'S NERVES WERE strung tight from the sharp vigilance required to ride through night wilderness. Bobcat, bear, and wolves were an ever-present danger. And while, from all accounts, the Indians had been subdued and moved further west over the mountains, at one time the Shawnee had camped in this area, and one could never be too sure. He had yet to see an Indian and wasn't quite sure what he would do if he did. He'd rather not find out alone, in the middle of the night.

It was early and the birds were up and chirping when he finally made it to the outskirts of Frederick Town. His eyes felt sand-filled and he knew he would have to get a couple hours' sleep before he could make the trek back to Christopher's home with a doctor.

Turning his equally tired mount onto a familiar street, Drake picked his way to the same inn they had stayed at before. He had to bang on the door several times before the sleepy inn-keeper finally opened it. It was the same man he'd convinced of his need for a private room (by reminding him what it was like to be a newlywed) and he remembered Drake well. Drake told the man of Christopher's accident, the need for a doctor, and his more immediate need for a few hours' sleep.

"Anything will do this time, good sir. A blanket on the floor, if needs be."

The man waved his suggestion away. "No, no, follow me. I have a bed in an attic room."

Drake was too tired to care that the statement meant sleeping in his clothes and sharing a bed with strangers. A couple of hours of rest and then he was assured that he could find the doctor.

AN ELBOW IN the ribs woke him. At first he thought it Serena and reached out, only to be met with the shaggy beard of his bedmate. Snatching his hand back he came awake and sat up. Groggily, he searched for the pocket watch he now owned. It had been one of the many trades he had made—from a gold watch, elegantly inlaid with tortoiseshell, to the plain pewter. But it worked. And truly, that was all that mattered in a place like this.

The morning light was bright with spring sunshine washing over the little town. Small though it might be, it bustled with an economical energy the Germans were known for. Having retrieved direction to the doctor's home, Drake set out.

A brisk knock on the knobby wood door brought round a stout woman with rosy cheeks and a wide smile. "Might I help thee?"

A Quaker—good. "Yes, ma'am. I was looking for the doctor. Might he be available?"

She nodded happily and motioned him in. He was led into a parlor and told, "Make thyself comfortable. I will get the doctor."

The wait was thankfully short. A middle-aged man with a well-fed belly, who looked utterly incapable of making the long ride on a wilderness trail, entered the room. He thrust out a hand with a friendly smile to match his wife's.

Drake introduced himself and then explained the situation. "Can you come? My wife is hesitant to set the bone herself, and I have no experience in such matters. I fear we might make it worse."

"Much swelling?"

Drake nodded. "At least twice the normal size."

"Well, there's no time like the present then. I'll get my bag and horse and meet you in front of the inn."

IT WAS NEARING dinnertime when they finally made it to the cabin. The trip back had been uneventful, and Drake was pleased it had only taken a little longer than the journey there. The good doctor was a surprise in more ways than one. Not only could he ride with astounding grace and forbearance; he was an excellent traveling companion, full of knowledge of the area, gossip, and tidbits of information about the inhabitants. Most amazing, he carried with him the best food Drake had had since leaving London.

"My wife is French," he'd explained, "and trained with culinary experts before I swept her off her pudgy little feet and brought her to this country." His obvious respect for his wife and her talents amused Drake. "A French Quaker? Was I mistaken in her speech in surmising her to be of the Friends?"

The doctor chuckled. "She dabbles in any and all social events. When she realized the Friends dominated the social life of the town, she joined them faster than I could gainsay her. They don't know it, but she only adheres to the language. We have plenty of French decadence in the other areas." His bushy gray eyebrows rose into his hairline suggestively.

Drake shook his head in wonder. "Do the Friends know?"

The man laughed so hard he almost fell off his horse. "If they know, they look the other way where she's concerned. Her cooking is prized at the pitch-ins. My suspicion is she could cook her way into any group."

After their lunch, Drake could only agree with him.

THE HOUSE LOOKED quiet in the midday sun as they approached, and a bad feeling rose from Drake's stomach as soon as they came upon it.

They took their horses to the barn, stayed long enough to fill the trough with feed, then hurried to the door. Serena met them before they reached it.

"Thank God!" Her eyes met Drake's, then the doctor's. "He is feverish and the break is terribly swollen." She rushed them inside and to Christopher's bed.

The next hour was a horror. The bone, hard to find in the swollen flesh that surrounded it, had to be set properly before it began to mend. Drake understood that much. Beyond that, he was hopelessly out of his scope of experience and dead tired.

After helping to pin Christopher to the bed, hearing him scream as the doctor—ruthlessly, it seemed—set the leg, Drake took refuge in the attic and collapsed on what was now Serena's and his bed.

THE DOCTOR STAYED the remainder of that day and night, taking his leave in the morning. He'd given stern instructions to Serena on how to care for Christopher. The fever was normal but must be watched; the swelling should go down in a week or two as the bone knitted. Christopher was warned to stay abed, leg elevated on pillows, and rest for several days, if not weeks.

Serena wanted desperately to believe the doctor's prediction that Christopher would be fine. She didn't know how she would cope if there were any permanent damage because of a foolish race. Penance seemed the only way to assuage her guilt. So she made an internal vow: From this day forward, Christopher would be her most determined concern.

Chapter Eighteen

omething was wrong. The feeling settled on him, heavy and filled with dread. Try as he might to dispel it with level-headed thinking, it would not leave.

Serena's actions bore evidence that Drake's world had changed somehow, was askew in a way that left him lurching on its deck. She was so busy nursing Christopher now, she had little time or energy left over for him. Worse yet, she seemed to be doing something no woman had ever done to him: She seemed to be avoiding him.

The thought that she preferred spending time with Christopher had raised its ugly head and shuddered its way deep within his mind. It chose the worst moments to rear up and demand notice—when they had a rare moment alone, when she lay soft and pliant on the makeshift bed in the loft beside him, when she sat by Christopher's bed while he waited lonely and alone at the kitchen table, the laughter floating from the room making his heart ache. Curse it, he'd always prized his independence! What had he allowed her to do to him?

Now he stood, looking at the cabin that he was supposed to finish a couple of miles from where his wife was spending time with another man, staring at it in disgust, trying to decide where to begin the work. Christopher hadn't understated it when he'd said it was a half-built cabin. It was only four feet high, rough logs stacked in a square with a hole for the beginnings of the door and another for the fireplace. It was worse than anything his people in Northumberland lived in, nothing but a small, dark box. An existence. He breathed hard through his nostrils and let his arm fall from rubbing his forehead to slap against his leg. He turned away with a scowl. At least the woods surrounding the land were lovely. After chopping trees all day, cutting the branches off with his ax to make the beginning of logs, he was physically and emotionally drained. He took a deep breath. He would just have to keep at it, try again to be more cheerful tomorrow.

Mounting his horse and galloping into the dense woods, he realized that this was his kind of evening. It was dusk, just before the hazy colors of twilight, the wind whipping through the trees and sending a spiral of new leaves to an early death. In the past, he might have gone for a night ride on a horse far more prized than Christopher's entire farm. Or he might have stood on one of the balconies at Alnwick Castle, puffing on a cheroot, soaking in the evening air and looking out over his land—a masterpiece of property.

Now he galloped through wildness. This land struck him as old in the ways of God but new, caught and fledgling, in the ways of man, trying to grasp how quickly everything was changing. It was bittersweet . . . but there would be no turning back. Man would eventually have his way.

A cool breeze that smelled slightly of wet bark and the greens and browns of the forest ruffled his hair and he smiled. Drake was suddenly thankful just to be alive. What if he *had* ended up in Newgate Prison? Or even a duke in London's crowded ballrooms? Could he feel any more connected to God and his own heart than he was right now?

God. Drake thought about Him often these days. A feeling much like he had experienced at meeting with the Friends crept in on him, like a shy bird not sure of its welcome. The wind seemed more alive all of a sudden, like it was full of breath instead of air. Drake took a long inhale of it, feeling a peace like he had never known settle into his insides, spreading until it filled him. A part of him, a deep part long unopened, strained toward it. He felt tears quicken at his throat. He looked up at the darkening sky, half afraid, half astounded. Completely captivated.

"Are You real?"

The wind quickened as if in response. He could only breathe it in, wondering if he might be close to his own death . . . or life as he'd never known it. Something new and strange. Everything within him strained toward it, wanting . . . what exactly, he couldn't put into words.

Another voice insinuated itself. *There's no one here but the wind. Foolish man! Who do you think you are? If there was a God, would He speak to you? Your own father didn't want you. He wanted to destroy you, remember? Now your wife has found another. No one wants you. No one could ever want you. Illegitimate. Unwanted. Unloved . . . Murderer.*

As he listened, anger, bitterness, and shame crept in on his peace. As thoughts surfaced he began feeling foolish, snapping his eyes back to the trail and the forest closing in on him. The peace faded a little more and then more, and some part of him recognized that he was allowing it away—that accepting peace meant believing in something he couldn't see or hear or touch.

In an instant of cognitive recognition, he knew he had to make a choice. What was truth? In his world of concrete figures and cold, hard facts, Drake had rarely allowed for sentimentality. There were a few moments when something cracked through—a symphony, a section in a book, his mother's face. These had occasionally pierced his veneer of control, but this . . . this was different.

And were he totally honest, it frightened him as nothing else ever had. Not the battlefield where he served as a commander in King George's royal navy; not his wedding day; not even his father's face when he'd cackled at Drake at the end. No, this was another kind of fear.

Fear of surrender.

The clearing came suddenly into view. Christopher's house sat bathed in twilight, looking almost beautiful in the eerie stillness. He rode carefully forward into the spilling of the ghost light, trying to quiet the clinking of the stirrups and the soft thud of the horse's hoofs, sensing . . . something. As he drew closer into the yard, the hair on the back of his neck lifted. His mount's ears pricked forward with a low whinny. Patting the animal's neck, Drake quieted him. Everything was still—too still. His gaze scanned the tree line, searching for movement. There, behind the house, he heard the whinny of a horse . . . or horses.

Suddenly a scream pierced the air. Serena! His wife was screaming!

Everything in him wanted to charge forward, but years of service to his king overrode any such self-indulgence. Dropping from the saddle, he tied his mount to the nearest tree, silently cursing his own feet when they slipped on wet leaves. He was long out of practice. Making his way through the shadows, he edged up to the front porch, climbed the steps of the painted wood planks, finally coming to one of the windows.

Two men, dressed in gray and homespun, were advancing on Serena. One was inches from her and gesturing with his hands, menacing laughter coming from his throat. The other was coming from Christopher's bedroom, a knife in one hand. A huge knife, coated with blood.

Drake checked his rifle. It was ready to fire, good for one shot. With every sense heightened, he studied the man talking to Serena. He was demanding something, but Drake couldn't hear. Then the scoundrel turned and he recognized Davis Lyle, one of their traveling companions to York. A hunting knife hung by a leather strap bound on his upper thigh, but he didn't appear intent upon using it; he seemed more interested in getting his hands on Serena.

A memory of the man leering at Serena and then watching them mount the stairs in the inn to their private room flashed across his mind. Lyle had turned and looked into Drake's eyes. Drake had never seen such envious hatred and lust.

The other man, then, must be Thom Patrick. A horse whinnied from behind the house, and Drake turned his head to peer into the night. Were Henry and Delana Trimble here, too? They wouldn't have brought a woman for such intent, would they?

He turned back to the window in time to hear Serena let out a cry as Lyle lunged at her. Lyle's hand gripped Serena's arm with brutal strength, wrenching it as he brought her close, his chest puffed out as he tried to wrestle Serena into an embrace. Drake sprung into action, darting for the front door. Just as he lifted the wooden latch he heard another sound—a startled grunt and a gunshot.

He burst through the door.

Serena stood staring, face pale, at Lyle, who lay at her feet, red spreading across his back. Drake quickly took stock of the others in the room, trying to make sense of the scene before him. Thom had turned and was running for the back door. Drake lifted his rifle, but the man was lightning fast and was out of range before Drake could draw an accurate bead on him. Drake lowered the gun and chased after him, running out the back of the house and into the yard some ways before he gave up and turned back toward the house.

Who shot Lyle? Serena? And the bloody knife. With a sick feeling, he turned around and ran back into the house for answers. Serena was sitting, shaking violently, her eyes wide and unseeing. He went to her first, checking for injuries and talking in a sure voice, but he didn't have time to comfort her.

Lyle was sprawled next to her, lying on his stomach with a huge, ragged hole in his back. A horrible sight. His shirt was becoming soaked in blood, his face still registering shock. Drake squatted beside him and checked for a pulse. He was already dead. Turning, he looked into the bedroom. Christopher lay just inside the bedroom door, blood pooling from a stab wound in his chest.

Drake went to the man's side. He was still alive and breathing, but very shallow. He picked up the first thing he could get his hands on and pressed the cloth into Christopher's wound. It was soon soaked, warm and red. "What happened?"

"They were going after—" he struggled for breath— "Serena."

Drake nodded, he had seen that much. "What did they want? Did they say?"

Christopher shook his head. "I do not know. Didn't have time to ask." He smiled at Drake.

Drake pushed a pillow under Christopher's head, hoping to help him breathe. He felt so helpless. The man was dying, and there was naught he could do about it.

"I called out to her . . . to tell her to give them money. I believe they were here for her." He stopped and took a few gasps. "When I heard her scream . . . I made it to the door with my pistol . . . always keep a pistol in the . . . bedside table." He paused again and Drake interceded.

"Do not talk. I understand." He looked into Christopher's eyes and felt a million regrets. This man could have been his friend. "You saved her."

Christopher reached out for Drake's hand. He struggled, summoning his strength. "Take care of her. Live here . . . it was always hers."

If burning coals were dumped on his head, Drake couldn't feel any more wretched.

Christopher's next words made it nigh impossible for Drake to breathe. "Now I understand . . . God knew." He smiled, and for an instant his face shone with an unearthly light. Then he looked up and past Drake.

Drake's heart speeded up until it pounded in his ears.

"Look! I see heaven. It has opened!" Christopher's eyes were bright and full of reflected light. Drake looked up into the beams that formed the ceiling of the cabin but saw nothing. Christopher made a sudden sound, regaining Drake's attention. Then the wounded man took one shallow breath—and breathed no more.

Drake heard a cry and turned back to Serena. She sat in a terrorized trance, unable to move away from the dead man but seeming to know that Christopher was gone. Gently Drake closed Christopher's eyes and then went to his wife. She sat, unmoving, until Drake gathered her into his arms. After a while, deep shaking overtook her.

DRAKE SAT AND held her, his mind working to make sense of it all. What did one do with two dead bodies . . . friend and foe. Finally he forced Serena to drink a little brandy. Steadier, she went to Christopher, kneeling beside his body. Drake watched as she put her hand on his head, touched his golden hair with her fingertips. A little sob escaped her throat and her hand rose to her mouth as she looked up at Drake. "Is he really gone?"

"Oh, sweetheart . . ." Drake went to her, wrapping his arms around her as she buried her face in his shoulder, beginning to sob.

"It is our fault!" She lifted her head to look at Drake, her eyes giant pools of tears. "We never should have come here."

Silently Drake agreed with her. They had brought the dragon's curse here. He had brought it. But her friend's death wasn't Serena's fault, and Drake couldn't let her believe it. "Never say that. Never think it." He cupped his wife's lovely face and lifted it until she met his eyes. "Christopher would never want you to think that, would he?"

She shook her head, sniffling. "No, he would not. But those men. It was Lyle and Thom Patrick." She started crying again, her gaze back on Christopher's face. "They followed us here . . . but why?"

Drake wasn't about to tell her the truth. She did not need to know a man's lust and what it could do. Not now. Instead, he prevaricated. "They must have thought we had money. At the inn, when we received the better room, they must have thought I had enough to pay for such luxuries."

"But they did not ask for money, they—"

"They just hadn't gotten around to it yet. They would have. It's the only logical explanation."

She lowered her head, nodding. Then she touched Christopher's hair. "God forgive them—" she bowed her head—"for I don't know how I shall."

She started crying again, and Drake hauled her into his arms. He gave her another sip of brandy and then insisted she go lie down on the cot in the loft. After she left the room, Drake gently wrapped Christopher's body with a sheet and laid him on his bed.

Looking at Lyle's body, crumpled on the floor in a bloody pool, he felt sick. It was all he could do to look at the man, yet he had to do so much more. Taking a fortifying breath he grasped the thin wrists, really looking at the dead face for the first time. He was so young, had such a long life ahead of him . . . and what had he died for?

Disgusted, Drake dragged Lyle's body out into the yard and then farther, as far as his strength would let him, to the end of Christopher's property. The man would have to be buried tomorrow but not, Drake vowed, on Christopher's land. The longer he pulled, the angrier he became. What had given this man the right to come after Drake's wife? To take Christopher's life?

As soon as he thought it, he saw the man he pushed over the balustrade of his Northumberland mansion. Suddenly it was as if he and Lyle were one. Drake flung his arms away as a ragged sound tore from his throat. He stumbled from the body, turned, and ran . . . away from the image . . . away from the ghosts.

Fear dogged him as he ran. He had not thought to bring a gun with him and the darkness descended with sudden menace. The wind blew through the branches of the surrounding trees, making threatening shadows in the moonlight. Sounds of the woods were suddenly loud and distinct. He shouldn't have left Serena alone so long. Stumbling, he ran toward the house.

Finally he came into the clearing, panting and slowing to a walk. All was quiet in the house, only a small light coming from the kitchen window where the fire burned. Drake crept quietly in the back door, hoping not to wake Serena. Heaven knew she needed to sleep. There would be wreckage enough to deal with in the morning.

Now, with blood on the floor waiting to be cleaned up, was not the time to deal with the coming demons.

Chapter Nineteen

They tried to make a home on the homestead of Christopher Kingsley's land. They tried to clean up the nightmare and pick up where he had left off. They tried to live Christopher's dream, but they both knew it wasn't working. Everywhere they looked were the efforts of a man they had both come to regard as more saint than human, more angel than mortal, more noble than either of them.

Drake slammed his fist down upon the small writing table, making the quill and ink jump. Serena jerked her head around.

"What is it, Drake?"

He stared at his hands. They were hardly recognizable. Deep calluses lined the palms, dry and rough, catching on Serena's clothing when he touched her. His face and upper torso had bronzed in the sun, growing lean and strong. A farmer's hands and body.

Something told him he should be proud—his was the body of a man who knew a hard day's work—but he was not. What he wouldn't give for the thrill of a contract being sealed, his scrolling signature at the bottom of a Parliament document to be read and considered by the king.

"Nothing. I am sorry." He forced a smile for her. The lie must be perpetuated—the fairy tale carried out to its bitter end.

She rose and came to him. Reaching around him she slowly opened a drawer in the desk, dug into the back under Christopher's papers, and drew out a letter. Staring at it in her hand a moment, she studied the address, then drew a deep breath. "I—Drake, I took thy letter from the postmaster. I think it is time for thee to open it." She held it out for him to see.

Drake stared at the letter as if it were a snake, coiled and ready to strike. "You've had it all this time?" He could not believe she'd kept this from him.

"Yes." She didn't say more, just held it out to him.

"You would have me open it," he stated, as if to make himself believe it.

She considered him a moment, then nodded, looking surer than she ever had. "Thou shouldst bring it into the light."

In the light. Nothing felt better in the light. Only in the dark recesses of his soul, hidden, could Drake stand this wilderness life. But Serena had changed since Christopher's death—something inside her had matured. Where there once was simplicity was now a grave serenity, a quiet strength. He found he could not fight against her this time.

Let it be as she said. Let them bring it into the light.

He took the letter from her hand and swiftly tore it open. Before he had time to give it a coward's thought he flipped the page open and began to read:

To His Grace, the Duke of Northumberland:

Wait . . . that was his father's address. Was this letter intended for his father? Drake flipped the envelope back over and reread the name. It was his own. "Drake Weston, Earl of Warwick" in flowing black scrawl. He took up the page once more:

Yes, dear friend, you read correctly. It is not too late to continue with your plan to grasp the dukedom. Much has happened since your flight. First of all, your servants saw the man trip and fall backwards over the railing of your balcony. They have testified that you did not touch him, and I believe this to be true. From your own accounting to me, you merely frightened him, which led to the unfortunate event. Furthermore, the man lived! He bled terribly, I am told, being cut in the head and having several broken bones, one being that nasty leg you described, but all have mended nicely since. All has been satisfactorily dismissed regarding this matter. Apparently, Judge Abbot was looking for you to offer you a position as royal advisor to His Majesty, at King George's request. They were somewhat distressed to learn you and your father had departed for a trip to the continent, as I explained to them. So you see, all believe your father still lives and that the two of you are even now enjoying a tour of the colonies.

Drake, you must see what this means. You can now return, leaving your father safely hidden in the colonies. It would further your original plan to bring home a wife and pass her off as your step-mother. After she conceives (hopefully on the voyage over), we will learn that your father has passed away . . . buried somewhere on the frontier, perhaps? Then you can marry the "widow" and run the estate until your son inherits. It is a superior plan to the original, if I do say so myself. No messy makeup and fake appearances. No gossipy servants or funeral to plan.

All you have to do is find the right woman. Good luck, your grace, my dear Duke of Northumberland.

Ever Your Servant,
Albert Radcliff

Drake's hands were trembling. The man lived. The man *lived!*

Just as his death had haunted Drake, so now his survival thrilled him. Drake folded the paper and placed it on the desk, but kept his hand over it, afraid it would disappear.

"What is it, Drake? Tell me everything."

He looked into Serena's worried eyes and wondered . . .

Did he have it in him anymore, the ability to deceive, to make his own wife an accomplice to such a lie? At one time he wouldn't have hesitated. Now . . .

Had he changed so much? He didn't know what to tell Serena, but one thing was clear: She could never read this letter. His hand closed around it, wadding it into a ball. With even strides he made for the fireplace and threw it in. He watched it catch and then blaze with yellow light until it was nothing but ash.

He felt Serena's arms slip around his waist, her head resting on his back. "I am sorry. I should not have asked thee to read it."

He turned, putting his arms around her, kissing the top of her head, his throat so raw, so choked with emotion he hardly knew what to say. "No, it was a good thing. I just did not want it around." Tilting her chin up to look into her eyes, he took a deep breath and then plunged in. "It told me two things, Serena. Two very important things. We have to go back." The first step. It was easier than it should have been.

"Go back? To Philadelphia? But Drake, why? I know thy heart dost not love it here, but if we give it more time . . . allow the memory of Christopher's death to fade . . ." She'd been talking fast, but slowed and, seeing his set eyes, her argument faded into silence.

"I have to go back to London."

She took a step back, out of his arms. "London?" Her eyes searched his face. "But . . . why? I thought thou couldst never return."

Drake stepped up to her again and grasped both her arms. "Dearest . . . the letter said . . ." He stopped and allowed the joy of it to fill him, to suffuse his face and eyes. "It's incredible. The man I thought I killed did not die! He lives! Serena, do you realize what this means? We can go back to England! I can take up my life again."

Suddenly, he realized it—all the consequences, advantages, and realities of being of English nobility. He wouldn't be cheating her! He would be giving Serena everything she deserved. Finally he would be able to shower her with all the wealth and status the world had to give. He could be her provider, protector, her husband in truth. He laughed again, squeezing her tight, lifting her feet from the floor and spinning her around in a circle.

Serena only grasped his arms, confusion in the lines on her brow. "But Drake, what does this mean?"

He set her on her feet. "Allow me to make the introductions." The words tumbled out, easy and sweet. Bowing his most elegant bow, he stated with relish. "Serena, dearest, your husband is a duke. And you are . . . a duchess. The Duchess of Northumberland, to be exact."

Serena backed away again. "Drake, stop it. Thou art frightening me." She *looked* frightened, and Drake could not resist a chuckle. "I am sorry, Serena. It must seem madness, but please, if you will sit down I will explain everything."

Pale and wide-eyed, she sat, hands clasped tightly in her lap, while Drake told her the truth.

Most of it.

He explained how, fearing for his life, he had fled London and boarded a ship as an indentured servant, how his money was stolen and his health robbed to the very brink of death. He told her the truth of how he came to be indentured. Then he told her about his life before the accident.

It was in this telling that the madness began.

He told her of the life he had lived, and the life they would now share when they returned to London as the Duke and Duchess of Northumberland. It didn't seem important that she thought him the duke and not his father. It was perfect really, now that he considered it. She was so innocent of the ways of the world. She would never understand what he had to do. But no matter, for it would be an easy deception.

After a few carefully chosen social events where she would appear with him as his stepmother, he would take them to Northumberland where she would give birth to an heir. The sooner she became pregnant, the better, of course. For anyone to believe the child was the duke's, she would have to conceive in the next few months. But Drake had little doubt he could make it so. They had time before the journey and the ocean voyage. Then, after the babe was born and they announced his father's death, the will would be read and circumvented by the presence of a legitimate heir.

And if Serena ever learns the truth?

He pushed the caution aside. He would convince her it had all been necessary. No . . . their *son* would convince her. What mother wouldn't do anything for her son to inherit such a title and estate?

Oh, indeed he was back. A changed and better man for his hardships, yes, but back and alive again, not buried in this wilderness coffin awaiting a slow, guilt-ridden death. He would make everything—his life and now hers—a dream come true.

SERENA SAT IN silence, unable to comprehend and yet knowing. It all made so much sense now. She had always known he was like no one else, had always suspected he was of the English nobility. But a duke. God help her, she had never entertained such a thought. And she, a duchess! She wasn't sure she even understood what that meant.

Sudden, overwhelming tears struck her. "I cannot be a duchess! I am still a Quaker at heart. I cannot go to London. What shall I do in London?" She looked up at him with all the helplessness that she felt.

He sat down beside her, gathering her cold hands into his. "Thou wilt make a wonderful duchess. Quaker or not, Serena, you are my wife and I love you. You must come with me, take your place in the world at my side. I will guide you."

"But . . . how does one be a duchess? Drake——" she stopped alarmed. "May I still call thee Drake? Is there some special address I should be using?"

Drake laughed. She was so delightful. "Of course you may call me Drake. Others will address us both as 'your grace,' but family and close friends use first names." He gathered her into his arms. "You have no idea how wonderful it will be. I have seen your world . . . now let me show you mine." He leaned back to look into her eyes. "Serena, trust me in this. Let me show you my world."

Something inside her said no, that this was wrong. But he looked so happy . . . and she hadn't seen that look very often, nearly never. She found that she would do anything to make it permanent.

Even ignore the counsel of her heart.

Chapter Twenty

LONDON

"Ow!"

Serena jerked as a pin stuck the delicate skin of her wrist. She stood, precariously balanced on a three-legged stool, while seamstresses swarmed about her. A "fitting" they called it. Serena wondered if the flames of hell would come now or later. Such decadence. Such luxurious fabrics, one yard of which cost more than her father made in a year. The laces and furs and jewels.

What was she doing here?

She was being fitted for a court dress, for her presentation to the queen of England. Never in all her wildest imaginings had she thought to someday be in such a place. Her hands brushed across the skirt of her gown as she stared at her reflection in awe. The underskirt, or chemise, was heavy, gold brocade with a lighter cream fleur-de-lis design. The overskirt and bodice were done in deep blue silk. The overskirt was draped back and away, providing a teasing glimpse of the magnificence of the chemise, gathering at the sides and attached in the back. The bodice was a triangular stomacher, the blue fabric inset with real jewels of amber, diamond, and sapphire. The magnitude of the wealth she was wearing made her want to shriek with both terror and delight.

The still-sane part of her thought of the poor she had seen in the streets of London, the orphans and the widows and the starving. The other part of her swelled with wonder and . . . something else . . . a feeling of astonishment that she could look so beautiful, like a princess from some faraway land, as though this dress revealed some part of her that she'd never known existed.

She blinked into the mirror, feeling like two different women, and wondered which would prevail.

Her stays were so tight she could barely breathe. Standing before the full-length, gilt-edged, peer glass in her own private dressing room—which was connected with the large bedroom she and Drake shared—Serena swallowed hard, gulping as much air as she could. *Don't let me fail Thee, God. If this is a test . . . I do not want to fail.*

"Your grace, could you turn?"

Madame de Bourbor, whom Drake assured her was the best dressmaker in all of England, demanded more than asked. Serena had little doubt what Drake said was true. Since their arrival she had had little choice but to trust his vast knowledge in every way. She might hardly recognize her husband these days, but she was sure *he* knew whatever it was he was currently about.

Her husband.

Serena attempted another deep breath and turned as directed, thinking of him, of this strange and glorious creature she had married.

Her husband.

A vision of him in his "duke's clothing" (as she thought of his raiment) rose to mind, sending a warm shiver over her. The changes in him since returning to London had been nothing short of astounding. It wasn't just the clothing or the extravagant townhouse on Berkeley Square, where they now lived. When

Drake asked her to let him show her his world, she'd had no idea the scope of such a world.

So much had happened since Drake read that letter.

They had sold the farm in the Shenandoah Valley to a nice Quaker family who promised to make of it all Christopher had hoped. It was hard to leave and yet a relief of sorts. They were meant for something different. Back in Philadelphia they had visited briefly with Serena's family, explaining everything that had happened. Her mother and father had showed little shock to find their daughter married into the English nobility, knowing all along that there was much more to their son-in-law than an indentured servant. They were saddened to see Serena off to England but acknowledged she must follow her husband. The two of them had sent Serena and Drake off with kisses of goodwill at the dockside.

The journey was much easier than the one Drake had taken over a year ago. With money, Serena learned, anything could be had. His name and title reinstated, Drake took charge. They boarded one of the king's own vessels, taking possession of a comfortable cabin complete with feather bed, servants to wait upon them, and French delicacies to dine upon.

Upon reaching London, her breath caught at her first sight of one of the world's largest cities. The harbor was at least as busy as Philadelphia's but different; it seemed busy in an ancient way, as though all knew their business better. The people here spoke in her husband's accent, even the dock hands, though their sound was more coarse. But they treated Drake with deferential bows and ran to and fro to fetch him his heart's desires. Serena realized something along those docks: Drake's title, just the name they called him, that alone generated respect. It didn't matter what he did or how he lived his life; he was a duke.

It was all so foreign. She'd clung to his arm like a child, hating that she felt so helpless, feeling that whatever ground she had gained, whatever growing up she had done after Christopher's death, was gone like a puff of smoke. This world was as unknown to her as the silversmith shop and the farm had been to Drake. Now *he* was the confident one. They were now in his world where they were sudden royalty and everyone around them bowed and scraped for no other reason than the accident of one's birth.

A hired carriage had taken them from the busy harbor, down the cobbled streets to Berkeley Square. On the ride Serena glimpsed the sorry side of London. Dirty children ran like rats in the narrow alleys. Dark and dank little houses lined the side streets, and everywhere were hucksters with their carts. It was such a frenetic place, so alive with the business of trying to make a living. Serena was appalled and enthralled by turns.

They had finally reached Berkeley Square, where the wealthy and titled resided in three-storied brownstone houses that lined the square. Like the king's own guards, the stately homes stood ready to cast judgment on any who didn't belong. Serena had floated through the front door of the duke's home, as if riding on a cloudy dream. The entrance was more of a salon than a hall. A polished black-and-white marble floor gave way to snowy white walls, complete with Roman columns and inset arched cases. Six gilt armchairs, done in gold and white velvet, flanked the walls. A black velvet settee with matching scrolling gilt edging sat against another wall. Chinese urns of dark-hued richness, as tall as she, stood guard on either side of an arched doorway that led to a short hall. A domed ceiling was intricately plastered, with a brilliant chandelier its central jewel. It was a room designed to impress and intimidate.

It accomplished both. Serena had been overwhelmed.

Further down the hall was a feast for the eyes, with landscape paintings in soft greens and blues, a thick carpet running its length. There was a library filled with alcoves of books, a sunny yellow breakfast room, and a gallery with family portraits and valuable works of art. The main drawing room was done in sapphire blue and gold. The ballroom boasted a huge domed ceiling. And in the back was a well-hidden kitchen.

Upstairs Drake had been eager to show her the master bedchamber and the deep four-poster bed with heavy velvet curtains. It was a dark, private world inside those walls of fabric and Drake had been more sure of himself there under that silk counterpane, had shown her things he seemed to have forgotten across the sea.

As smooth as water running over a rocky outcropping, that was Drake's manner now, and as powerful as a waterfall. Serena marveled at how well it fit him. She no longer wondered at his black moods and stony silences of the past—all was explained in the reclaiming of his identity. This man, so sure, so confident, but now with a hard-won kindness and new appreciation for those things beneath his notice before . . . this was the man she had married. If she thought she loved the shadow that Drake had been, she was ensnared, spellbound by the real thing. Gorgeous . . . powerful . . . confident . . . he was any woman's fantasy.

And he was in love with *her*.

She had no doubt of his love. He proved it a hundred times a day since they had moved into the brownstone bearing the ducal seal above the front door. Each day held new surprises, planned and executed with exacting care—all for her. Today she would be fitted for a new wardrobe, then take a curtsy class, something she'd only been convinced was necessary by a detailed description of her presentation to the queen. A short rest time would be followed by an intimate dinner with Drake. That evening they were to attend an opera at the Theatre Royal in Drury Lane. Serena had never even seen a play, and tonight she was going to the opera and sitting in a private box with her husband, the duke.

It was all as in a dream.

SERENA DESCENDED THE stairs a little breathless, still trying to get used to the confining stays and tight bodice of her evening gown. She felt as though she'd been transformed into someone else while she was sleeping. She wasn't sure she liked it—or more accurately, was afraid she liked it too much. What kind of woman wore finery such as that in which she was draped? What kind of woman wore her hair elaborately coiled, with one long, provocative curl dangling over a shoulder.

She gripped her heavy skirt with one hand, lifting it above the stairs and grasped the railing tight with her other hand. So intent on traversing the stairs, she did not see Drake standing at the bottom, awaiting her. When she finally reached the landing, she looked up and gasped.

"Thou frightened me!" She laughed and then looked down, feeling suddenly shy. "Thou hast been waiting long?"

Drake stood speechless. Admiration—and something else Serena could not quite identify, pride perhaps—showing from his eyes.

"Turn around," his deep voice commanded softly. "I would see all of you."

She turned slowly, holding back a delighted laugh. Her gown was gold, the color of the amber flecks in her eyes, with a green-and-gold-striped underskirt and matching puffed sleeves. Emeralds hung from her ears, swaying provocatively and catching the candlelight from the wall sconces. A choker wrapped around her neck and tiny tear-shaped jewels sparkled from her hair. It had taken the combined urgings of her personal maid and the housekeeper to convince her it was acceptable to wear such a low-cut gown in public. Elegant gloves covered her arms to the elbows with an emerald and gold bracelet on one wrist and a Chinese fan dangling from the other.

"I knew you would be beautiful dressed as my duchess, but Serena, I am speechless. The men will adore you and the women will envy you." He spoke the last in an underbreath, as though to himself. Then he held out her deep-black satin cloak with ermine fur trim and continued. "There are a few important instructions I would give you before we enter the theatre."

"Instructions?" She turned toward him.

"Nothing to fret about. I shall explain in the carriage."

The night air was brisk, but Serena barely had time to feel it before she was ensconced in a well-sprung carriage complete with fur lap robes. Drake slipped in next to her, seeming too big, too alive to be confined in such an enclosed space, even one so richly appointed as this.

As soon as the carriage swung into motion, Drake turned to her with a smile. "Serena, dearest, what I am about to tell you may seem odd . . . wrong even, on some level, but let me explain marriages of the nobility."

Serena nodded, listening and vowing to follow his instruction to the minutest detail.

"I shall introduce you as Serena Weston, Duchess of Northumberland. When asked about your parentage you should reply that you were born in the colonies and lived in Pennsylvania. No need to mention that you are Quaker—that shall be discovered soon enough. Also, very, very important. Do not refer to me as

Drake or your husband." He smiled at her. "Always refer to your husband as 'the duke,' such as, 'the duke and I met in Philadelphia,' or 'the duke is a most generous husband.'" He winked at her. "And this is very important, Serena. We shall go to social functions together and sometimes even sit together, but it is not fashionable for husbands and wives to be affectionate or even overly friendly with one another in public."

"But—"

Drake took hold of her hand and kissed the back of it. "I know it seems dreadful, but we shall make up for it in private. Just treat me as . . . a brother, perhaps, when we are with others."

"A *brother?* That is preposterous. However will I do it?"

Drake just laughed. "It is not so hard. Watch the others, my dear; you will soon see what I mean. And if in doubt, then just remain silent and observe. For the first weeks, that will probably be wisest."

Serena nodded. She had been tutored in the basics of comportment since arriving on their London doorstep, but she still had much to learn. Best to lean upon Drake in the treacherous social waters of the ton.

The theatre was magnificent, complete with columns and a domed ceiling with a tiered glass chandelier seemingly suspended in midair from a great height. Light sparkled from wall candelabras and sconces, showering glittering raindrops of light on the people and their elaborate costumes.

Drake ushered her into their private box, her eyes slowly adjusting to the darkened theatre. They had an excellent view of the stage, curtains still drawn as the opera had yet to begin. Below them were crowds of people. Serena was hard pressed not to gape in astonishment as she spied a scantily clad girl selling oranges and being pawed at by overzealous men. The woman seemed not to mind the attention as she took their coins and giggled. Ribald comments flew back and forth between the men and women, whose bosoms all but fell from their low-cut gowns.

Drake leaned close to her ear. "Serena, I would like to introduce you to someone."

Pulling herself from the sights, she stood and turned. An older gentleman with kind eyes and a ruddy face stood at the entrance of their box. Advancing, he bowed, taking up Serena's hand.

"May I present Lord Albert Radcliff," Drake said with a smile.

"My lord, it is so very nice to meet thee." She saw his surprise at the "thee" and wondered if she shouldn't have said it. Should she perhaps drop the Quaker speech—if she could, so ingrained in her it was. No, such silly thoughts! She wouldn't change her speech for Drake or anyone. She had changed enough as it was.

Some of her joy fled as shame filled her. Yes, she had changed. Had she already strayed so far from The Way? Was her soul in jeopardy?

Albert apparently read her stricken features and tried to smooth things over. "How delightful. Drake, you did not tell me she was a Quaker." He nodded, jowls shaking. "Highest regard for the Quakers . . . yes . . . such solid people."

"Thank thee, sir." Serena decided she liked him. "I hope thou art not the only one in London to feel so."

Before Albert had a chance to respond, three men and a beautiful woman entered their box. Serena watched Drake's face for clues as to their identity. She wished later she had not been watching quite so closely. Recognition flashed in his eyes as he saw the blond woman. It was not the kind of look one wanted to see in a husband's eyes for another woman. He recovered quickly, though, and made the introductions.

He pulled Serena close. "May I have the honor of presenting the Duchess of Northumberland."

The woman, Maria Louisa Chamberlain, bowed, as befitted Serena's station, yet disdain dripped from her as thick as the diamonds she was wearing. With her blond hair and flashing blue eyes, she captivated the other men in the box with a skill Serena could only marvel at. When the woman addressed her, Serena was hard pressed not to stutter in response.

"Fresh from the colonies?"

Gathering inner courage, Serena offered a sweet smile and nodded. "Yes, Philadelphia."

The woman glanced at Drake and then back at her. Serena was shocked to see pity in her eyes. "It must be difficult, being newly married and the duke having stayed—"

Drake interrupted her with practiced smoothness. "I am doing my best to keep her entertained."

Serena jumped at Drake's interruption. There was an almost threatening undertone to his statement that Serena didn't understand, but apparently the woman did, for she gave him a conciliatory look and a short "I see."

Serena knew there was much more being said than what she had heard. Attempting to draw the woman's attention back toward herself she asked, "Thou hast been friends with the duke for a long time?"

The woman's eyebrows raised. "I would hardly call us friends." She glanced at Drake and smiled a slow smile. "But I am on more . . . intimate terms with other members of the family."

Turning back to Serena, she tossed her head and smiled. "You will find many among us jealous of the time your stay in London affords you with those others."

Serena felt as if some other language, some code perhaps, was being spoken. Her confusion must have shone from her eyes as she looked to Drake, for he was quick to step in.

"Sheath your claws, Maria. The duchess is unused to such frays, and you would do well to make some allowances."

Maria pouted at him and then shrugged a nearly bare shoulder. "You cannot blame me. It is so very easy."

"All the more reason for restraint." He sounded like a stern father lecturing a child.

Maria turned to one of the gentlemen who had entered with her and, with a bored sigh, indicated her desire to leave. The three men gathered themselves in response, bowing to Serena and telling her outrageous lies—how ravishing she was and how they should like to call on her and take her riding in the park. Confused at such offers when they knew she was married, she could only smile and nod and remain silent.

When they left she leaned against Drake's arm for a moment, then looked up into his eyes. "Whatever did all that mean?"

His warm laugh washed over her as he turned her to her seat. "You will get used to it. Now, let us sit. The opera is about to begin."

During the performance, Drake watched Serena from the corner of his eye. The glow from the stage bathed her face in creamy light, lending an aura of luminosity to her skin. Her delight in the production only added to his enchantment.

Stop it, you fool!

He forced his gaze back to the actors. He mustn't look at her like a lovesick calf! The world, his world, believed she was his stepmother . . . and it was going to be harder than he thought to pull it off. One thing was made certain tonight: He would not be able to keep her in society long. The women would eat her alive and have her believing all sorts of things about him—some true, but many exaggerated. He'd never really cared before, but now he suddenly didn't want her hearing the worst of his past. He rather liked her devotion.

How long do you think that devotion can last in a climate such as this? The thought plagued him, his mouth pressing together in a tense line. He pushed the unsettling question away, doing his best to convince himself there was no reason for worry. Nothing could diminish Serena's love for him.

He only prayed he was right.

Chapter Twenty-One

Drake attempted to immerse himself in his old lifestyle, taking fencing lessons, managing vast estates needy from his long absence, visiting his club, and escorting Serena to very select social engagements—those with limited conversation, where his need to leave her unattended was unlikely. While all this kept him busy, he was, still, somehow restless. In fact, were he honest with himself, he'd have to admit it was all . . . empty.

Rather than relishing his position and wealth as he had in the old days, now, when he rode in the seedier parts of town, he noticed the wretched urchins, the beleaguered mothers, and the downtrodden men who found escape in a bottle of spirits. Just yesterday he had shocked his valet by inquiring if the man had a cold after he had sneezed several times.

Had he changed so much? After all, he still felt the satisfied rush of accomplishment when he received, earlier in the week, news of a successful shipping venture. It was as if he had become two men, and he didn't know how to reconcile them into one whole.

Frustrated, he redoubled his efforts in the one direction he was sure of—Serena. He had promised to show her his world, and now he did so with the grandeur of his dreams. There were flowers overflowing from every vase in the house, jewels that were exclaimed over as if they were the first she had ever seen, clothes and furs and every bauble and delicacy he could put his hands on.

He knew she loved anything he gave her, but lately she looked a little perplexed when some new trinket arrived, as if she sensed the dam was threatening to break and flood waters about to flow, full force, upon them.

Drake feared it was so as well.

It was the strain of it all, he told himself as he leaned his head into his hands at the desk in his library. They had to be so careful. *He* had to be so careful, forever on guard, fielding questions and comments about the duke, smoothing any blunders Serena unknowingly made. Furthermore, she had yet to conceive. It was perplexing at best, fast becoming alarming.

He had asked a time or two if she'd thought it possible she was with child and received only shy smiles and a shake of her head. They both wanted it, and he knew she was pleased that he seemed to be anticipating it. But it wasn't happening fast enough for his purposes. Everything hinged on her getting pregnant.

Picturing her face made his stomach do an odd twist, a reaction becoming more and more frequent of late. That Serena had not yet become suspicious was nothing short of miraculous. There had been many occasions when his explanation of some flippant comment made by a man or woman of their set had sounded absurd even to his own ears. But she always believed him.

She was so naïve and so very trusting.

And you are so very deceitful.

He couldn't have imagined a year ago that he would experience even a pang of guilt in this situation. He would have stayed the course with single-minded determination and no consideration of how Serena might feel when the truth came out. But now . . . he was haunted by it.

Someday it was going to all come crashing down around him, and Serena, wife of his heart, would no longer look at him with those trusting, adoring eyes.

But someday wasn't now and so he continued the tightrope act, playing the dutiful stepson in public, the doting husband in private.

If he could just get through the next week. The social season and the trials it brought were almost over, thank heaven! One more ball tonight, and then he could whisk her off to Northumberland and Alnwick Castle.

Home.

He glanced down at a pamphlet about the latest innovations in agriculture and cultivation and tried to make himself concentrate on it as he had meant to do this afternoon. But naught stilled the voice whispering in his heart. A voice of concern . . .

And conviction.

SERENA'S HANDS TREMBLED. She dropped the letter as if it were on fire and sat down. She couldn't believe what she had just read. How old was this letter? Did Drake know of its contents? Why was it still here, in this desk that had belonged to Drake's mother?

She scanned it again, trying to make sense of it. It was a love letter. One of the most eloquent expressions of love she had ever read. And, dear heavens, it was from a Richard Weston to Helena,

Drake's mother. She concentrated, trying to remember every detail Drake had told her of his family. She remembered him saying his mother had died when he was a young boy. Hadn't he also said she was sickly and sad? Yes . . . and no wonder if she had loved her husband's brother, as this letter suggested.

Richard Weston. Very little had been told to her about him other than the fact that he was the youngest of the three brothers and now lived in Bristol. She picked up the delicate parchment and opened it, scanning the lines:

As to the child, he should remain of that household and become the next Duke of Northumberland. We must be brave and strong for him, for his future inheritance. Nothing can be proven and my brother will have little choice but to accept him. Dearest, we must endure for his sake as together we could give him nothing.

Was Drake the son they spoke of? Her head swam with the implications. Did he know? And then another question gripped her: Should she show him the letter? Were there others in the desk that may be less cryptic? She had found this one while searching for paper to write a letter home. The top drawer had stuck, and after giving a mighty pull, she had jerked the entire drawer out into her lap. As she lifted it to put it back in place, she discovered a secret compartment in the back of the drawer. After a little prying, it opened. Inside lay this lone letter.

The desk was a treasure of hidden drawers, false backs, and lovely workmanship, but though she rummaged through it with frantic thoroughness, looking for anything that might shed more light on Drake's family, she found nothing. If there had been other letters, they were hidden in another place or destroyed long ago. She would simply have to question Drake about his family.

Perhaps, together, they could discover the truth.

A LOW SHRIEK jolted Drake awake and into a sudden sitting position. The foggy haze of the intense nightmare surrounded him, leaving him unsure for the moment what was real. His heart was pounding as if he had run the length of London and his body shook in a cold sweat. What had made that sound? He realized it must have been him.

Serena sat up and touched his arm. "What was that sound? Was it thee, Drake? Art thou all right?"

He wasn't sure if he could answer. He had to get some air. Pulling back the coverlet and then the bed curtain, he climbed out of bed, his legs weak as a baby's. The chill of the night air hit his naked body like a bucket of cold water, helping to pull him back into reality. Hurriedly, he pulled on his dressing gown and finally attempted to answer her.

"Just a dream. I'll go down to walk it off. Go back to sleep, Serena."

The moonlight fell into the room through the tall windows and into their cocoon, revealing the worry on her shadowed face. "Art thou sure? I could get something for thee."

He shook his head, putting on slippers. "I'm all right. I will be back shortly." He wasn't sure that was true, but he had to be alone.

His steps led him into the library, his sanctuary and place to think. The window hangings were drawn and the fire almost dead, lending an eerie darkness to the room that normally wouldn't have bothered him. Setting down the candle he carried, he stirred up the embers and added a log, trying to dissipate the chill in the room—and the chill clinging to his mind.

He poured a glass of amber liquor, then sat in the armchair behind his desk and let his breath out in a rush. As his eyes closed, the memory of the dream rushed back over him.

His father, again, trying to pull him down into the flames. It was so real, always so real, but this time there had been more. Other souls were there, in the distant blackness, screaming for him to help them. Their cries were like nothing he had heard on earth—guttural sounds more animal than human. Gone was any trace of dignity or self-possession. He could just make out their arms reaching, their hands clawing, wanting either to pull him in or secure his help in getting out. He didn't know which. He knew only that it terrified him.

He inhaled sharply as he remembered being able to smell them. Even now, the stench of brimstone and burning flesh clung to the insides of his nostrils. He'd seen his father in that darkness—a darkness so dense and alive that it seemed to crawl over him. Ivor had watched Drake, eyes glittering, hate and pain twisting his face. He clawed into the air, trying to reach Drake, trying to drag him into the torment of that dark nothingness.

Shivering, Drake opened his eyes and rubbed a hand over his face. The liquor was a long, slow burn down his throat, making his stomach warm and bringing a small measure of comfort. But the dream remained, so vivid that he felt his heart thudding loudly in his chest.

This was Serena's fault. His fingers gripped his glass as he felt the first real anger at her since their marriage. All those questions at dinner . . . about his parents and their relationship. And then she had brought up his Uncle Richard, as if she knew something and was trying to validate it. He didn't like it. Why couldn't she let the past stay where it belonged?

Buried.

His head dropped back onto the high back of the chair, his eyes closed. The notion that the dream meant something, that his father was telling him something from the grave, wouldn't leave. Was his father in hell? Was he truly trying to pull him down into some ghoulish, eternal nightmare with him? All he knew for certain was that the old man was still haunting him, still trying to ruin his life. "Why?" Drake gritted out into the dark room. "What do you want?"

A log fell, sending a shower of sparks and a sudden spurt of flame shooting up the chimney. Drake swung around, staring at the dancing blaze. "Go ahead. Tell me! What do you *want?*" He was shouting now, but he didn't care. He wanted answers. "Why won't you leave me alone?"

Empty silence was his only answer. The abyss mocked him, for he had no control over it. It could haunt him at will, especially in the vulnerability of sleep.

Drake's face twisted. "Whatever it is, you won't get it. We shall see who has the last laugh when my son inherits everything. Then we shall see who wins." His words sounded powerless compared with the horror of the nightmare—a little boy's bravado in the face of a monster.

Impotent fury filled him. Drake stood, ready to fling the glass in his hand at the fireplace, but he stopped. Carefully, quietly, he set it down on the desk. He could not let a cold body in a grave have such control over his emotions ever again. But as he stared down at his shaking hands, he suddenly felt helpless to fight it. He was cold and hot at the same time. Terror and stark panic sent him to his knees on the thick rug.

"If there is a hell, there *must* be a heaven!"

His body quivered, sweat glistening on the skin beneath his dressing gown. Taking a deep, spasmodic breath he dropped his head, suddenly longing for peace—so thick he could almost touch it—the peace he had found in the Quaker meetinghouse.

Serena. She always brought him peace. Standing, he stumbled from the library and went in search of his wife, his safe harbor, his reason. He would bury himself in her serenity and there, as always, find his haven and his hope.

Chapter Twenty-Two

Lady Chamberlain paced the marble floors of the entrance, her red heels clicking out her impatience. She would not leave until she got to the bottom of the mysterious Duchess of Northumberland. There was something disturbing in the way Drake looked at his stepmother. If she knew anything, she knew a man in love when she saw one! What she didn't know was how far their little farce had gone, but she wasn't leaving here today until she found out.

All these years, waiting for Drake to notice her. And now, just as the bloom was fading from her face and form, he chose someone else? A woman married to his father! Her gloved hands balled into fists at her side as she remembered when, years ago, she had been the most sought-after woman of the ton. Drake had insinuated a relationship then, but not the one she'd wanted, so she played hard to get.

When Drake's interest cooled toward her, others had taken note and dropped back as well. Now at thirty, she was practically on the shelf. When she thought of the offers she had turned down . . . it made her want to stamp her feet and scream. Now those eligibles were married with babies, and the younger bloods coming behind them did not want her. She would be forced to marry an old widower with children not her own to raise.

Her eyes narrowed. Someone was going to pay for that.

She may not have any power over Drake, but she certainly could get her claws into a backwater provincial who didn't know her way around a London puddle, much less the sea of Lady Maria Louisa Chamberlain's world. Serena Weston was hiding something, and Maria Louisa was determined to find out what it was and use it to maximum advantage.

She would have Drake yet.

Finally the butler came back and intoned that her grace would see her in the blue drawing room. She had never been inside any of Drake's homes. Her eyes devoured the elegance, and she felt her temper flare once more into her cheeks. Taking a calming breath, she stepped through the doorway, nodded dismissively at the butler, and studied the seating arrangements.

She entered the room and took a seat with her back to the wide windows. Facing the entrance, she sat on the edge of her chair, carefully arranging her skirts. The chit had better not keep her waiting! Maria Louisa doubted the duchess even understood the nuances of a well-timed entry or exit, so she couldn't credit Serena with duplicity and yet, she knew better than to underestimate one's opponent.

It wasn't long before the duchess entered, a little breathless and very pretty with those pure eyes and rosy cheeks. Maria Louisa had to admit the child was attractive. Stifling a curled lip, she pasted on a gracious smile and purred, "Why, your grace, you look as if you have been running. I do hope you did not hurry on my account."

Serena's smile broadened. "Oh no," she laughed. "Drake and I were riding early this morning and only just returned. We ride every morning, before the crowds begin." Her sigh was positively dreamy. "'Tis one of the best parts of the day." She pulled her hat off as she spoke and with it some of her pins. Long, golden-red curls cascaded around her shoulders. What man wouldn't long to bury his face in that resplendent hair?

Maria Louisa dug the nails of one hand into the flesh of the palm of the other. How could anyone be so happy? It was preposterous. And it was time to wipe away the innocent's grin. "Drake . . . hmmm . . . you *are* close, the two of you, yes?"

Serena blushed, that dreamy look on her tilted face. Aha! There it was. They were having an affair. It wasn't the first time she'd heard of a man doing so with his stepmother, and it would not, she was sure, be the last.

"Shall I ring for tea?"

Clearly this young woman had never held court at a morning calling session. Another mystery. Why was it that no one ever called on the young and mysterious duchess? She should have been a delectable diversion to many of the ton.

"Of course, one should always provide refreshments for callers." Maria Louisa stated it with upraised brows, as if reprimanding a child.

Serena only agreed with a smile, going to the door to nod at the waiting footman. She seated herself across from Maria Louisa and laughed. "I have callers so seldom, I suppose my manners are a bit rusty." Then, looking Maria Louisa directly in the eyes, she asked with humble sincerity. "It was so nice of thee to come. Art thou well, Lady Chamberlain?"

She looked as if she really wanted to know, really cared and liked her. Maria Louisa scrambled for a moment, trying to gain a foothold. Hmmm, mayhap she *had* underestimated this woman.

Recovering, she smiled, cocking her bright-blond head to one side. "I am wonderful . . . but concerned, your grace."

"Concerned?"

The duchess was all innocence, and Maria Louisa wondered if she was being played the fool. "Yes," she plunged forward with her plan. "There have been . . . rumors." She let the word fall heavy into the room.

Serena's brow puckered. "I am sorry, Lady Chamberlain, but I do not understand. Rumors about what?"

Maria Louisa fidgeted with her gloves in her lap, feigning reluctance. Finally she looked up with sad knowing in her eyes. "About you and Drake, your grace."

Serena laughed. "Please, Lady Chamberlain, let us dispense with this melodrama and be frank with one another. What, exactly, art thou trying to say?"

Maria Louisa ground her teeth. This woman's head must be made of stone. Changing tactics, she glared at her. "Your grace, scandalous rumors are flying that—" she fanned herself, showing the impact of such news on a true lady—"with the duke in the colonies, you and the earl are having an affair!"

SERENA LOOKED AT this beautiful woman, a woman obviously mad with jealousy, and felt pity for her. "As difficult as it may seem to understand, my lady, the duke married me. We have no need to have an affair."

Lady Chamberlain looked ready to burst a vein. Her blue eyes widened and then she sputtered, "You dolt. Of course the duke married you. I am not referring to the duke, but to Drake— the earl."

Serena shook her head. "Drake is the duke."

Lady Chamberlain looked confused for a long moment, then stood and pulled on her gloves. "I cannot fathom why the duke married such an addle-brained, untitled colonist. A mere child who can't even keep track of the difference in names and titles of her own husband. Let me put it simply for you. Ivan Weston, your husband, is the duke." She was nearly shouting now. "Drake is the *Earl* of Warwick and heir to the dukedom . . . and *he* is going to be *my* husband, so you may kindly take your hands off him and keep them off!"

The woman stormed out the door, almost running over the butler, who was loaded down with a one-of-a-kind mandarin-blue Chelsea tea service.

Serena stood in numb shock. Her brain couldn't seem to function.

The butler came into the room and set down the tea service. "Is anything amiss, your grace?"

Serena turned toward him but hadn't heard him enter. "No . . . no. Please go . . . and shut the door behind thee."

When he had left, Serena sank down on the settee, her hands limp in her lap. Lady Chamberlain thought she was married to Drake's father. The words pounded into her brain but made no sense. Everyone thought she was married to Drake's father.

Everyone thought she was married to Drake's father!

Oh God! God, please . . .

Trembling she slid to the floor, her head in her hands. Why had he lied? Why would he tell them such a thing?

Random thoughts flitted through her mind, trying to connect themselves, trying to make sense of it all. Drake wasn't Ivor's son. Drake had nearly killed a man and ran to America. Ivor was dead. Or was he? Could he be in the colonies as Lady Chamberlain said? If so, why would Drake lie about his father? Drake said he was the duke. Wasn't he? If not, who was her husband? So many questions. And only Drake, gone to his fencing practice, could give her the answers.

Was there ever a greater fool than she? She stared at the beautiful room. Christopher's image rose in her mind. She could have had a life with him. He would still be alive had she chosen him and their simple Quaker life. She could have chosen safety, but she had not. She had chosen this world. She had chosen the lies, the deceit . . .

She had chosen Drake.

Chapter Twenty-Three

The coach ride from London to Bristol was making Serena sick. She lay back against the thin seat and fought for breath in the stagnant summer air. The swaying was dizzying. The man across from her devoured a meat pie with dripping enjoyment, making her avert her eyes and press the back of her hand to her mouth.

Combine these discomforts with the smells of the hot, cramped bodies of her fellow passengers and it was all she could do not to retch—again. Every few hours, she had had to beg the coachman to stop so that she could throw up on the side of the road. It was a condition her fellow passengers found increasingly annoying, but not so annoying, Serena reasoned, as vomiting into their laps.

She wondered vaguely and not for the first time if she was coming down with something. But she had felt so much better at the small inn they had stopped at last night that she didn't think so. It must be a traveling sickness of some sort. She had never been on such a long journey in a coach before.

Dressed again in her Quaker gray, with a dainty white lace cap atop her hair, she had adopted her maiden name of Serena

Winter and was traveling as a widow. In truth, she didn't know what she was. Mayhap a widow. Had she married a duke, a dead duke, an actor? She flushed with anger and shame every time she thought of it.

After picking herself up from the floor of that elegant drawing room that she no longer felt she had any right to be in, Serena had packed her bags. Taking only the most simple gowns and belongings brought from her childhood home, she had decided to set out for some answers. Aside from Drake, there was only one man in all of England who could give them to her. The man of the letter. The man who might be Drake's real father. Richard Weston.

Exactly where he lived and how she would find him was still something of a mystery to her, but she supposed she would figure that out in Bristol. This wretched sickness had not been in her plans though, and she wondered in what condition she would arrive in the coastal town.

Some hours later Serena jerked awake to the sudden stopping of the carriage. In the darkness there were sounds of a river. Her stomach, thankfully quiet for the moment, surprised her with ravenous hunger. She climbed out of the tight space of the coach with her fellow passengers to find herself in Bristol on King Street, standing next to an inn whose sign read *Llandoger Trow.* With its white stone and rich, yellow light pouring from the many four-paned glass windows, the place looked warm and welcoming. Serena breathed a sigh of relief.

Inside, she ordered her supper and a room, using a portion of the small stash of coins she had taken from Drake's dressing table. She was told she would share her bed with three other women. After being treated like a queen for the last few months, she was amazed at the difference in the way people were treating her now, all because she wore different clothes and acted like someone of middle class. People were mostly friendly, though, and with tired resignation she ate her meal and finally dropped into an exhausted sleep.

The next morning brought more nausea, but not as bad as on the coach. The aftereffects of traveling, she supposed. Finding Richard Weston turned out to be easy, as he seemed to be very well liked and respected. Serena was heartened by this, reminding herself that she had had no other choice. She certainly would not have been able to question Drake and believe a word he might say to her.

She walked the short distance, paying a boy of about twelve to carry her trunk for her. The town reminded her of home. A shipping port, Bristol was situated on the River Avon, just as Philadelphia faced the Delaware. The docks in the distance were busy, crews loading and unloading the tall, masted ships. Black-headed gulls soared with quiet grace overhead and the air smelled of damp moss and fish, causing her to feel the first real pangs of homesickness since her arrival in England.

She looked up into the sky as she walked along, pretending for a moment she was on a Philadelphia street and walking home after a day of painting by the shore. The sky reflected the blue-gray waters with filaments of scattered clouds, providing a pretty setting for the many spires and towers of tall churches and cathedrals. Bristol was a town of churches, she thought, with a sudden, intense longing for her brushes and canvas.

She stopped in front of a white stone house on Queen Square, located just where the innkeeper had directed her. It was a handsome house, rising three stories, with arched, fancy stonework around the door and windows. Serena had expected something grander after the lifestyle of the nobles Drake had shown her, but she supposed this was not London.

Mustering her flagging courage, she lifted her hand to knock. It wasn't very long before an elderly gentleman opened the door.

"Yes?" He squinted at her.

Serena gave him her most sunny, confident smile. "Good day, sir. I am Serena Weston, wife to Drake Weston, and I have come to call upon Lord Richard."

His wiry white eyebrows wiggled up and down as he considered her identity. He bowed awkwardly and motioned her in with one arm. "You're the new duchess, then? Drake's finally gone and gotten himself a wife?"

Serena nodded, entering the hall. "Is his lordship at home?"

"Yes, yes," the unconventional butler stated, but not before he moved closer and studied her face. "You're a young one!" he barked out and then seemed to remember that he shouldn't have said such a thing. He backed up into the hall. "Sit down, your grace, whilst I fetch him." He cackled when he said the last, shaking his head and smiling at his own thoughts as he left her alone in the small entry.

Serena saw the low, wooden bench the butler had pointed out but preferred to remain standing. The entry was small and poorly lit, making it hard to see where the butler had gone. Looking about, her eyes caught a painting through the open door of a drawing room just off the entry. Curiosity drew her into the room. She moved toward the stone fireplace where the portrait hung. It was lovely. *She* was lovely. A tall, willowy woman with long dark hair. She stood in front of a long-legged, brown thoroughbred, its mane decorated with red braided ribbons, as proud and pleased as his mistress. The woman wore a blue riding habit, white ruffles frothing at her neck. A matching blue hat with long, black feathers dangled from one outstretched hand. The artist had so superbly captured the mood that Serena could imagine the plumes of feathers swaying in the breeze and the woman laughing at something being said. In the distance looked to be pinkish-purple fields . . . of heather? Serena wondered if it was painted in Northumberland and had a sudden overwhelming desire to see the place.

"She loved to ride."

The deep voice startled her, so engrossed was she in the painting she had forgotten where she was and why she had come. Turning, she faced a man who must be Richard Weston.

He was shorter than Drake and a bit stocky in his middle age, but in the face, and especially the eyes, she could see the family resemblance. Serena turned back to the painting. "She is lovely. Who is she?"

The man's smile held deep sorrow. He walked into the room, came up alongside Serena, and pondered the painting with her. "Well, your grace, if you are who my addle-brained butler claims you are, that woman, had she lived, would have been your mother-in-law."

Drake's mother. Of course. Drake had her smile. Serena turned to this man, whose voice held the pain of lost love, and held out her gloved hand. "And thou art my uncle?" She smiled, wanting to cheer him and not knowing why exactly.

Richard took her hand and bowed over it. "As you say." There was a twinkle in his eyes that made Serena immediately like him. She had made the right decision in coming here.

"Please sit down and I'll ring for some tea or—" he grinned at her again— "attempt to do so."

Serena sat on a striped settee and laughed. "I do see what thou meanest, my lord. Thy butler seems a bit . . . aged?"

"Call me Richard, please. And yes, the poor chap has been in my employ for so long it would feel as if I were letting my own father go. I have, mind you, tried to bribe him into retirement with a substantial pension, but he would have none of it." He laughed and inclined his head toward her, the epitome of a conspirator. "Truthfully, he was so offended when I hinted he could no longer perform his duties that he didn't talk to me for three weeks. As he answers the door, it was a rather long three weeks."

Serena laughed and then hurriedly closed her mouth as the object of their conversation entered the room.

After the butler left, having to repeat the request for refreshments to himself several times, Richard took a seat across from her. "So you are Drake's wife. Did you travel alone, my dear? Tell me, how did all this come about?"

He seemed so genuinely interested and caring, so reminiscent of her father, that she felt a sheen of tears threaten her vision. Blast these emotions that rose up so suddenly, so overwhelming these days! She blinked and looked away for a moment, struggling to compose herself. "'Tis a long story. Dost thou want the whole of it now?"

Richard nodded, understanding in his eyes. "Is that not why you've come?"

She supposed it was. And it did seem right. But he was a stranger, and she felt little trust for anyone at the moment.

It took a few false starts, but by the time the tea and cakes arrived, Serena had done her best to tell the story of her meeting and marriage to Drake. She told it from her own perspective and from what she had believed true at the time. Now it was time to ask if any of her beliefs were true.

Blushing, she described the letter she had found in Helena's desk, then went on to tell of Lady Chamberlain's visit and the strange inaccuracies between what the ton seemed to believe and all she had been told.

"I could not ask Drake. But I thought that thou might knowest . . . the truth. I must discover the truth."

INSIDE RICHARD WAS railing at himself, for all the stupid mistakes he had made, for the courage he lacked—courage such as he saw in this gentle Quaker woman. He had been shocked at first to realize that she was a Quaker. The Drake he knew would never have chosen such a woman. But after hearing her story and spending time in her company, he understood. Understood so very much. And he was glad for some of it. Glad Drake had stepped into the shoes of the poor and the enslaved . . . even if it was only for a little while. And glad heaven had sent him this angel, whose wings had been clipped but could be mended and sent out to love his son again.

His son.

How to tell her?

But then, she already suspected. That letter . . . he had wondered whatever became of it. It was the only one he had ever written to Helena. He'd thought it thrown into the fire or dissolved in the tears he knew it had caused, destroyed just as surely as it had destroyed their love. He would forever mourn those misbegotten decisions of his youth and the wreckage of human life they had caused. But how to tell this sweet girl, his daughter-in-law?

He had been staring sadly at her for some time. Seeing the tears she held at bay, he remembered her question. "Truth? I must tell you, Serena, my dear, you are the first to have asked for it." He looked down at his hands hanging limp between his knees.

"I thought Drake might come here one day, as you have, demanding answers. But I hadn't expected this." He smiled at her again and took a fortifying sip of tea.

"Since you have been so brave as to seek it out, I will tell you. What I know of it, anyway. Helena and I met just before she married my brother, Ivor. She had been betrothed to him for years, a most desirable family alliance, you see, but she had never met him." He gazed at the painting as he continued. "When she came to Alnwick, in Northumberland, she was so young. We all were, looking back on it. She was innocent and my brother . . . well, let's just say he was much older and experienced of the world. She had ideals about marriage that he had no intention of fulfilling. He told her so, and she tried to end the betrothal. By chance or fortune, I met up with her one night in the garden. I had only seen her from afar and hadn't fully appreciated her effect on me until that night. She was . . . so full of life. I was enchanted, and she was disillusioned and vulnerable. Together we . . . consoled one another."

"But you said you loved her."

"I did, as only a twenty-year-old who thinks himself a man could. But I didn't understand the cost of such love, or even the meaning of it, until it was too late." He took another sip of tea. "The marriage went ahead as planned. I was . . . we were both heartbroken. She swore to me she would have nothing to do with him, but we both knew it was a lie. A month passed and Ivor left for one of his many excursions abroad. She knew by then that he went to gamble and dally with his current mistress. He had many mistresses over the years and wasn't very discreet about it. It was then, while he was away, that she begged me to come for a visit. I did, and as you may have suspected, fathered Drake that long wonderful month we were together.

"We both pretended it would never end. And that it was perfectly natural for me to be there—right, even. We convinced ourselves that we were a world apart, not needing or wanting the outside. We hoped my brother would never return, but he did. And it didn't take him very long to guess that we had been together. I suppose it was written on both our faces. He threw me out with a broken rib and more than a few bruises." Richard shrugged. "I can't say that I blame him. Helena was his wife and I never should have touched her. I received a letter from Helena a month later saying she was with child. She said Ivor had threatened to beat the child from her body if she didn't assure him the babe was his. Helena lied the best she could, but we knew. We both knew the child was ours. There had been signs even before I left."

He stood, unable to sit still a moment longer as the terrible memories assailed him. "When I wrote that letter, the one you read, I thought I was doing the wise thing. The noble thing. I convinced myself that the best I could do for my child was to relinquish all rights as his father and allow him to grow up an heir to the dukedom. I had watched my brother, groomed since birth for the position of wealth and power he would someday reign over and . . . I was envious. I thought if my son could inherit that world, it would be worth the sacrifice of Helena's and my love. What choice did we have really?"

He swung around to face Serena again, unable to keep the harsh tone from his voice. "But I *did* have other choices. Choices Helena hinted at, but I was unwilling to see. Choices involving hardship and lack and hard work. I could have taken them both away . . . to the colonies . . . to Holland . . . somewhere. I could have made a life for the woman I loved, and for my son. Instead, I choose the comfort of cold familiarity."

There. It was out. As ugly in revelation as it had been within him. "Serena, I tell you what I have admitted to myself many times in the dark lonely hours since: I was a coward."

"No—"

Richard stopped her.

"If that were only the worst of it." He looked back at Helena's portrait. The same portrait he looked at every day, silently begging her forgiveness. "She wasted away . . . slowly . . . like a flower whose petals dropped off, one by one, leaving a thin and lifeless stem. Until that, too, turned pale and dead."

The pain sliced through him as he set free the truth he'd held back all these years. "I am responsible for her death."

SERENA COULD SIT no longer. Striding over to Richard Weston, she placed a hand on his shoulder. "Sir, thou must not torture thyself like this. Thou mayest have made some mistakes, but only God knows to what degree thy choices affected her life. She might have died in Holland, onboard a ship to the colonies— any number of things could have happened. Thou only played a part. Like Drake and I, we are both responsible for where we now stand. Helena made her choices, too, and I am certain she would not want thee to carry this burden thy whole life." The tears she had held back during the telling of the story now spilled forth. "Thou must forgive thyself."

Richard stared into her clear eyes. "Does Drake know what he's found in you?"

She thought he had, hoped he had. Believed with all her heart he'd known how rare their love was. How it needed to be cherished and protected.

But now . . .

Now she could only bow her head and fight back the sorrow that threatened to overwhelm her. Sorrow for what Drake's mother and this good man had lost. And for all she feared she had lost as well.

Chapter Twenty-Four

It was a relief, telling all of it to someone. Like a weight had been lifted and now his head felt light. Richard laughed, a little self-conscious. "But you didn't come here to hear all of that, did you, Serena. You want to know if Drake is telling the truth about his identity." He hated to tell her he didn't know, but he must.

"To the world and to himself, Drake is the son of Ivor, the Duke of Northumberland and his only heir. I have not seen my brother in many years. Honestly, I don't know whether he is dead or alive, but if he died I can't imagine why I would not have been so informed. I would have certainly attended his funeral. So . . . that leaves a very big question. If, indeed, Ivor is dead as Drake told you, why doesn't anyone else know about it?"

Serena wondered aloud, "But why would he lie to me about his father? And why would he pretend to society that I am his—" she nearly choked on the words—"father's wife and not his own."

There was the pain of it, betrayal and hurt in her eyes. Richard wished he had some answer that would erase that look, but he didn't. "Only Drake can answer those questions. You will have to face him at some point. You know that, do you not?"

Serena shook her head. "How can I believe anything he tells me?"

Richard walked closer to her. "His game is up, my dear. I believe he will tell you the truth now. Whatever he is playing at, he had to have had good reason. Drake is not one for frivolous undertakings, as I'm sure you're aware. He's a careful man, a planning man. He will have compelling reasons why he's done this to you."

Serena searched his eyes. "How compelling can they be? To pretend I am his stepmother? It is . . . it is disgusting!"

Richard could only agree with her. "Does he know where you are?"

She shook her head. "I—I left suddenly, without any thought beyond finding thee." Her eyes grew round. "I did not even bring any money beyond the coach fare. Might I stay here tonight?"

"Of course. For as long as you wish." He smiled at her. "You may find yourself tiring of an old bachelor like myself, and when you do, I will escort you back to London. You'll not have to face him alone, Serena. It is past time the truth about my part in all this came out."

"Yes, Drake needs to know who he is. He thinks he knows, but there is something missing. He is so . . . restless. But I cannot go back there. Not now." Helplessness and fear shone from her eyes. "Perhaps never."

He patted her shoulder. "A day at time. That's how we'll manage this." He knew of what he spoke. It was how he had lived the last thirty years of his life.

DRAKE PACED BACK and forth between the bedchamber and Serena's dressing room. Stopping at the mess in front of her armoire, the mess he had made days before while searching her room, he cursed. Where to look next?

His worst fear had come true. She had left him.

He lashed out by pulling more jewel-encrusted gowns out unto the floor. Kicking them aside, he studied the contents of the empty shelves. Where had she gone? How could she leave without even coming to him and demanding to know what he'd done? Why hadn't she asked him if all Lady Chamberlain said was true?

When he thought of Maria Louisa Chamberlain, the vicious smile in her eyes as she told him about her little conversation with his "stepmother," Drake ground his teeth. Whatever Serena had believed from that conversation was enough to drive her away. By the time he arrived home, she had vanished without a trace. The servants had not seen her leave and had no knowledge of where she went. Her dressing room looked, at first, untouched, but upon further investigation Drake found a few things missing. That's when he started to panic. It would be so like her to take only her belongings from before . . . before her life with him.

Slowly it had sunk in that she'd left him. Three days now with no word, no clues. Every avenue of questioning had turned up nothing. When he thought of her alone in London, so naïve, without money and his protection . . . his stomach lurched. It was as if the earth had opened up and swallowed her.

He stared into the room, scarcely able to move or put two thoughts together to form a plan of action. What else could he do, aside from this wretched waiting?

Pacing back to Serena's desk he sat hard in the chair, staring at the top. She hadn't even left him a note. He opened the top drawer again, staring at its emptiness. As he began to close the drawer once more, he heard a piece of wood rattle in the back. He frowned, then pulled the drawer all the way free and set it on the top of the desk. Further investigation revealed the desk had a false back. The wood had come loose and, with a little prying, it easily opened. There in the corner lay something that he pulled out. A crumpled page. He smoothed it out, staring at the yellowed paper. Could Serena have found this?

He read it.

Then he read it a second time, and then a third before he slowly laid the paper down on the drawer and drew a deep breath.

So. It was true.

He was illegitimate.

Something inside him shifted and then slipped into place, like a wandering thought now finding its resting place. Richard's words from the letter rolled about in his mind, how he'd urged Drake's mother to allow their son to be raised as Ivor's rightful heir. Drake could understand such a request; it was what *he* would have done. It was, in a twisted way, what he was trying to accomplish now. Richard had not wanted Drake to bear the stigma of illegitimacy.

Drake expected to feel searing pain at the truth. It was a shameful state of being, illegitimacy. Yet, as if he held a mental poker, he gently prodded his emotions and found there wasn't anything of the sort there. Curious, all thoughts of Serena suspended in this new moment of identity, he explored his feelings and found only dumbfounding relief.

Ivor was not his father.

It was as if some chain that had held him fell away. He stood, light-headed with the freedom of it, and took a deep breath. The man he had tried to please, had tried to mold himself after, was not his father! He didn't have to be like him. He didn't have to be the Duke of Northumberland.

But he *wanted* to be the Duke of Northumberland, didn't he?

Drake couldn't answer that question right now, but just the fact that he had thought it brought many other questions to mind. Turning back to the desk, he focused once more on the most important question.

"Where are you, Serena?"

He looked at the letter again. Wait a moment . . . that night at dinner, she had asked him all those questions about his family. About his uncle. She *must* have found this letter. Of course! There was no other place she could have gone. She didn't know anyone in London, hadn't made any close friends—he had seen to that. She must have gone to his uncle's—no, his *father's*—home in Bristol. He would check the coach stations first thing in the morning. If they yielded any clues to confirm his suspicions, he would follow her and tell her everything.

He could live with the truth of his birth. And, he was realizing, he might even live without the title of duke.

But there was one thing he would not, *could* not live without.

Chapter Twenty-Five

There was no denying the truth.

In the two weeks since coming to Bristol, the morning sickness only worsened. She could no longer blame it on traveling. She was with child.

Standing over the commode, Serena waited for the retching to stop. Sweat beaded on her forehead as she wondered if she might faint. "God help me not to faint," she prayed, already on her knees, the cold, hard floor beckoning to her.

Weak but feeling temporarily better, she struggled back to the bed and pulled the covers to her chin. She would like to be angry—angry with Drake for stealing the joy she knew she would have felt about this child. But however rightfully deserved, she couldn't muster the energy. Sleep, that's what she needed. Just a few more hours of sleep.

She had just closed her eyes and settled deeper into the downy pillow when the door opened and the maid Richard insisted on assigning her curtsied in.

"Pardon, your grace," Dolly whispered, bobbing her head up and down like a pigeon. "Lord Richard wished me to ask if ye would be dining with him this mornin' or havin' breakfast in your chamber again?"

Serena roused herself enough to lift her head. "Oh dear, no breakfast please." Just the thought of food made her stomach queasy. "I am not feeling just the thing this morning . . . again."

The maid nodded and dipped again. "He said if you weren't feeling well, to ask if a doctor should be sent for. I think he is worried about you, your grace."

Serena gave her a weak smile. "No doctor, but have Richard come up at his convenience. I do need to speak with him. And wake me ten minutes before, so that I may dress."

She had been putting off telling him. As a bachelor she doubted he suspected, but it would be obvious soon enough and she wanted to tell him before he guessed.

Richard arrived a little while later with a soft knock. She was wearing a dressing gown and cap, sitting up in the bed, her back propped up with pillows. When he entered she smiled at him and patted the mattress beside her. He had been so kind. How would he take the news that he was to become a grandfather?

"How are you feeling?"

She laughed a little at the anxiety in his eyes. "Not so bad, now. I am so very sorry for putting thee and thy household to such a degree of trouble. I—I am not unwell, really."

He took her hand. "Are you overcome with sadness? Is there anything I can do?"

Serena shook her head. "Richard, I am not depressed . . . I am with child." There, she'd said it. She watched the emotions— first surprise, and then utter delight—cross his face.

"You are certain?"

Serena nodded. "My mother had seven of us, of which I am the eldest. I have seen the signs many times before and am quite certain. The babe will be born in the month of May, I believe.

Richard squeezed her hand, laughing. "Spring. That's wonderful!" His brow creased. "It *is* wonderful, is it not? Are you happy?"

She nodded. "Yes, I–I used to daydream about having a child with Drake. I used to think about how I would tell him and imagine his reaction." She smiled sadly. "My dreams never envisioned this. I know I shall have to talk to Drake soon. This is not something I can keep from him."

Richard shook his head. "I expected him to find his way here by now. I know you said you left no clues, but I thought perhaps . . . he would find us out."

"I suppose I will have to write to him. Much as I dread it."

"Let me write to him on your behalf. It's the least I could do."

Serena was relieved, but unsure. "Let me think about it. We shall decide tomorrow."

Richard nodded. "You must rest. I had planned a little excursion that I thought you might like this afternoon, but you should stay abed."

Serena brightened. "Oh no, I feel much better. 'Tis only in the mornings that I feel so unwell. The remainder of the day I only feel as if I have been run down by a carriage." She grinned at him. "Please, I would love to get out and enjoy some fresh air."

"Very well. Meet me downstairs in an hour and we will go. I think you will enjoy this."

DRAKE RODE A fresh horse as he galloped toward the little seaside town of Bristol. It had been years—decades, even—since he'd seen it, and he wondered if his memory would serve. He tried to drum up a picture of Richard. He had only seen him once, when his grandmother, the dowager duchess, had died. He cringed remembering how he had treated Richard, rather like he was below Drake in rank and status, which, at the time, he thought was true. Richard had been younger and much quieter than his father, but he'd had a kind smile for Drake. Now Drake would see him in a new light.

Drake was hardly a mile from the town when he came upon a coal mining site. Coal, he knew, was becoming more and more important to England and new uses were being discovered for it all the time. With the rise in demand had come the need for people to work in the deep tunnels in the earth.

Curious, he turned his horse toward the site. As he rode into the miners' camp, he had to wonder if his eyes were deceiving him. He felt as if he'd stumbled upon a poor village in Africa. Men, women, and children—many of the latter naked and covered in black from the coal—swarmed the camp. As he neared, there was a sharp cry to his right. Drake turned his head and saw a young boy of about ten being set loose from a metal girdle. Long, thick chains hung from the girdle between his legs and lay for many more feet in a pile on the ground. Behind him, attached to the ends of the chain was a large tub full of black coal. Had the child dragged that load of coal out of the mine's tunnels on his own? Drake could hardly tear his eyes away from him, so strong was his shock. Outrage boiled within him as he rode over and dismounted in front of the boy. Drake could see the boy's bloody hips through the torn shreds of a cloth he wore around his waist. Naked, stark pain shone from his sunken eyes.

"What is the meaning of this? You men, do you use the backs of children for work such as this?" He stalked over to the tub and lifted one side. It must have weighed over two hundred pounds.

A man, standing naked except for the rag that hung from his lower body, looked up into Drake's eyes. Old eyes, tired as the earth he had been working in, stared back at Drake. He coughed suddenly before he answered, and Drake's heart sank to see black spittle in the man's hand.

"The boy'll be aright. He's new is all, sir."

Drake's eyes swept the community, taking in the details, each one piercing him as nothing he had ever seen—and Drake had seen much. Poverty, filth, the dregs of humanity—he had seen it all. And yet this sight gripped him as nothing before.

The men stared back at him, frozen by his presence, as though he were some other being—a god, perhaps—and they couldn't make out what he was doing there. So many children, some looked as young as five, their eyes ranging from lifeless to wretched. The women were as bad off, one round with child and so tired, swaying where she stood, that he found he could not continue looking at her. The men were at least men! They could handle hard, even terrible work . . . then he really looked at them, saw their misshapen bodies—short, stooped, with long arms that seemed almost deformed despite bulking musculature from the years of pounding the earth. Drake wanted to sit among them and cry.

He walked back to the boy. The lad stood in front of him, shivering in spite of the late summer heat. The cloth that hung about his waist was wet and dripping dirty water onto the thin patch of grass below his bare feet.

Drake squatted down. "What is your name, son?"

"Robbie," he said in a frightened voice.

"How long have you been working in the mines, Robbie?"

"About three months, sir. Came over with four other lads from Gloucester."

"Why did you come? Are your parents here?"

He shook his head, his hair a ragged crop of brown. "They died in a fire, my da and mum. Me and some boys heard of the work here and decided it was better 'n the streets."

Drake nodded, stood, and patted the boy on the head. Looking at the men around him he asked, "Where is the overseer? I would speak with him."

One of the men pointed toward the town. "Gone to hear the preacher, I expect. Word just came that George Whitefield is preaching in a field north of town. Not enough room for all that wants to hear him in those fancy churches, I guess." He motioned to the people around the camp. "Most of us are headed there. We were quitting early today. Most days we are in the mines twelve, fourteen hours and don't come out till dark. But Mr. Henley, he said we could quit early today and go and hear the preacher."

Drake took a long breath. "How many children would you say work in these mines?"

The man shrugged. "I guess about thirty, countin' the older ones. About twice as many women." He squinted up at Drake. "You never seen a mine before, mister?"

How could Drake tell this man that he was a partner in several mining companies? It sickened him to think that those might be like this one. "Not firsthand." Drake looked around again. "Are they all like this?"

The man shrugged. "I guess so. Can't rightly say. This is the only mine I've worked in." He pointed to a stooped man. "'Enry, over there, he's a well traveled sort. Worked in all kinds of mines."

Drake nodded to the man. "Thank you." He looked at the boy again. "I would like to take you to a doctor in town. Will you come with me?"

The boy grinned up at him, showing surprisingly white teeth against the dirty face. "I wouldn't want to miss the preacher, sir. Can we go there first?"

How could he disappoint the first light he'd seen in the lad's eyes. "Of course."

Drake questioned the "well traveled" Henry, heart dropping as the man confirmed that, yes, this was the typical condition of the mines. Then he looked into the main tunnels, gauging their size and depth. There was no doubt in Drake's mind. Something drastic had to be done. The air was dank and probably full of gases. He would not be surprised if lung damage showed up early and permanently. Some of the tunnels had standing water. And, so he was told, the further down one went, the worse the conditions became. Disgusted, Drake made his way back to the boy. Lifting him onto his horse, he mounted behind him. The boy moved stiffly but didn't complain as he grasped the gelding's mane and smiled up at Drake.

"I've dreamed of riding, sir. We're so high off the ground."

Drake looked into those deep brown eyes and felt some piece of a wall inside him crumble. His childhood . . . his life, so full of self-indulgence, every desire gratified before he had had the chance to really feel it—it all seemed so horrifying in the face of this child's simple joy.

He didn't want it anymore. He wanted something *real,* something important to live for. He wanted to help someone.

Starting with this boy.

IT WASN'T LONG before Drake and his new charge began to merge with the streams of people going to hear George Whitefield. There must have been thousands riding and walking and driving carriages toward the vast grassy clearing. Curious now, Drake directed his mount over toward the main crowd.

Thousands sat on the warm grass, listening to the young man who was already speaking. Amazing how well the man's voice carried. He stood upon a large, wooden platform, hands upraised, hair blowing in the breeze. Drake felt himself pulled in by the man's voice, so full of fervor and authority.

Drake dismounted and helped Robbie down to the grass.

Whitefield was speaking of his own life, how he had joined a group of young men at Oxford University called the Holy Club. They were diligent, holding to a disciplined life of early devotions, journaling to examine their spiritual life, fasting, and visiting the prisons and poorhouses. They read voraciously and studied every translation of Scripture. He asked the audience of miners, farming men, and townspeople if they didn't think such a man would please God?

The crowd shouted a hearty "Yes, preacher!"

But the young man shook his head.

His eyes flashed, so piercing and bold Drake thought they were directed right at—and through—him. Whitefield told them that even after such efforts, he still felt something was missing. Drake nodded inwardly. He knew that feeling.

Whitefield's voice rang out. "I believed that, somehow, I was not doing enough. And so I took a new resolution upon myself, to work harder. I even stopped attending the Holy Club, for fear

I loved it too much." His words brought to life the image of nights spent in sweaty prayer, of eating less and less to the point of constant fasting. This young man gave everything he could to the poor.

"One frosty morning," he said, "after hours of prayer outdoors, I realized one of my hands had turned black. I scarcely cared, but my friends urged me to my bed, and there I lay for the next seven weeks."

Drake was appalled and, at the same time, admired this man's devotion. He looked about him, saw the engrossed faces, saw how quiet all around him were, how they strained to catch every word.

The preacher began laughing. It was as if joy bubbled up within him and overflowed. Robbie laughed too, looking up into Drake's face. Those around him smiled, and a few laughed for no apparent reason other than basking in Whitefield's joy.

"While I lay on my bed near death," Whitefield went on, "unable to do anything to please God, I began to hear God speak. *If any man thirst, let him come to Me . . . '* The words pierced my whole being and I broke, crying out, 'I thirst!' It was so simple—absurdly simple." Whitefield's voice rang out like a liberty bell. "To finally be saved by such a simple prayer. And then . . . I laughed. And once I began laughing, the floodgates of heaven burst upon me.

"Listen, now, my friends, to Ezekiel 36:26: 'A new heart also will I give you, and a new spirit will I put within you: and I will take away the stony heart out of your flesh, and I will give you a heart of flesh.'"

Tears streaked the blackened faces around Drake. Some stood, but many had fallen to their knees and were crying out, hands lifted to the heavens. Drake looked down at Robbie—the boy's eyes shone, full of hope. A deep shaking started within Drake, frightening him with its intensity.

Then he, too, collapsed to his knees in the grass. His heart rushed so in his chest, he thought he might die. Eyes closed, he saw his life, all the events leading to this moment. He saw his mother, glowing and smiling down at him, so very pleased. He saw himself as a child playing in a stream, with his shirt and socks hidden on the bank so he wouldn't be caught. He saw his father, Ivor, a stern face glaring down at him. But then he saw beyond the face into his father's eyes—and saw Ivor as a frightened little boy.

And then he saw *her*. Serena. A bright light illuminated her face and then faded, and he saw her as warm and living and real. He could almost reach out and touch her. But she vanished, replaced in his mind's eyes by the coal miners and the filthy wretchedness of the children, of Robbie—

And suddenly, Drake knew.

His mission was as clear as if God had spoken it aloud. In those few moments, everything fell into place: the man he had tried to be and the man he was created to be. It was as though a key were turned, a locked-up place opened, and all the people, all the events that led to this moment suddenly made sense as never before.

Throwing his eyes open, he gulped in air. The preacher was praying for the souls of all those in the audience, and Drake grasped hold of that prayer with all that he had. *Yes.* The word resounded within him. *Yes! Yes!* His spirit soared, his hands lifted toward heaven without any fear or shame.

Save me, Lord Jesus. Save me, too!

God's response came, swift and sure, and Drake had never felt so light . . . so alive.

So deeply, deeply loved.

Chapter Twenty-Six

Drake rose from the damp earth, laughing. He couldn't seem to stem the tide of joy that had overtaken him. He hugged Robbie's thin, broken frame and felt nothing but overwhelming love for the lad. He would help him. He would help them all.

It was then that he saw her. Serena. Across the way, sitting in a carriage beside Richard.

His father.

At first Drake didn't know if she was real or some further apparition of his mind. But everything within him silently called out to her, *Serena! Wife of my heart.* And as he stared, he knew. She wasn't in his mind, she was here! *I'm sorry. I am so sorry.* He stumbled toward them, forgetting all but the woman before him.

When he was but a few feet away, she turned her head and their eyes locked. He saw her inhale sharply, shock on her face, and then Richard saw him too. Drake traversed the crowd, desperate to reach her, watched in despair the hurried gestures she was making, asking Richard to take them away.

"Wait!" He stumbled, righted himself, and then began to run. "Serena . . . wait!"

The glossy black carriage flashed in the sun as it turned and spun away, jostling over the bumpy ground.

He tried to catch them, ran after them, then slowed to a walk and finally stopped. "I am so sorry!" He said it to the wind, but not with despair. He would find her and beg her forgiveness. He *would* win her back.

It took a little time to find his horse and Robbie. The boy chattered about Whitefield's preaching all the way into town.

The Bristol doctor was not surprised by the boy's wounds. After examining Robbie and putting salve where the chains had worn the skin raw, he took Drake into the outer room and spoke in low anger. "He will be lucky to live to see twenty. I must tell you, sir, the cases only get worse, and the little girls . . ." He shook his head.

"I do not imagine many of them even seek your care."

"No, they don't. Not until it's too late." He motioned toward the closed door where the boy lay. "What he needs is rest and decent food. The children that work these mines are so tired, they fall asleep while walking home at night and their parents have to go and search for them alongside the road. They haven't the strength even to eat. They sleep all day on Sunday to rest for the week ahead. It is absolute barbarity."

Drake could only agree. "I plan to see the king hears of this. I will speak to Parliament myself."

The doctor squinted at him. "You are of the nobility, then? Good, good, we need men like you to take up the cause of these children. I would be glad to help . . . write up my findings, appear before Parliament, anything at all."

Drake patted him on the shoulder. "Yes, any cases you can document would be helpful. The boy can stay here overnight? I have other business that needs attending, but I would like to check on him tomorrow."

"Certainly. He will be given the best care."

Drake handed the man some coins and returned to the boy. He picked up Robbie's bony hand and squeezed it, something he wouldn't have done even yesterday. "You stay here and rest, Robbie. The doctor is going to take good care of you."

"But sir, if I don't return, they'll dismiss me. I have to have work."

Drake shook his head, near tears. That the child wanted to go back proved how destitute he really was. "No, you won't be going back, Robbie. As soon as you are able, *I* am going to give you a job, a good job, with plenty of food and a good place to sleep at night. And you will go to school. You will learn to read and write and do sums so that someday you can have a life of your own choosing. Does that sound fair, son?"

"Fair, sir?" Robbie's eyes filled with tears. "It sounds a dream, sir."

Drake nearly lost his composure but pulled himself together and smiled down at the lad. "Good." Drake ruffled his hair. "Now rest and I will see you in the morning."

DRAKE STOOD OUTSIDE the front door to his father's house. He took a deep breath, said a little prayer, and knocked. His father answered, his face impassive and impossible to read.

"Come in, your grace, we've been expecting you." He gave a slight bow of his head as Drake swept past him into the hall.

"Please, call me Drake." Suddenly a new thought occurred to him. "For all I know, you were the one to come up with the name . . . did you?"

There were many questions in that query. Richard shook his head. "I told your mother to name you David. I always thought to have a son named David."

"You never married, then? Never had children?"

Richard shook his head. "You are my only child."

There, it was said. Out in the open at last.

Drake didn't know what to say.

"I am sorry."

Richard hesitated. "You found the letter, then?"

He moved further into the hall, where the lighting was better, so that he could see his father, read his reactions to all that was said. He studied Richard. The man was a good four inches shorter than Drake, a little round in the middle, his face softening around the jaw line, his hair gray at the temples. He was a little amazed to see that his resemblance to Ivor was by far more pronounced.

"Yes, I found it. Are you certain?"

Richard motioned him into the salon, and poured them both a drink. He looked to be seriously considering the question. Sitting across from Drake, he finally inclined his head. "Your mother was sure. That was enough for me."

Drake nodded. "I seem to look more like my uncle then, and after being raised by him . . ." He couldn't seem to finish the sentence. A hard lump immobilized his throat.

"Drake, I'm . . . sorry. I made choices based on the paltry experiences of a twenty-year-old. I—I made mistakes."

Drake nodded briefly, then taking a deep breath asked, "May I see my wife, sir?"

"Of course. I'm sorry we ran out at the meeting, but she . . . wasn't prepared. You gave her quite a shock. Did you enjoy George Whitefield?"

Drake couldn't help his smile. "More than I can express. I had heard of him and the near riots to hear him preach. Now I understand why."

Richard nodded. "Word is, he will be here in Bristol for a few weeks and preach every day. I plan to see him, and I believe Serena does, too, but I will let you speak with her. Oh, here she is now."

They both stood as Serena walked into the room. Drake turned, setting his glass down too hard on the table in front of him, the sound in the sudden quiet startling everyone. His wife looked pale and tired in a simple blue dress, her hair pulled back with a few curls hanging down her back. More distressing was the sadness laced with longsuffering that now looked back at him. He hated that he was the cause of it. He went to her and reached out for her hands.

Serena turned from him, walking over to stand beside Richard. Her greeting was cool. "Good day, your grace."

Drake walked back to his chair. "For heaven's sake, Serena, do not call me that."

Her chin lifted as did her beautiful reddish-gold eyebrows. "Why . . . art thou not a duke, perchance?"

He supposed he deserved that. Bowing his head, he acknowledged it was time to tell the truth. He had rehearsed many different versions of the truth on the way to Bristol in an effort to discover his best advantage. Now, seeing her, all the words fell away.

She couldn't have chosen her position better. She stood behind the settee, his father seated in front of her like guard and protector. He hated that she felt need of one with him. But that, too, was his fault.

"Serena, there is one thing you must understand before I tell this story. One fact that can never, ever leave your mind."

She nodded and he was intensely glad. She wanted him to explain it, which meant she still loved him. It gave him the courage to continue.

"From my first memory I was raised to be a duke. There was never a time when it was not reminded to me, never a moment when the weight of such a title didn't sit upon my shoulders. Ivor directed my training from the least inconsequential activity, such as how to hold my fork, to the most complex economic schemes. More than that, he taught me how to think like one of highest-ranking men of the nobility, just beneath royalty. His example ingrained in me how to regard humankind as my servants and, if there was no need I had of them, how to let them fade into the background like a piece of furniture with no thought to their well-being or even that they were a living being. It wasn't a life-style, Serena; it was a mind-set, and one I adapted to and even thrived on with amazing success. It was, and to some degree even after all I have experienced in the last years, still is what I am today. And whether you would like to admit it or not, it is part of why you fell in love with me."

Her face whitened at that, her hands gripping the back of the settee, but she wanted the truth and now she must have it, barefaced and cold as it sometimes was.

"One night, several months ago my father died." He gave Richard an apologetic look. "I regret you were not informed, sir. You will comprehend why in a moment." His attention shifted back to Serena. "I also regret that we, my barrister and good friend Charles and I, read the will before Ivor was even laid in his grave. It sickens me now to see how ruthless I was. Nevertheless, it was done, and that was the night the madness began. The will stated that I was completely cut out of any and all inheritance."

Richard and Serena exchanged shocked glances, which was understandable. For a father to cut his son out in such a manner . . . it just wasn't done.

"At the time I couldn't begin to understand why he would do such a thing. Now I realize, Ivor knew I was not his son and, in a preconceived revenge, that had I not been the object of, I would have greatly admired, he trained me and painstakingly prepared me for a position in the world that he intended to rip away at his death. Needless to say, I was outraged. Enraged is more precise. And so I concocted a plan to marry secretly, as my father, and as quickly as possible produce an heir, who would then be introduced into society as my sibling. A brother, I was told, might inherit all, and I was determined to *have* it all even if it be through a son. I thought whatever woman I married could easily be bought with the title of duchess."

Serena gasped. "Thou only married me to——?"

"Of course not!" Drake calmed his tone. "You, my dear, were not planned at all." He took a deep breath and told them about the man who had tried to blackmail him—the man who Drake believed had fallen to his death from the edge of the railing. Drake watched Richard's face for the expected revulsion, but instead found only sad understanding. Then Drake described his flight to America and his meeting with Serena.

Serena had lowered herself to sit next to Richard. "What happened to make thee decide to bring us back to London and go through with this plan?"

Drake's hand formed a fist by his side. "I was a failure in America. I couldn't do anything well, not smithing, not farming.

Serena, I was dying inside a little more every day. Couldn't you tell?"

She offered a slow nod. "I knew thou wert restless, unhappy even. I have never seen thee as happy as when we came to London."

Drake nodded, stood and paced. "When I finally read the letter, I realized all was not lost, that we didn't have to just survive there in the wilderness." He looked into Serena's eyes, willing her to understand. "I realized that with a little deception, I could give you the world—*my* world. The one I knew I could succeed at. The one I was ruler of. Serena, I did it for you and for our children."

"No. For *thyself,* Drake." Her words burst out, suddenly fierce. "I was happy a farmer's wife."

Drake moved to squat in front of her. Taking her limp hands into his, he looked deep into her eyes. "Were you? Why then did you not marry Christopher?"

SERENA INHALED AS his meaning drove into her.

Why *hadn't* she married Christopher? Her words claimed one thing, but all of her actions proved another. Thinking back, she was suddenly heartsick. Once the shock of discovering her husband's true position had worn off, she had secretly delighted to learn she was a duchess. She had been living in an excited hum ever since meeting Drake—it was like being intoxicated all of the time, only reliant on excitement instead of a bottle of spirits. Drake made her feel alive and somehow free. Being a plain Quaker woman was never what she really wanted. Drake had awakened her, awakened all her dreams beyond that simple life.

She'd hungered after the forbidden fruit, she'd eaten it, and now she knew . . . she knew the good and evil that was within her.

The shock of those thoughts had her head spinning and her mouth tightly closed. One question, though, screamed in her mind: Had Drake consulted her before leaving for England, would she have agreed to his plan? She hadn't wasted any time helping him escape when she thought he would be tried for a murderer.

Richard rose and handed Serena a glass of water. "Drake, I believe she has had enough shock for now. It's not good for her condition, you know."

"Her . . . her condition?" Drake frowned, looking at her.

She met his startled gaze. "I had hoped to tell thee later. But thou wilt be happy to know that thy plan is nearly carried through." She couldn't help the bitterness that crept into her voice. "I am with child." She didn't know what response she had expected, but his whole face lighting with genuine joy had certainly not been one of them.

"Are you certain? When did you know? Do you feel faint? Women faint when they are pregnant, do they not?"

He was gushing. The bold, proud Duke of Northumberland . . . was gushing.

Serena stared at him, marveling at how he looked without the usual veneer of control that always stole the joy from his face. She smiled, unable to ruin the moment with all her misgivings. "I am sure and I am fine. I may not faint, but be careful treading near me in the mornings. I may retch upon thy shoes."

He smiled, the usual steel of his eyes softened and bluer. "I will make it right. Somehow . . . I promise."

"How can it be made right?"

"I will go to the king and tell the truth."

"The truth?" Even that didn't seem enough to untangle such a web of deception. "The world thinks me thy stepmother. Will think this babe thy brother or sister."

"You will be risking your neck if you tell the king all you've done." Richard's tone sounded as anxious as Serena felt. "The king will not take this lightly."

Drake nodded and then sat next to Serena and gripped her hands. "I won't lie to you again, Serena. Telling the truth means changing our lives. At best, the scandal will be . . . monstrous. I . . . we . . . will assuredly be banished from polite society. I may lose everything—the title, all the estates, the wealth. I may lose my life and leave you to raise our child alone." He gripped her hands. "We must risk everything to tell the truth."

She stared at him, unable to answer or put to words the churning thoughts within her. All she knew was the full force of the price of loving him. "Thou hast decided, then."

Drake nodded, solemn but firm. "It is the only way. I will throw myself on the mercy of the king—" his eyes looked up at the ceiling—"and the mercy of God. And we will hope, Serena. Hope that it will work toward our good. Can you stand with me in this?"

She felt his conviction down into the innermost parts of her, despite her anger, despite her hurt. Something had changed him, and as she looked into those blue eyes, everything in her urged her to say yes. To walk this path out with him.

Yet she was afraid. Her eyes, once opened, could not close again in blessed innocence. What had she done, trying to nail down to an ordinary life such a man as this?

"Yes. We will tell the truth."

And, God help me, live with the consequences.

Chapter Twenty-Seven

Serena stood in the hush of the anteroom to the council chamber of King George II, staring at a painting of a hunting scene without really seeing it. She and Drake had left immediately, traveling back to London and the justice of a volatile king. Drake spent several days getting his affairs in order and attempting to provide something for Serena should the worst happen.

Today, a bare week after returning to London, he had received his summons to attend the king. And he had gone eagerly, ready to make known to the world that he was little more than an illegitimate son of a third son of a duke. He went knowing he could be facing death, and yet, to Serena's amazement, he seemed at peace.

It was a peace Serena credited to God. In the past weeks, Drake shared his heart and all that happened to him while hearing George Whitefield speak. They went everyday to hear the young preacher and Serena too had experienced a new birth. Had given herself up fully to God.

But still, she was afraid. Was this new Drake someone she could trust? His motives seemed so pure these days, and yet she felt she didn't even know him. Tears started to well up, blurring the painting.

"Dash this pregnancy!"

She wiped her tears away. Now was not the time for weeping. She must be strong. This meeting was about to dictate the course of their lives. She took a shuddering breath, readying to stand beside her husband, no matter what he deserved. Later, if he escaped this horrid tangle with his life intact, then she would consider their future and how she must proceed. Staring at the painting, she muttered the prayer that had become a salve to her mind: "Please, God, have mercy on my husband."

The minutes dragged by, her pulse racing and then slowing so that she thought she might need to sit down. The room was nearly empty, many of the members of court purportedly out on the green viewing a flock of swans recently brought in from Germany for the king's pleasure. Serena was glad. What little she knew of court life was intimidating in the best of circumstances. The questions and looks and behind-the-hand whispers had the room been crowded would have been excruciating.

DRAKE WAITED IN the growing silence.

He had stated his case, told of Ivor's will and his plan to prepare Drake for the dukedom and then destroy the man he had raised as son. He told the king that he believed himself to be the son of Lord Richard Weston and produced the letter as evidence. And then Drake told His Royal Highness of his own diabolical plot to take back that which he'd believed stolen from him.

Finally, he asked the king for mercy, explaining that his Quaker wife was with child and his only desire now was to be a good husband and father and somehow provide for them in his homeland of Northumberland.

The king sat thinking and staring at Drake with beady eyes. Drake felt the hardness of his chair, his body straining to stand and pace.

"Your father—Ivor, that is—was a rascal and a liar." The king's statement carried sudden heat. "He and Robert Walpole had more than one fierce battle. Ha! But you—you have tread on the sanctity of the law and acted with vile greed."

Drake nodded, but kept his mouth safely closed. *I will not defend my actions. I am in Your hands, God.*

The king peered at him intently, and Drake felt a trickle of sweat run down his back.

"I shall have to consider what will be done with you. In the meantime, it would please us to see you consider your ways in the tower."

Drake bowed low. "In the tower, my sovereign." The words repeated themselves in his mind, numb but ringing. "Is there anything I can add to my defense?"

The king waved him away. "I have heard enough for today." He turned to the guard at the door behind him. "Have this man escorted to the tower." The bellowed order echoed about them.

Drake stood, shaking, and felt the guard grasp his upper arm and pull him toward the door, felt the newfound, untried foundation of faith waver, felt the old self rear its protective head to be noticed.

Upon entering the anteroom, Serena's terror-filled gaze slammed into him, and again he felt the blow of his betrayal and its consequences.

"A moment with my wife," he begged the guard.

The man turned indifferent eyes upon him, then nodded, letting go of Drake and summoning additional guards to do the actual transport.

Drake hurried to her side, taking up her hands in a tight clasp. "It's not the worst yet, my love. The king wants to consider the matter and is having me bide my time in the tower until a decision is made. You must pray . . . and wait. I will not see you again until the matter is settled."

Serena looked up into his eyes, tears glittering. "I had not thought of this. I thought at the least we would know."

Drake nodded. "Nor I." Two guards were coming toward him. "I love you."

The men grasped his arms, escorting him away.

"Yes," she managed back, though the word was tight with sobs. "Yes!"

SERENA TOOK A deep, fortifying breath and opened the door, leaving the sanctuary of the quiet walls of the townhouse. She knew what awaited her in the society of London. She had endured their scorn, their accusing or pitying stares for the past twenty days and she would endure it again today.

Liddell, her driver, a burly man who looked and acted more a guard, helped her into the carriage. At least there had not been anyone waiting outside her door. Many days she'd had to fight through the press of the curious and scornful to traverse the path to her carriage. So many seemed glad to see one of Drake's class receive their comeuppance. She hadn't allowed it to stop her, though. Every day she went to the palace and requested audience with the king. And every day she was turned away.

She stared out the window at the now-familiar streets, the shops and houses, as they crossed London, a city she had never dreamed she would ever see.

"Why me?" she whispered aloud. She talked to God often these days, almost exclusively. She sought Him as she had never known she could, and she knew deep within her one thing: She must fight for Drake's life. It was her destiny to be his help and his hope . . . his *petit chevalier,* as he'd called her so long ago. If she never did another thing for him for the rest of her days, she would know that she had carried out her mission on earth concerning Drake Weston.

They swung up to the entrance where the guards tipped their tall hats at her with something like respect from their stolid posture. She nodded at them, no longer fearful in the familiarity of such routine.

The anteroom was also well-known, now crowded with members of the ton. Here, too, Serena rarely found a friendly face or heard an encouraging word. They all seemed hungry for the downfall of one of England's greatest. Serena knew they hated what Drake had done, making them believe he was someone worthy of their respect because he held the title of duke. She knew they remembered how they had acquiesced to him and could only imagine how bitter that memory must be now. They'd bent their frame to an illegitimate son.

Albert and a friend or two of Drake's were sometimes present to lend her support, but as she looked around she realized none were present today.

That suited Serena's mood. Today she felt the stirrings of a battle within her. Her eyes swept over the people of the room, flashing in her conviction, silencing a few and challenging others. With regal ease—learned from Drake, yes, but rooted more in the rightness of her mission—she approached the king's inner chamber.

"I would request audience with the king." She stated it in a firm voice to the standing guard, ignoring the vicious chuckles in the background.

He nodded, as he had nodded to her every day. "Yes, my lady."

She wandered away from the door, toward a window alcove. The request could take some time to issue, so she sat on a cushion and closed her eyes, blocking the room and focusing her attention on the only other thing that mattered these days: her baby. As she thought of the babe inside her, she placed one hand on the small mound hidden beneath her voluminous skirt, drawing comfort and strength. The warm sunlight filtered through the tall window at her back, warming her with its intensity, relaxing her with its heat. Suddenly, she felt movement. A fluttering on the inside of her like a leaping heart, but lower, deep in her belly. She smiled with the joy of it. She had never felt the babe move before.

"Something funny, Serena?"

The voice cut into her dream world, and her eyes fluttered open and focused on Lady Chamberlain's smirking face.

Serena dropped her hand, not wanting to reveal her pregnancy. Drake had told the king of their situation, but she did not think the entire court had learned of it. Just as well. She could withstand their scorn but didn't want any of it to sully their child.

When she didn't immediately answer, Lady Chamberlain lifted her chin. "I would not think you would have anything to smile about, my dear. Such a tragedy your life has turned out to be."

Serena didn't want to use any of her resources crossing verbal swords with this woman and so only nodded. "As you say," she returned with gentle dignity, borrowing the phrase from her husband.

The woman huffed and, thankfully, strode away.

A commotion at the door gained the crowd's attention. Voices could be heard inside the king's chamber. The guard searched for and found Serena's gaze. With a hand he beckoned her forward.

"The king will see you now," he murmured when she reached him. She could feel those behind her straining to hear every word.

"Very good." She gave a confident nod, then swept into the chamber, a richly appointed room that she had never been allowed to see before. As she did so, the strange, confident fight stirred within her.

The king sat on a raised dais, upon a throne of gold. The chair beside him was empty, but the king's advisors and attendants stood about him in differing postures. Serena approached the throne and immediately sank into a perfect curtsy. She waited, as she had been taught, for the king's permission to rise.

When it came, she stood silent while the king studied her. She knew she looked fine, being dressed every morning in the elaborate manner of full-court dress. She was accustomed to the styles now and felt more natural in them.

"You are a most persistent wench."

Serena dipped her head at the king's forceful comment. "My cause is great, Your Highness."

"Well, I can see why he married you. The talk of your beauty was not exaggerated."

He seemed to be talking to himself in the matter and Serena remained perfectly still.

"I suppose you have come to beg for your husband's life, eh?"

Serena again nodded. "With thy permission, I would like to put the begging into words, sire."

He chuckled and waved his hand at her. "Yes, yes, go on."

She had practiced what she would say, but as she opened her mouth, new words sprang to life. "When I first met Drake Weston, he was not a duke. He was barely alive and a haunted man. I did not understand at the time the demons he fought, but in the time since, I have become intimately acquainted with those demons. They are the ones who say a man's worth is based on the status of his birth, not his character or being one of God's creation. Drake suffered from the belief that without his position in society, he was as nothing."

She took a breath. "Sire, I have not known nobles and kings before now, but I have known noble men. My father is one such man, and even though he is to the world a silversmith, I must tell thee that there is no other man on earth that I would value as highly as a worthy man and friend." She allowed a little smile, then paused. The king smiled back, though whether from being drawn into her words or from the shock of them she didn't know. Still the action bolstered her courage.

She sank to her knees. "My husband, Drake Weston, may no longer be a duke, a member of nobility by birth, but please hear me say that through his trials he has faced his demons and become a noble man. Sire, I plead mercy on his behalf. Please spare his life."

The king studied her, his face stern. "As you have so little admiration for the nobility, I assume you plead only for his life."

"Yes."

He paused, steepling his hands to his chin, and then smiled, a mischievous light in his eyes. "Yes, yes," he nodded to himself. "Lady Weston, you have suffered much through this ordeal. I understand he lied to you, and you only recently learned of this will and the plot to outmaneuver it—" the king waved his hand in circles—"etcetera, etcetera." He paused, letting the moment loom over them. "If the choice were yours, what punishment would *you* give your husband?"

Serena paused, hearing the suspended breath in the room. She knew that to all present she was only a commoner. What the king had just asked was unheard of. She opened her mouth to answer as she knew Drake would want her to answer, taking full advantage of the opportunity for reinstatement, and then found she could not say what was not in her heart.

"I wish to live in Bristol, by the sea, as it reminds me of my home in Philadelphia. I wish to raise our children together, near their grandfather, whom I have grown to love and respect. I wish my husband to do what he has told me is now in his heart: to help the miners and their children and bring reform to laws that allow such innocents to work in appalling conditions. I would not ask for titles or wealth, sire, just the opportunity to live out our lives together."

There was a flutter of activity and excited voices when she ended her impassioned speech, but the king silenced all with a raised hand. His eyes seemed to pierce into her, seeking to burn away any untruth.

"And do you think this would be Drake's request, if given the choice?

Serena couldn't lie. "Nay, sire. I think he might prefer death to such a quiet life as I've described."

The king laughed again, long and loud. Waving over a tall man in a green velvet costume, he commanded. "See that it is done exactly as Mrs. Weston requested. I have a feeling she is aright, and this will be more of a punishment than death." With that he dismissed her.

Serena rose and walked out of the palace for the last time, slightly stunned. And confused. Had she just gained an enormous triumph . . . or a life sentence for a husband she was no longer certain she knew.

SERENA HAD RUN to the townhouse window every time she heard a carriage clatter by, hoping it was Drake's. They had told her he was to be released straightaway, that he could return to her, a husband reclaimed. But as the shadows grew deeper in the room, her eyelids fluttered closed.

She jerked awake at the creaking of the front door. "Drake?" She rushed into the foyer.

Then into his arms.

Serena broke into sobs, her shoulders shaking while he crushed her to him. She could feel his tears dripping into her hair.

"Oh, Serena." He cupped her face with his palms.

She looked up into his eyes, those blue eyes that she hoped so long ago would wake up and look at her just so.

Just as they looked at her now. "You saved me. Once again." He laughed a little, the crinkles around his eyes deeper, his face thinner.

"No. God saved thee."

Drake looked to the ceiling and then back into her eyes. "Yes. But you helped Him."

They walked into the sitting room, hand in hand, lingering, touching, making it real that they were together again.

"Was it terrible?" She sat down close to him.

"The image of your face kept me sane. I thought of you when I couldn't bear it." He paused. "And I prayed. I prayed constantly."

She could see it in him, a strong rooting having taken place.

"So," he studied her, "we will live in Bristol?"

"Art thou disappointed? I could have asked for anything, but I found only one thing in my heart."

"No. I am thankful to be alive, with you in my arms again. Nothing else matters."

Serena hoped that would remain true when the shock of being set free wore away. And when she told him what else was in her heart: that she was not ready to be his wife in truth yet. That she needed time to heal, to trust again.

"Drake . . ."

Alarm rose in his eyes at her tone.

She breathed deep, praying for the words. "I need time."

"Time for what, sweetest?"

"Time for all this to settle. For my heart to heal."

His brow furrowed, and a glimmer of fear entered his gaze.

"When we return to Bristol, I am hopeful that thy father will allow me to stay with him for a little while, until I have sorted this out within myself."

His eyes widened. "What are you saying, Serena?"

"Just that . . . I love thee, but I am not ready to live with thee again. Not yet."

Anger settled on his brow, but he held his silence.

Mustering courage, she went on. "I know it will be difficult. For me, too." She lifted her chin and gave him a melting smile. "But we have dealt with difficult things before. At the end of this, I will know how to truly become thy wife. Please, Drake, I need this time."

She could hardly bear his sadness as he turned away from her, and it took all her will to stay seated as he rose and left the room.

She slept alone that night, wanting so much to go to him, but knowing that she couldn't let herself. Because more than one night was at stake. Their lives, their happiness . . . it all rested on one thing.

Serena's holding to what she knew was right.

EPILOGUE

rake stood on the threshold of his father's house, a bunch of wildflowers in his hand, the brim of his hat gripped in the other. She had hinted to give him an answer today. It was a question he asked since that first week after being back in Bristol.

Was she ready to be his wife again?

His initial response to her demand to live without him had been anger and disbelief. He had thought to convince her otherwise. It hadn't taken him long, though, to realize how serious she was. After leaving her with his father, whom Drake resented for having urged Serena to follow her heart in this matter, he retired to the lonely, if sometimes crowded, bed of a local inn. With that one decision she turned the tables on their relationship, and they'd begun a lengthy and—if Drake was to be honest—most illuminating courtship.

He came every Friday, spending the weekend with them after a long work week as a partner in a new bank that he founded. He thrived on the challenges of turning a silversmithing business into a clearinghouse, securities investor, and lender to the community.

Now he was fast becoming a political voice in the community, having taken up the cause of the miners and child labor. Robbie was his personal assistant, valet, driver, and anything else the lad seemed able to do. He was so eager to learn, his body now healed and filled out with good food, his language taking on Drake's cultured, clipped tones. The boy was forever making Drake smile or laugh out loud with his quick wit. It was humbling, having Robbie at his side when the boy was not in school—a practice the lad resisted and Drake insisted upon.

Now, as Drake banged at the door of his father's home, he smiled. The last year in Bristol had wrought such changes in them all. It *had* been hard, but well worth it.

The door opened to reveal his father's butler. The man rarely remembered who Drake was these days, so Drake reintroduced himself each time he called. "Drake Weston to see Serena."

He watched while the man thought through the names and then nodded, his eyes bright with humor for some reason.

"Into the blue drawing room with you, then," he intoned, motioning the way to Drake as if he had never stepped foot into the house and didn't know the way.

Drake handed over his hat and strode for the door. It was closed. He suddenly felt nervous. What if she rejected him? What if today, when asked the question, she turned him down forever?

Taking a deep breath, he opened the door and then stopped. The room was so dark.

"Surprise!"

"Happy Birthday!"

Calls and happy voices rang out toward him. Candles were brought forth, and suddenly the room was ablaze in soft light.

He turned this way and that, seeing his father, new friends and business associates—and her.

Serena stood to one side, their three-month-old daughter in her arms, a broad smile making her face glow in the candlelight.

Today was his birthday. In his eagerness to see her he had forgotten!

She swept over to him, trading baby Hope for the flowers. "For me?" Her smile deepened and she buried her face into the sweet petals. "So many beautiful colors! I shall paint them tomorrow before they fade." She had just finished a portrait of Drake cradling Hope in the crook of one arm. It was one of the many paintings she had completed in the last year.

He shook his head at her. "I can't believe you've done this."

"And why not? 'Tis a special occasion, a birthday." She winked at him, and he accepted this new, flirtatious side of her with growing amusement. It had been showing itself more often since Hope's birth.

His longing for Serena rose until it was almost painful. Blocking it out with a bark of laughter, he stared down at his daughter, kissing the top of her downy blonde hair. "How is my sweet one today?"

"Smiling all of the time, but she misses you." Serena had dropped most of the thees and thys from her speech. As she became more of herself, she left anything false behind.

Drake looked deeply into his wife's eyes, aware how closely they were being watched. "I hope to remedy that soon."

Serena answered back with a knowing smile. "One must never lose hope."

THE PARTY LASTED for hours, and while Drake enjoyed himself, he was glad when the last guest had left. His father, a man he'd grown to love over the past year, had taken the baby upstairs to her cradle.

He finally had his wife all to himself. "Thank you, Serena. It was so . . . surprising . . . and wonderful." He stood with his back to her, pouring punch into a small, delicate cup. He felt her come up behind him and press into his back, wrapping her arms around his waist and leaning her head against him.

"You are welcome." The words were a soft purr—and a shock rushed through his body when he felt her lips at the back of his neck.

Growling, he turned and swept her into his arms. Bending low, he devoured her mouth. She held nothing back, returning the kiss with equal passion—which spoke well of a year of hard-won trust between them.

Gasping, she pulled back, laughing up into his eyes. "Are you going to ask me?"

He was almost afraid. What if this were some cruel setting for his downfall? But no, Serena would never do such a thing. She may not be a Quaker or a duchess, but she was a warm, wonderful woman of many hidden depths and talents and kindnesses. If Drake knew anything about her at all, he knew she would never be cruel.

He took a deep breath. "Will you come home with me? Be my wife in truth?" He had asked it before, but this time his eyes filled as if he anticipated her reply. It was in the air—a feeling of triumph—as though he had climbed a mountain and now stood at the summit overlooking a new world.

"The house is ready?" Her smile teased. "No half-built cabin in the wilderness?"

Drake laughed, squeezing her tight. "Your palace awaits you. And might I add, it is perfect." It was. He had overseen every detail of the three-story brick home and was inordinately proud he had earned every cent for it from his own careful investments.

"Then I think—" she paused, and he could see her battle sudden tears of her own—"that I am ready to love the dragon again."

He shook his head. "No . . . no more dragons, I promise."

She cupped his face in between her hands. "Oh Drake, do you not see? You will always have a little of the dragon in you, and you should. It will aid you in your mission to change some of the atrocities of our world. And what lies between you and me . . . it no longer matters. For you see, dragon or no, I have become a knight." She smiled through her tears. "Your *petit chevalier,* in truth. I first protected the dragon, but God has tamed him. And I have always loved him. So breathe on, and make your fire. For I am not afraid."

They cried together then, staring into each other's eyes. It was the end of one thing and the beginning of another. And Drake had no doubt. The love between them had been tested, purified by God's fire, even as the smith refines his silver. And now . . . it was ready to be poured forth, molded into their story.

Drake leaned toward her lips, brushing them with his. He might not know exactly what life held for them, but he knew one truth without a shadow of doubt.

Together, they could be anything.